THE
FINAL
COUNTDOWN

**A novel by Martin Caidin
based on a screenplay by David
Ambrose & Gerry Davis and Thomas
Hunter & Peter Powell; based
on a story by Thomas Hunter &
Peter Powell and David Ambrose.**

BANTAM BOOKS
TORONTO · NEW YORK · LONDON

THE FINAL COUNTDOWN
A Bantam Book / August 1980

ISBN 0-553-12155-3

Published simultaneously in the United States and Canada

Bantam Books are published by Bantam Books, Inc. Its trademark, consisting of the words "Bantam Books" and the portrayal of a bantam, is Registered in U.S. Patent and Trademark Office and in other countries. Marca Registrada. Bantam Books, Inc., 666 Fifth Avenue, New York, New York 10019.

PRINTED IN THE UNITED STATES OF AMERICA

0 9 8 7 6 5 4 3 2 1

DECEMBER 7, 1980

There is a storm approaching that your ship's computer says is impossible . . . Within a second the bottom of the ocean drops and the hair on your neck stands up as a tunnel of water envelopes you, hurling your ship from front to back and whisking jets along the deck like model planes . . .

DECEMBER 7, 1941

The sea is calm at once . . . But the sun is twelve hours further behind you and the only radio you can receive is a public broadcast from the President . . . Franklin Delano Roosevelt. When the recon planes you've sent to base at Pearl Harbor report a fleet of Japanese bombers forming to attack, you face a decision that cannot be made . . . and the Final Countdown has begun!

RICHARD R. ST. JOHNS PRESENTS

KIRK DOUGLAS   **MARTIN SHEEN**   **KATHARINE ROSS**

JAMES FARENTINO

in

THE BRYNA COMPANY'S PRODUCTION of

THE FINAL COUNTDOWN

Starring
RON O'NEAL and
CHARLES DURNING
as Senator Chapman

Directed by
DON TAYLOR

Produced by
PETER VINCENT DOUGLAS

Executive Producer
RICHARD R. ST. JOHNS

Screenplay by
DAVID AMBROSE & GERRY DAVIS
and THOMAS HUNTER & PETER POWELL

Story by
THOMAS HUNTER & PETER POWELL
and DAVID AMBROSE

Director of Photography
VICTOR J. KEMPER

Music by
JOHN SCOTT

Associate Producer
LLOYD KAUFMAN

Edited by
ROBERT K. LAMBERT

Executive In Charge of Production
JOHN W. HYDE

This book is for a fellow time traveler
Vern Renaud

THE
FINAL
COUNTDOWN

☆ 1 ☆

An airfield under the harsh midday sun is like a concrete desert, spliced with lines of asphalt, and spider-webbing of paint and stenciled numbers and letters, and all manner of buildings bleached in shimmering heat. The naval air station at Hawaii might never have been near the island paradise of the island name. A bone-white runway stretched for two miles beneath the pitiless light in the sky, lying on a line that was exactly east-west. At one end of the runway, a great slab-winged metal bird stood locked against its brakes, trembling from the subdued power of mighty engines. Inside the Plexiglas-domed cockpit the crew in brain buckets and pressure suits and hoses and lines enjoyed cold air streaming about their bodies. For the moment they were poised, men and machine a single entity, waiting for release by radioed voice from the control tower. The two crewmen glanced idly to one side where a big helicopter stood on the ramp, great overhead rotors turning, obviously on standby. They saw the reason. A long black limousine driving slowly toward the waiting chopper. The pilot of the powerful Grumman Tomcat fighter turned his attention back to the runway. Brisk winds, scattered clouds at four thousand, some haze on the horizon, and nice bright blue above that. A good day for winging it through

1

the blue. His headset cracked with the voice from the tower.

"Tomcat One Zero One, wind two seven five at fourteen knots, cleared for immediate takeoff, make straight climbout."

The F-14 pilot nodded imperceptibly to himself. "One Zero One rolling." His hands moved only slightly, but thunder screamed a dinosaur cry as the engines went to afterburner and spat angry tubes of bright flame behind them. Flame in one direction, knife-edged fighter in the other, and a breathless rush along concrete, an effortless sigh away from hard surface, and in moments the fighter was a dot and its thunder a fading hoarse whisper.

The helicopter crew had seen plenty of fighters leaving earth behind. They were more interested in two vehicles. That long black limo with darkened windows. You couldn't see in but the people inside saw out clearly. The limo stopped a hundred yards away and didn't move. From the other side of the helicopter another vehicle approached. A naval staff car. It slowed to a halt well clear of the rotors. The front right door opened and the chopper crew looked with open curiosity at the civilian who emerged. The co-pilot nudged the man by his side. "Stranger. Ever see him before?"

The pilot shook his head. "Uh uh. Mystery man. All I know is we're under priority orders to wait for him, be nice, you know, the kid gloves treatment, and then move out when he's aboard." The pilot thumbed another button, called to a crewman. "Higgins, get your butt out there and give that civvie a hand. Bring him aboard pronto."

"Yes, sir." Higgins unhooked his communications line from the helicopter and dropped to the ground. By the time he reached the civilian the staff car was gone. The stranger studied him. "I'm Warren Lasky. Apparently you're my transportation to, uh—"

Higgins threw him a casual salute. "The skipper's

expecting you, sir." He gestured to Lasky's side. "Is that your only bag, sir?"

Lasky nodded. "That's all." Higgins's showed the question on his face. It was damned peculiar. A civilian gets dropped off on the flight line all by his lonesome, a large and fast helicopter is waiting for him, they're on a priority mission, and the man has only this one small bag. Higgins studied the newcomer. Nothing special. Slacks and a sport jacket, open shirt, no hat. A man in his thirties, trim, an air of solid self-confidence. Higgins nodded, then extended the flight helmet he was carrying. "Mr. Lasky, if you'd put on the brain bucket before we get to the chopper? That way we can plug you into the intercom system as soon as you're aboard."

Lasky took the helmet, but for the moment he paused, studying the long limousine. He squinted in the sun for a better look at the big car. It didn't help much. He could make out the outline of a driver behind the wheel, and behind those darkened windows there was a silhouette of some kind. Obviously someone was studying them. Lasky turned to the crewman, the question showing on his face. The man shrugged. "I don't know a thing about it, sir. We'd better go."

Lasky gestured impatiently. "Be with you in a minute." He stared at the parked car. More intrigued than ever he started toward the vehicle. He hadn't gone a few steps before the front door opened and an enormous man stepped out with a surprisingly lithe, quick movement. Lasky understood immediately; he'd seen enough skilled bodyguards to recognize the signs. The big man stood before him. "Sorry, sir. No closer."

"Why not?" Lasky demanded. No response came from the other man. He looked impassively at Lasky and his message was implicit: don't cross the line. The unspoken message even said "please," and that came through in body language because that walking bludgeon could afford the courtesy. They held the standoff for several moments and then the other front door opened. Lasky looked with renewed interest at the second man approaching him. The walk was easy, the gestures friendly. This was Mr. Smooth, decided Lasky. Gray suit, vest, shoes gleaming in the sun, perfectly groomed and a right touch of a shock of white hair. He had executive written all over him and if his smile wasn't genuine, it was certainly practiced, polished, and perfect. The businessman stopped directly before Warren Lasky and extended a hand.

"I'm sorry for any seeming discourtesy," he said in a voice as silken smooth as any old-time radio announcer. "My name is Harold Elliott, and I'm executive assistant to Richard Tideman." He paused to let the message sink in and Lasky quickly got the message. What the hell—*he* worked for Tideman, and in the same thought he realized he'd never seen Tideman. Or, for that matter, had he ever seen so much as a picture of the man who alone owned, managed, and directed Tideman Industries with an iron hand. Then he dismissed the thoughts because Elliott's smile was getting almost as bright as the sun.

"Mr. Tideman is here," Elliott said as if to confirm Lasky's own thoughts. "He expressed a personal desire to see you off in the helicopter." The conversation ended there, like punching a tape player to OFF in the middle of a song.

Lasky strained to see better, but the bright sun and dark windows thwarted his effort. "That's Richard Tideman, himself? In the car? Look, I work for him. I'd like very much just to meet the man."

Elliott mixed his smile with a slow shake of his head. "I'm sorry, Mr. Lasky. That won't be possible. Neither is it necessary. Perhaps you didn't hear me. As I said, *he* came here to observe *your* departure."

The bodyguard hovered near by and Lasky recognized all the signs of futility. Lasky nodded slowly, then shrugged away further attempts. "Well, at least he feels I'm important enough to be sure I made it." Elliott smiled, said nothing. "Thank him for his interest," Lasky added, turning back toward the waiting helicopter, quite calm about the strange incident, but inwardly seething with questions. Why would the big man himself come down to a naval air station just to *see* Warren Lasky get into that helicopter? He could have gotten all the confirmation he wanted by radio or telephone or personal report. Too much here wasn't visible. At the helicopter, the whirling rotors hurling wind at him, he slipped on the brain bucket, adjusted the straps with the help of the crewman, and climbed into the capacious cabin. He turned for a final look at the black limousine before the crew slid the door closed. The big car remained where it was, the bodyguard and the aide to Tideman standing where he'd seen them before. Lasky had a definite view of the dark silhouette behind the rear windows, and that was all.

He pushed it aside as the crewman directed him to his assigned seat on the canvas bench running along the helicopter cabin. He strapped in as the crewman hooked him up for intercom. "How do you read, sir?" came into Lasky's earphones. He nodded. "Loud and clear. Thanks."

"Very good, Mr. Lasky. We'll be taking off in a few moments. I think you'll enjoy the view."

Lasky looked about him, felt the chopper vibrating as the pilots fed power to the engines and the great rotors above spun ever faster. He heard the tower clear them for a rolling takeoff from their present position. "Ah, Helo Eight One Three, you're clear for five hundred feet down the harbor."

"Roger that. Eight One Three is lifting."

More noise and vibration and the ground beneath Lasky fell away and behind him as the chopper lifted into the wind, tilted for an immediate turn, and soared easily to 500 feet. Lasky had a last glimpse of the black limousine and two small figures standing by the car, and then he turned his attention to the warships and other vessels in the naval harbor. He leaned closer to his window, turning in his seat for a better look at one warship in particular. A memory to time: the memorial to the *U.S.S. Arizona*, ripped apart by bombs and torpedos on a horrifying Sunday morning. December 7th, 1941. Lasky knew the dead crew had been entombed within the shattered carcass of the great battlewagon. Painted, kept gleaming as a memorial to the nation's war dead, it was also packed with tourists.

Then they were across the last beachline beneath them. The crewman stood before Lasky, an embarrassed look on his face. "Sir, I forgot. Your life vest? Would you let me put it on, please?"

Lasky grinned. It was obvious from the look that this was one crewman who'd just gotten chewed out by his pilot for a memory lapse. He released his belt and put on the Mae West. He felt better for it. They had a lot of open water to cover before they'd touch down—at sea.

☆ 2 ☆

The paper rolled slowly from the curving print tube, extending across a set of mechanical arms that held it away from the machine for instant drying. Several men stood about the relay printout that was picking up signals directly from a meteorological satellite that was at that moment passing within a thousand miles of the great aircraft carrier. The men listened to the mechanical fluting and the gentle rustling of paper. A red light blinked on and a chime sounded, and with those two signals an automatic paper cutter released the sheet for the large roll within the metsat receiver. An officer picked up the printout and glanced at the jetstream pattern, idly noting cumulus buildups and other weather flows. Nothing unusual. He started from the weather center, headed for flight operations, and paused as a bulkhead speaker rattled.

"Attention all hands, attention all hands. There will be a launch test-firing of the Harpoon missile system from turret five at seventeen hundred hours. This will be a live firing. Repeat, this will be a live firing. All hands stand clear of the turret five area. All hands—"

The officer blanked out the announcement; with the weather good he wouldn't be involved in the missile test. He left the weather center and went down a short passageway to operations. Inside the ops room, he carried the satellite picture to a bulletin board,

7

smoothed it against the self-sticking surface, and closed a clear Plexiglas sheet over the picture. The officer made his first real study of the photograph and frowned at a black smudge over an area free of clouds. He opened the Plexiglas and tried to rub away the smudge. "Damn it," he muttered quietly. "Got to do something about that facsimile system." The smudge shouldn't have been there. The ocean area was clean of any weather disturbances.

Other men joined him to study the picture. "Looks good," one said. "See that cirrus? It's high and thin. No sweat."

Another voice agreed. "Yep. No cumulus, no build-ups, and the old man will be pleased. They're calling for full optical track and recording all the way."

"Good. We stay on schedule."

A finger tapped the Plexiglas. "What's that black area over there?"

"Just some crap from the machine, looks like."

"Uh huh."

"Okay, mark it off." Lines from a grease pencil began to cover the Plexiglas overlay as the men marked wind patterns, upper jet streams, cloud movements; it all went down on a list at the side of the chart.

A weather officer shouldered his way into the group. He stood hulk-wide among the others. The nameplate on his uniform read L/CDR JOHN ARTHUR, but no one used his name. He was a full-blooded American Indian and he was known throughout the great ship as Black Cloud. Not too many men knew whether his name came from his Indian family or because he so often offered up so much stinking weather. Little matter; he'd carried the handle a long time and he enjoyed it.

"Looks neat," Black Cloud said. "We can confirm in the clear for the next twelve hours." He tapped the board. "These the latest numbers?"

"Right," a lieutenant responded. "Severe clear out there. Winds out of the north at four knots."

"Just like Miami Beach in the posters," Black Cloud remarked. "I'm going topside with the poop. The old man wants this report in person."

Black Cloud walked briskly along what appeared to be an endless passageway that was punctuated by oval-shaped watertight hatches—known as knee busters. He could have been in a subterranean chamber of a great city and in one way that's what it was like aboard a great warship. Some men moved in his direction and a steady stream of men passed in the opposite direction. Black Cloud nodded or gave fast greetings to the ones he knew. He took a narrow, fast-moving escalator to a higher level, stepped off, turned to his left, and began to climb a zigzagging series of metal steps. The higher he went the more he liked it. He liked the sounds. A subdued hum; almost a muted chorus. Not from the machinery that could be heard down in the engine rooms or along the propeller shafts or in the maintenance shops. Up here it was all honey-smooth. Powerful electronic systems, radar shacks, computers. The war center, the place where the head honchos ran the whole works. This is where Black Cloud wanted to belong.

He entered a wide and spacious bridge complex, blinking with the unexpected glare of sunlight streaming through the great angled windows of the ops center, from where the carrier received its commands of life. All about him were men at their stations, some standing, others strapped into seats with helmets on their heads and thin lip mikes by their mouths. The crew was made up of the usual mix found aboard a carrier this size: most of the men were U.S. Navy; there was a contingent of marines on special duty—security, aide to the captain, and top staff officers—and there were a handful of civilians. There was a quite babble up here, the crosscurrents of information and decisions and command. Black Cloud worked his way through to a corner where he saw the captain sitting in an airliner-type seat that was flanked on either side by the great windows. Not only was Captain Matthew Yelland privy to every area within the ship though electronics contact, but from where he sat he enjoyed the satisfying view of watching his ship working. Looking down on the expanse of a magnificent aircraft carrier is both an enormously rewarding and a humbling sight. This carrier had more power in its innards than did most large cities. It carried enough firepower in its aircraft and ordnance systems to match everything turned loose during the Second World War by *all* combatants. Triple that, mused Black Cloud, or increase it by a factor of a hundred, when you considered some of the really big thermonuclear warheads. The flight deck reared eighty feet above the waterline, and the *Nimitz's* huge nuclear turbines deep in her belly provided enough power for her computer-designed hull to outrun even a destroyer. Any time you can get a warship of 140,000 tons in that kind of shape and with that speed, you have in a single package the equal of an entire nation's fighting arsenal. *Nimitz* was all that and more. Black Cloud pushed off his sudden mood of introspection and focused his eyes on the captain who was silhouetted against the stark sunlight glare behind him.

The weather officer stood quietly waiting for the captain to turn. "Ah, the veritable Black Cloud himself," Yelland said, not unkindly. "From the looks of things, Commander, we might just be calling you White Cloud today." He raised an eyebrow just a hair. "I hope, that is," he added.

"Yes, sir." Black Cloud unrolled the weather satellite photo facsimile and clipped it to an information board by the captain's seat. The old man studied it with an experienced eye. "Looks good," he said, and then a frown crossed his face. He brushed a finger over the smudge in the otherwise clear ocean area. "What's this?" he queried.

"Nothing to do with weather, sir. It's in the machine."

"I don't like it, Commander." Captain Yelland looked into Black Cloud's eyes. "When you leave here, the first thing you do is get that smudge maker of yours cleaned up. A smudge can kill you. A speck on your windshield can kill you. You can't tell it from a fighter coming head on at you."

"Yes, sir," Black Cloud said. He cursed to himself. Goddamn that Stark. He was supposed to clean that triple-damned machine twice a day. He obviously hadn't done it and here was Black Cloud getting his ass reamed for something he didn't do. Well, he'd ream some butt himself.

He was saved from further chewing when a speaker came alive. "Notice to the bridge from radar. We have Helo Eight One Three from Pearl twelve minutes out at present speed."

The captain nodded to Black Cloud. "Leave the chart here. Thank you."

"Yes, sir."

Captain Yelland turned to his officer of the deck, Lieutenant Artemus Perry. "That chopper we've been waiting for is coming in. Take her into the wind, Mr. Perry."

"Aye, sir." Perry spoke to the man at his side. "Come to course one four six."

"One four six it is, sir," the helmsman confirmed. The wheel he turned wasn't remotely like the helm of ships from the past. It didn't turn anything directly but sent electronic signals to a computer that in turn commanded its own powerful servomechanisms. A man stood on the bridge and moved a wheel with gentle finger pressure and giant electronic-mechanical slaves did his instant bidding. The carrier began her turn, a city of steel easing onto a new course to point directly into the wind. Far in the distance the pilots of Helo Eight One Three saw the great warship commence her turn.

The crewman in the helicopter cabin looked through the window with Warren Lasky. "That is one hell of an impressive boat," he told the civilian. "I've served aboard a lot of carriers, but that one makes the word huge seem silly."

The Sikorsky eased steadily from the sky, the pilot holding just enough speed to close steadily on the carrier, his aiming and touchdown point already marked by flashing strobes. They felt the turbulence nibbling at them as the air swirled behind the great ship, saw the landing signal officer watching from his control booth. The LSO made certain, helicopter or not, the pilot was using the mirrored landing system. Everything was on the line, and the chopper gentled her way down to the deck. The instant the helicopter stopped, crewmen snapped restraining cables to the landing gear and signaled the pilot to cut power. They shut down quickly and the great rotors began their slowing motion.

Inside the cabin, Lasky released his belt and doffed the Mae West. He removed his helmet, handed it to the waiting crewman, and took his small attache case to the doorway. He stepped onto the deck and was stunned with the powerful wind—the speed of the carrier adding to the surface winds so that he was in a meaningful gale. Before he could say a word to anyone, an explosion assailed him. Out of sight but obviously close by a jet fighter was running up to full power, and the noise crashed against his eardrums. So loud was the jet cry that Lasky stumbled. Loudspeakers tore at his hearing and he heard words about clear to launch and then another explosion as the fighter went to afterburners, flame screamed, the catapult thundered and the jet, on the other side of the helicopter, was hurled away from the carrier deck. He could hear again.

"Put that chopper on spot four. Get the lead out. Move that machine!" Another loudspeaker. Men seemed to be running in all directions. Lasky hurried away as a tug clamped onto the helicopter and it started moving. A man with his face concealed beneath a helmet and visor beckoned to him. Lasky went forward, fighting the wind. They stopped by the side of the carrier deck island, which loomed beside and over them like a great vertical wall. The crewman started to speak but his words vanished in a sudden new blast of jet thunder. He motioned Lasky closer and shouted into his ear. "Who are you?"

"Warren Lasky!" he shouted back.

"You a civilian?"

"Yes!"

"Through that yellow door over there!" The crewman was gone. Lasky blinked. The helicopter was rolling away and he saw across the deck. There were other warships far beyond the carrier. He squinted. Unless his eyes were playing tricks on him, there were also fishing trawlers out there. Russian, by the looks of them. He turned his attention back to his immediate surroundings as a small yellow truck roared past him, narrowly missing running over his foot. The world was ignoring him and then that omnipresent voice, magnified a hundredfold by the powerful amplifiers, crashed about him again. He had the strangest feeling that he was cast in the *Wizard of Oz*, standing in the great hall while the omnipotent voice railed and boomed against him: "On the flight deck. Attention the flight deck. Get that man with the case the devil off. What's he doing there? Move it, move it! Get him clear before he gets killed!"

A hand gripped Lasky's arm. He turned to stare into the smiling face of Commander Dan Thurman, who gestured to Lasky to follow him. They walked together to an open door by the island structure. Abruptly they were out of the wind and Lasky felt he could breathe and talk once more. "Jesus!" he said. "It's a madhouse out there."

The navy officer laughed and clasped Lasky's hand. "I'm Dan Thurman, exec officer. Sorry we missed getting you just when you touched down. How was the flight?"

"Oh, fine, fine." Lasky turned back to look out across the ocean. "Those trawlers. Russian?"

"Sure are."

"What are they doing out here in the middle of an American task force?"

Thurman laughed. "One thing's for sure. They don't do much fishing. Look; save the questions for later. Let's get you squared away right now, okay?"

Lasky nodded gratefully. He was damned glad someone was immediately in charge. "Okay, Commander. Lead on."

He had a brief moment to study the other man. Thurman stood a good six feet two inches. There was something about the man, and then Lasky understood. If you could hang titles on people, then this man would be known as "Navy all the way." He was immaculate, even spotless in the midst of all of this bedlam, he moved with the easy grace of a man in excellent physical shape, and he radiated a confidence that could be born only of command for a long time. Thurman paused as a bull-necked marine in starched uniform and white peaked cap came up to them, snapped a salute to Thurman, and reached for Lasky's case. "Corporal Luther Kullman, sir. I'll carry your bag." He snatched it from Lasky's hand and stood back, waiting to follow the two men.

Thurman nodded to Lasky. "Your first time aboard *Nimitz*?"

"My first time aboard a carrier, period," came the honest reply. "Everything out there seems like mass confusion."

"Anything but," Thurman reassured him. "I—" He held back his words as that amplified stentorian voice boomed through the open doorway: "Secure from flight quarters. Secure from flight quarters."

"Just a little ways from here you can hear yourself think," Thurman said. "Just follow me, Mr. Lasky. It gets easier quickly." Lasky followed, sandwiched in between the commander and the stocky marine taking up the rear. He could feel the carrier turning again as he worked carefully to sustain his balance. He didn't know that at that same moment he was being discussed on the bridge.

☆ 3 ☆

From the bridge Captain Matthew Yelland had watched the helicopter land, had seen Lasky emerge, confused and startled, finally to be led away by the hand of his executive officer. Jesus Christ. And he'd had to hold up *his* ship and this whole damned strike force just to wait for that skinny civilian popinjay down there. Yelland sighed. He was the oldest man on the bridge and even if his looks belied his years, he'd never see the better side of fifty again. That didn't matter much, either to him or the navy. His face was grizzled-tough, his eyes so piercing as to be a menacing blue if the mood behind them inspired that kind of thinking. He was a pilot's pilot, a veteran of jet fighting in Korea, and a hellbuster in Vietnam before a Sam missile screamed up through low broken clouds and tore apart his fighter. For eight years he'd been through every hellish torture thrown up by the North Vietnamese. He'd been from one prison camp to another, dragged through towns and villages by chains, incarcerated in tiny, bone-bending wooden cages, and then buried alive in the Hanoi Hilton. For eight years they burned him with cigarettes and broke his bones and pulled out his nails and they never broke him. His story was legion within the ranks of the flying navy and marines; thus the dismissal of his age to run this leviathan carrier. One waited to meet

16

Captain Yelland, prepared for a man stooped from a broken back, prepared to look at skin weathered and yellowed, and instead faced a solid physique, those piercing eyes, a commanding voice, and above all, a mind honed through years of experience and survival. Prison torture broke most men. For Yelland it had been the ultimate test and he emerged with his body in agony and his mind exquisite with its knowledge of survival. He had become a minor legend, an inspiration, and even the younger enlisted men, who might have followed the currently popular tendency to sneer at tradition, venerated Matthew Yelland.

Now, seated in his special chair from which he had an eagle-eye view of the sweeping carrier deck, he was totally within his element, using eyes, ears, mind, and a vast battery of instruments and devices with which to sustain the pulse beat of his enormous floating city. He took special enjoyment in the marriage of the old with the electronic new. The bridge was a masterpiece of modern science and electronic engineering, but the helm was mated to a wheel that was physically an exact duplicate of the wheels from older, even ancient vessels (notwithstanding its connections to computerized and electronic systems), and there was one other touch hewing to tradition, and to which Matthew Yelland demanded absolute obedience. If you were in uniform you by God wore the headpiece that came with that uniform—*always*. The headgear was absent only if you were a civilian or a guest to whom such apparel was normally not worn.

Yelland looked across the flight deck again, calmly studying small figures of men moving and placing fighters, bombers, reconnaissance planes, helicopters and cargo aircraft; watched elevators dropping below the top deck to mid-deck storage hangars and workshops. Small huffer trucks darted about, looking all the world like metallic beetles serving metal birds that were always kept ready for sudden flight. Then the deck was again clear, and Yelland turned to several technicians surrounded with sweeping control consoles. Yelland adjusted a headset and lip mike that was kept open always to the communications monitor on the bridge. "Give me Pri-Fly," he said easily.

"Aye, sir," came the immediate response. A pause, then the confirmation. "Pri-Fly on, Captain."

"Pri-Fly, this is the captain. Continue fixed-wing recovery."

High above the flight deck of *Nimitz*, almost at a dizzying height above the great flat expanse of the carrier, perched the control tower, filled with equipment similar to many such installations on land, but with everything arranged with painstaking compactness. Two command chairs dominated the activity within Pri-Fly—the control tower. These rested in dead center of the tower, with the left seat occupied by the air boss and the right seat by his assistant. Their view commanded not so much the entirety of the great deck—that aligned with the ship and the second, angled deck—but towards the stern of the great carrier, from which direction aircraft would approach to land. Air boss at this moment, on this watch, was Commander Virgil Anson and the man in the adjacent seat, Lieutenant Douglas Blake. Anson had just received the command from the captain, barked a quick, "Aye, aye, sir," into his lip mike, and nodded to Blake.

"Okay, the old man wants them in. Let's bring the CAG aboard."

Blake nodded in turn, picked up a small mike hanging on the armrest of his chair, and spoke into it. His words carried to hundreds of men on and within the great warship. "Tomcat One Zero One . . . Charlie Now. Repeat, Charlie Now."

At the vessel's stern the landing signal officer and his crew judged the position and sliding, descending energy curve of the approaching Grumman Tomcat with practiced and unblinking eyes. They had been in this same position for literally many thousands of approaches of all manner of aircraft, from small liaison ships to howling fighters and bombers, and they knew from every movement, every slip, just what might be in store for them. Because every landing on a carrier was *not* a landing. It was an act of deliberate violence, a controlled crash, and the harnessing of enormous energies so that a fighter impacting with the deck would be snagged, hooked, and locked into place instead of ripping down a flight deck and either throwing itself into the sea or, much worse, plowing into other aircraft and unnumbered men and transforming the unholy mess into violently exploding flames.

In the front seat of the Tomcat, its wings now swept fully forward, flaps and lift devices extended for maximum lifting energy at the slowest speed possible, gear down, arrestor hook down, everything "in the green," Commander Richard Owens studied the slanting, pitching deck of his water-based airfield as it expanded with his closing speed. Owens was more than another pilot coming onto *Nimitz*; the tall, prematurely balding veteran of 340 missions in Vietnam was also the carrier's CAG—air wing commander. As such, the LSO and his team was as much on the razor's edge of performance as the pilot needling his howling steed toward them. Owens flew with the master's touch, the fine hand of the man who wears an airplane as much as he flies it with caressing, knowing motions on the stick, feet slaved to his mind on the pedals, his left hand on the throttle so that with barely more movement than instinct, he could play enormous burning energy with a magician's dexterity. Every tiny movement, every twitch, brought its answer in a new movement or angle of the Tomcat fighter so that Owens was literally orchestrating his own speed, descent, and motions from side to side to match the "visual sound" of the carrier that seemed to rush up at him. And then he was *there*, the space be-

tween winged killer and enormous deck flashing
away, squeezing together, and the Tomcat smashed
with violent force on the aft section of the flight deck.

At this point in a landing—on a landing field on
hard ground—a pilot was expected to chop his power
and kill off the thrust that shoved him forward. Not on
a carrier. As the Tomcat banged its gear onto the deck,
the tail hook trailing behind and beneath the fighter
caught the Number Three restraining cable. The two
men in the Tomcat were hurled forward, their bodies
snagged taut by their harnesses. At the same instant
Commander Owens, instead of chopping his power by
jerking back on the levers, slammed them forward
and went to maximum thrust. The Tomcat struggled
madly to break free—and if it did, that constantly
available power meant that Owens could slam his
slab-winged killer back into the air if the cable let go
or if anything went wrong with the restraining system.
It didn't. Everything worked. A crewman in a bright
yellow jacket ran before the now fully restrained Tomcat. In direct view of the pilot he gave the signal to
cut power. Pri-Fly saw it all with a good sense of comfort; they always breathed a bit easier when the CAG
was about to walk instead of fly.

Captain Matthew Yelland watched the recovery operation of his CAG with unvoiced pleasure. He knew
Dick Owens well; they'd served and flown together
many times in the past. He watched the Tomcat freed
of its restraints and guided swiftly to a safe parking
area. Yelland turned slowly in his seat. Something
tugged at his consciousness. A feeling. Less than that,
perhaps. Some ancient instinct starting to rise in the
back of his mind like a wraith of thin smoke curling
into his thinking. Then he identified the feeling and
realized, at the same moment, that it didn't have a
damn to do with his subconscious. *Nimitz* steamed
well in good weather, just as it had been forecast.
Moreover, that forecast had covered a very wide ex-

panse of ocean and sky, and they would be in good weather for a minimum of two to three days. *Should be*, he corrected himself. Because if it were true, then what the devil was that gray haze on the distant horizon? A trace of annoyance showed on Yelland's face to mirror his inner feelings. He didn't like things that weren't neat and orderly and all in their place. There should be not so much as the vaguest hint of anything beyond severe clear for many, many hours to come. Gray haze was there. It shouldn't be. Something was— well, *different* would have to do for now. Yelland turned to his officer of the deck.

"Mr. Perry."

"Sir?"

"Am I mistaken," Yelland said slowly, "or did Black Cloud bring to this deck a very definite forecast this morning for clear skies and lots of sunshine?"

Lieutenant Perry glanced far ahead of the warship. He'd seen that gray haze as well, and he was also aware the captain had long noticed the strange effect on the horizon. "That he did, sir. But right now, with whatever it is out there, I'll bet he wishes he'd brought you bad news."

Yelland rubbed his chin. That was the rub, all right. He'd never known Black Cloud to be wrong about the weather. *Never*. And with the facilities at his disposal, including an astonishing array of weather satellites in high orbit above the earth, this kind of mistake was so wrong that—

Yelland gestured impatiently. "Mr. Perry, let me see that weather sheet again, please."

No longer observed by the captain, Dick Owens sat in the cockpit of the Tomcat as it was secured in its assigned parking position. He went through the routine of shutting down the complex fighter, disengaging himself from air hoses and oxygen lines and communications hookups. He safetied the ejection system, finished his shutdown checklist, removed his brain bucket, and released his restraint harness. He climbed slowly down from the fighter, his radar intercept officer, Lieutenant Yancy Miller, following him from the rear cockpit. Deck crewmen moved about them steadily as the two officers walked toward the looming island structure. They stopped to scan the horizon far ahead of the carrier.

"Either I'm crazy," Owens said slowly, "or that is a storm building out there."

"Yes, sir," Miller confirmed. His brow furrowed. "I don't get it, Commander. We've been upstairs and we didn't see a thing. Blue sky around the end of the world. And now. . . ." He shook his head.

Owens offered a wry look. "From what we heard the forecast, and I do repeat the word, forecast, we could look forward to 'hot and dusty' for a couple of days."

"They got 'wet and dusty' in the book, Commander?" Miller countered.

"Funny, funny," Owens said, but he was smiling. "C'mon, let's debrief. I want a hot shower."

Warren Lasky walked alongside the exec officer through what appeared to be endless steel tunnels in the bowels of a city that hadn't quite yet settled down on its foundations. For a brief time they'd walked in silence, the marine escort following them like a great silent bulldog, until finally Dan Thurman made it clear through easy conversation that he was willing to accept in a friendly fashion this hastily delivered civilian.

"We're all pretty much in the dark about you, Mr. Lasky," Thurman said for openers.

"Warren."

"Good. It's Dan." They nodded their acceptance of a more personal status. "What I meant," Thurman went on, "is that your means of arrival is, ah, unusual. One man in a chopper delivered to a ship at sea—and if there's any kind of emergency, I'm sure I'd know about it. And," he added with emphasis, "I don't."

"Neither do I," Lasky told him, and his candor showed through. "They said get your tail out to that boat—"

"Ship. A sub's a boat."

Lasky grinned. "So I fail the old salt test. Like I said, I'm in my office playing chess with a computer and I get this Class A priority that says move it, buddy. Just take your necessary work papers and computer tie-in equipment—"

"All that's in one attache case?"

"Uh huh. I was also told clothing and personal articles would be provided for me on the ship."

"They are," confirmed Thurman. He pushed on the business end of things. "You're with Tideman Industries, right?"

"Four years now."

"What's your field? Your specialty?"

"Systems analyst," Lasky said.

Thurman threw him a sideward glance. "That's another way of saying efficiency expert, isn't it?"

"And another way of saying efficiency expert," Lasky said drily, "is that you're a son of a bitch fifty miles from out of town."

"Nice riposte," Thurman acknowledged. "I won't deny my curiosity. But I would sure appreciate a very straight answer to a question."

"Shoot."

"What are you looking for?"

Lasky stopped and so did Thurman. The marine waited dutifully behind them. "You want it straight from the shoulder, Dan?"

Thurman nodded. His eyes were cold. "Cards on the table."

"I'll tell you the absolute truth. *I don't know.*"

"That's crazy!"

"I never said it wasn't. I was ordered to get to the

navy base, I was driven to a helicopter, I was flown out here, and I was told I'd be met by the executive officer of the *Nimitz*, who would take me to the captain of the boat—sorry; ship—and that I was to wing it from there."

Thurman shook his head, smiling. "It's ridiculous, but I believe you."

Lasky didn't return the smile. "Commander, I'd like to be friends with you. So let me tell you one thing straight out. Don't let the civilian clothes mislead you, and don't let my love affairs with computers lead you astray. I don't lie. *Ever*. About *anything*. If we're going to get along, please keep that in mind."

Thurman looked at him with undisguised astonishment. He nodded slowly. "We're almost there. Let's go on."

They walked onto the bridge and for several moments Dan Thurman played it slow and cool. He stood by Warren Lasky, keeping Lasky between himself and Captain Matthew Yelland. It was an old ploy of theirs. The bridge even at its quiet moments was minor official mayhem, and if the captain even *looked* busy you kept your distance and waited until he specifically noted and then acknowledged your presence. By standing quietly but in full view of the man who ran *Nimitz*, Dan Thurman was giving his boss a brief but vital interval in which to make his immediate first judgments of their visitor. And Thurman, as Yelland's chief alter ego, knew very well the captain was as much in the dark as anyone else with the presence of Lasky. Finally Thurman received the imperceptible nod and as he led Lasky forward, Yelland turned in his seat to greet them. Yelland clasped hands strongly.

"Mr. Lasky, I hope your trip was a pleasant one," Yelland said for openers.

Lasky nodded. "It was all that and more," he said pleasantly. "A bird's eye view of Pearl Harbor, the

Hawaiian coastline, an impressive panorama of our fleet, and a delightful view of those Russian trawlers." Lasky nodded to the front of the carrier. "It would also seem that despite what the helicopter crew told me, the weather is going to be something less than balmy."

"You're observant," Yelland said slowly. "I like that. What else did you see?"

"A vast cloud of noise, mass confusion, hysterical movement, enormous power, and great numbers of people wearing uniforms of strange colors and markings, all of them dashing about doing things I don't understand, and doing it so well it convinces me I am very much the neophyte in your midst."

Yelland couldn't help the laugh that burst from him. "Officially, then, Mr. Lasky, welcome aboard. I've never heard a better description of a carrier in my life. But you're right. You *are* the neophyte among us. Everything that takes place about you, from the intolerable of the nuclear reactors to a sailor's dreams of a pretty girl, has its time and place for *Nimitz*."

Lasky turned his gaze to the horizon. Gray haze had been slowly but definitely transforming into ominous darkness, and they could all feel a definite reaction of the great carrier to seas under growing disturbance. Lasky, not too pleased with the willingness of even Captain Yelland to brand him as neophyte, no matter if the term had been self-inflicted, took the opportunity to jab. "Well, sir, it's good to see you're as human as us landlovers about not being able to forecast the weather."

The frown came again to Yelland's brow. "I would enjoy a contest on that issue, Mr. Lasky, but from what we can both see, I would lose hands down. Well, let it hang for the moment." Yelland gestured at several other men, who approached at his signal.

"Commander Ross Damon, our operations officer." Yelland nodded toward Lasky. "Commander, Mr.

Warren Lasky. He will have access to all command and operational centers of this vessel, except, and only except, if his personal safety is compromised."

"Yes, sir. Mr. Lasky, welcome to *Nimitz*." They shook hands.

"And this is Lieutenant Artemus Perry, officer of the deck."

"Nice to have you with us, sir," Perry said, shaking hands.

"You may not think so later," Yelland thrust into the exchange of niceties. Despite himself, Lasky felt a growing like for this crusty old man of wars past.

"Why not, Captain?" Lasky asked, meeting bluntness with its own cudgel.

"It's obvious, Mr. Lasky, you're not here on a pleasure cruise. It's equally obvious you were sent here under the highest priority I have ever seen given to any civilian, and that includes the secretary of the navy and the president of our country." Yelland's friendly view had retreated behind those devastating blue eyes. "You were preceded with a coded message, and in the highest code we have, that this vessel, and this entire task force, was to alter course and be certain that you would be delivered by helicopter to this flight deck, and then brought here to meet me. Which is what we are doing right at this moment. Which gives me the opening for my next question to you."

"Yes?"

"What in the hell are you doing here, who are you, and what are you looking for?" Yelland demanded.

"Thurman, here, asked me the same question," Lasky responded.

"Give me the same answer, then."

"I don't know."

The silence held heavy, making all the more evident the growing reaction of the carrier to a more turbulent sea. Finally Yelland found his voice. "That's ridiculous, Mr. Lasky."

Lasky didn't offer a smile. And he didn't fidget. "With all due respect, Captain Yelland, it is the absolute truth. You know my name. I'm what my company calls a master communicator with computer systems. I design, communicate with, and improve upon them. Systems analysis is the field. That's who I am and what I do. I am employed by Tideman Industries. They designed and *built* this carrier. *I* designed its computers. And as to why I'm here, well, the orders came directly from Richard Tideman. In writing, and with the highest priority. My orders were to get from my office to where I'm standing right now, and Captain, let me tell you one thing more. I do *not* know why I'm here."

Yelland sighed. He appeared a bit mollified with Lasky's response. "I must say that is the damnedest reason for holding up an entire task force. Just so a man who hasn't any idea of why he's here could get here in the first place."

Lasky held down laughter that wanted to burst free with the obviously contradictory aspects of the moment. "Captain, may I ask *you* a question?"

"By all means, sir."

"I was scheduled, today, to be in a special meeting of the National Security Agency in Washington. Not substituting for Tom Hyde on this whacko mystery cruise. No offense, captain, but I'm as miffed and puzzled as you are. So *who* outside of Tideman Industries signed the orders that turned the navy upside down?"

Yelland held Lasky's eyes for a long moment. "Mr. Lasky, as much as it pains me to say this, the orders came from the White House. I—" He hesitated as a sudden gust of wind howled audibly. He looked at angry skies and whitecaps that had seemed to appear from nowhere. He made a sudden decision. "Mr. Lasky, we'll attend to the mysteries later. Aside from all else, forgive my seeming rudeness. It's not intentional. I would consider it a favor if *you* would consider yourself a guest with us and accept the hospitality of this bridge."

His words took Lasky off balance. "Why, of course, sir."

"Good. Dan," Yelland said to Thurman, "please square away Mr. Lasky in his quarters. When that is done, he is free to return here on his own schedule. Forgive me, Mr. Lasky, but I must attend to a storm that doesn't exist."

Lightning punctuated his words. Lasky looked about him. The same brooding reflection, the same deepening sense of mystery about this storm that so obviously affected Yelland, was reaching to the other members of the bridge.

"Yes, sir," Lasky said, amazed with his own willingness to address Matthew Yelland with full military courtesy.

☆ 4 ☆

Lasky walked alongside Corporal Stanley Kullman, moving down a long and straight corridor lit by strips of fluorescent lights and seemingly stretching to infinity. It wasn't a steady walk for *Nimitz* had developed a motion quite different from what Lasky experienced when he first set foot on the carrier flight deck. But the marine ignored the rolling and pitching motions and Lasky did his best to emulate his guide.

Kullman glanced at his charge. "Sir, you've been assigned to navigator's in-port cabin. I don't know why they call it that," he added self-consciously, "because why would anyone need a navigator when you were on shore?"

"Tradition, corporal. The navy's great on tradition. It floats in huge jellied seas of tradition."

"Yes, sir," Kullman said. There came a pause while he digested what he'd heard; then he dismissed it. "Uh, anyway, sir, your cabin connects with CAG."

"What the hell's a cag?"

"Commander Air Group. But we call him air wing commander. That's—"

"Hold it, corporal. CAG aren't the initials for air wing commander."

Corporal Kullman stopped, seemingly thunderstruck. "I never thought of that, sir," he said hollowly.

"I'm sure no one else did, either," came the retort.

"Good old tradition. Keep moving, will you? I've already banged so many knees on these hatches I'm about to fall down. By the way, I assume CAG is a living, breathing human, since he requires a cabin?"

Kullman struggled to run the mental race and barely made it. "Uh, yes, sir, sure. That's Commander Richard Owens. I think you were still topside when he landed in that Tomcat."

"I remember," Lasky said, nodding. "My God, man, how much longer is it?"

Kullman pointed. "Right down there, sir." They stopped before a door with the number B3284. Kullman opened the door and led the way inside. It was surprisingly roomy, to Lasky's unexpected pleasure. A single bunk, an unusual desk with all manner of lights and plug-in connections, closet lockers, wall speakers, and even a comfortable armchair. Yet it was intended and had been used for work as much as for private occupancy and that greatly satisfied Warren Lasky. "Sir, I'll be waiting just outside while you get squared away. If there's anything you need, just holler, will you?"

"Got it, corporal. Thanks."

Lasky opened the closet. Jesus, they *had* been given a priority on him! Six sets of slacks, three flight jackets, even two flight suits. Several sweaters and other articles of clothing. He went to the dresser across the room. Just as he had come quickly to expect. Underwear, socks, shirts, shoes, waterproof boots—the works, and everything marked in his name with his size. Someone had radioed in all the data from Tideman Industries and a couple of very expert, very fast people in the quartermaster had selected, or modified, everything to Lasky's exact size. He returned to the desk, opening his attache case. Good! One of those desk plug-in connections was to the aircraft carrier's computer system, which, he knew, would be available to him on a "time allowable and noninterference" basis. Although for the life of him he still didn't know what the devil he was supposed to be doing here.

He walked to the bathroom door. It carried a small sign that read HEAD, and only the association brought back an oblique memory that navy jargon held sway here. He opened the door and stepped inside. Comfortable shower, a sink with two cabinets; the usual stuff one might expect aboard a ship, but this was upper-level officer country, and the design and fashionings were what he might expect aboard a cruise vessel instead. So much the better. He started back to his own cabin when an unexpectedly long, shuddering roll tipped the deck beneath him, and the door to the adjoining cabin swung open. Lasky looked into the cabin—he remembered: CAG, and that would be Richard Owens who lived here. His eyes widened slightly.

Owens, whoever and whatever CAG might be as a pilot, was also very obviously an intense, devoted student of history. Military history as a dominant theme, Lasky observed, from pictures of sea and air battles of World War II taped on every available inch of bulkhead space and onto lockers and cabinets. Without thinking of what he was doing, drawn instinctively to what was clearly an outstanding effort, Lasky moved slowly into Owens's cabin. Model airplanes and warships poked out from beneath masses of paper. Heavy tomes of history were piled up against cabinets and were stuffed beneath the bunk. On the desk rested an electric typewriter and sheets of manuscripts and notes to each side. A bulletin board over the desk bulged with notes. Lasky stood by the desk and read the manuscript cover. *The Pacific at War.* Beneath the title was the author's name. Richard T. Owens, USN. Lasky turned the page slowly. More and more fascinated, he finally sat at the desk, wrapped up in what was clearly a brilliant and incisive work. Twenty minutes later he was still there, unmoving, totally absorbed—not hearing the slight sound of the door opening from the passageway. The first he knew of anyone else's presence was an icy jab.

"Anything else you'd like to see?"

Lasky turned, startled. "Oh. I didn't hear you come in."

"That's damned obvious. There are some personal letters in the lower left drawer when you're finished."

"Jesus, I didn't . . . I mean—" Lasky rose to his feet. "Owens?" He tapped the manuscript cover. "The same, right? Richard T. Owens. The author of this, well, I've never seen anything like it." His words rushed on. "Look, I apologize. I didn't mean to intrude. The ship tilted, and I was in the bathroom and the door was open, and I'm a bit of a history buff myself, and oh, shit. I'm Warren Lasky and I was assigned the cabin next to yours and I've screwed things up before they even started and I really *do* apologize." He extended his hand. To his enormous relief Owens shook firmly, then stepped to one side and tossed his flight gear onto his bunk.

"You're new here, then," he said after a pause.

"New? The paint behind my ears isn't even dry."

Owens chuckled. "Okay, I think I understand. But you'd best understand something, also, Mr. Lasky—"

"Please. Warren. You know, prying neighbors and all that."

Owens laughed aloud this time. "I was trying to explain to you—and I don't know your background—is that those of us who go to sea rate the most important personal possession aboard a ship to be our privacy. Probably because we get so very damned little of it."

Lasky gestured, feeling helpless. "Commander, I understand and—"

Owens waved it away. "Once is good enough for me. I believe you."

"Then I'll tell you something else, Commander. I'm more than just a buff on Second World War. I wrote my thesis on that war and the manner in which it contributed to the emergence of the first cybernetics systems as dictated by global military requirements."

"Am I getting the opening paragraph, mister?" There was a glint in Owens's eye that tried to hide a smile.

"Oops. Got carried away there," Lasky admitted. "No; no speeches. I just wanted to repeat that you are *very* good at your history. The way you mesh events into a geopolitical situation no matter what the military impression . . . well, if you fly as well as you write history, then you're the Red Baron for sure."

"You fly, Mr. Lasky?"

"Only in a fanciful way. I'm a hell of a passenger, though."

"You mentioned cybernetics before as a thesis, if I recall."

"Right," Lasky confirmed. "I talk to computers and they talk to me."

"And you're a historian also."

"Heavy amateur."

"You sound like you cross a lot of lines," observed Owens.

"Precisely. Cross, recross, trip across, hatchweave and thatchweave."

"What exactly *is* your job?"

Lasky smiled. "You've heard the expression think tank?"

"Sure." Owens was a bit deprecating. "I've heard of them. Kind of a sanatorium for the seriously overeducated."

Lasky laughed. "I'll use that at the right time. But it goes way beyond that. I'm master computer controller for the Tideman Institute. Maybe you'd recognize the name easier if I said Tideman Industries."

Owens whistled. "Tideman built this floating city, if I recall."

"They did just that."

"And we're run by a master computer system, and you're—" He stabbed a finger at Lasky.

"Yep. That's me. I designed the thinking cap for *Nimitz*."

"What brings you aboard? Problems with the big brains?"

"None that I know of. Frankly, and I've already told this to Captain Yelland, I don't know why I'm here. Hush-hush orders, very mysterious. Get your ass out on the waves, and a big chopper brought me here, and I arrived just before you fell down on the flight deck in that Tomcat of yours."

Owens nodded slowly. He wasn't wasting any more words than he had to. Not now. Not after he'd learned who, and what, this civilian was before him. "What would you say described your job on an everyday basis?"

Lasky looked at Owens with an instant new respect. The semantic presentation of that query reflected one hell of a fast mind. "My job with Tideman, and wherever they send me, is simply to look at the way people—like you, for example—do things, and if I can then think of any, well, alternatives is a good word for it, I write 'em down and anticipate their effects, and I submit a report."

"You're on *Nimitz* now. On the high seas and not in some think tank or department store computer center. You think you'll find some changes here?"

Lasky didn't back off an inch. "Commander, there are always alternatives." He motioned to Owens's manuscript. "And you of all people know that."

Owens nodded slowly. "Well, I can't deny that if—" The telephone interrupted him. He snatched it up, said, "Yes, sir," several times, looked strangely at Warren Lasky, and finished the conversation with a hard look on his face. "Right away, sir," he said and returned the phone to its cradle. "That was the captain," he said carefully. "Your presence is requested on the bridge as soon as possible. I'm to bring you there personally."

Lasky had a blank expression as a response. "What's happening?"

"From what I can gather, the forecast for today was bright and clear."

"Yes. I was also told that."

"Our met officer is gnashing teeth and tearing out his hair. Because according to him, this storm is impossible."

"It's more than that," Lasky said, not asking.

"Yes, it is. All communications are going to hell in a handbasket, and those computers you designed, Mr. Lasky, are on the edge of insanity. The captain said they are *rejecting* all data input about this storm."

"That means the computers refuse to accept the data as real. But the storm *is* out there."

"That's your problem, mister. Shall we go?" Owens clapped his hands to his ears and winced with pain. "Holy Jesus! It feels like an icepick in my ears!"

"I—I don't feel anything," Lasky said, worried at the pain he was seeing.

Owens shook his head. "Gone now. But for a moment there . . . wow. I hear higher than most people, and whatever that was, I've never heard it before on this carrier." His face took on a grim look. "I don't know what the hell's going on, but we'd better shag it. If we can, we'll stop off at the weather office on the way to the bridge. Let's go."

☆ 5 ☆

Captain Matthew Yelland, strapped into his command chair on the bridge of *Nimitz*, felt the hair rising along the back of his neck. The lifting of his nape had something to do with the barometer going crazy— going *up* instead of down in this storm exploding into being about them. It had to do with the feel of the sea and the tremors nudging their way through the carrier. It also had a lot to do with several decades of experience and a life saving instinct that comes only through many years of slipping a single wave's length away from imminent death or disaster. *Nimitz* was hammering itself through a heavy sea that couldn't exist. This weather had never shown any indication of existence on the charts; it didn't have a hint on the satellite photos; even the other instruments seemed to have been blind to it. More than that, every other ship in their task force had been absolutely silent about the deteriorating weather. They had spread out because of the storm and now *Nimitz* was out of touch with anything else afloat in this part of the ocean, including those pesky Russian trawlers that shadowed them day and night.

Whatever was happening stank to high heaven. Matt Yelland had learned long ago that the starkly unusual can swiftly churn itself into the starkly dangerous. *Nimitz* could handle the rough sea. But the sea was supposed to be calm. More than that, dusk was approaching and he could smell rain in the air. He looked up at the low dark clouds scudding along swiftly and he cursed at storm demons that had no business showing up unannounced.

Several men came up to him. "Owens. Good. Damned glad you're here. And Mr. Lasky. Don't waste any time, if you please, sir," Yelland said without pause. "Right over there," he pointed. "A separate cubicle. Eddie Duncan is in there. He's a computer expert, but right now he wants to cry because our computers act like they're stoned on acid. Get in there, Mr. Lasky, and see if you can sober tham up."

Lasky nodded. This wasn't fun and games. These people were deadly serious. He left immediately for the cubicle, went inside, introduced himself to Commander Eddie Duncan. "You're Lasky. The captain said you were an oracle from Cybernetics Mountain. I hope that's better than Disneyworld." Duncan crashed a fist against the communications console. "Talk to them if you can, damnit! Because they're telling me that, based on everything they're taking into their data banks, we and this whole bloody carrier don't even exist any more!"

Lasky studied Duncan only for a moment and sat down before the master console. Lights flashed and flickered insanely before him. If anything, that was a good sign the computer was about to suffer a nervous breakdown. Lasky's fingers flew along the communications keys. Musiclike sounds fluted through the room and as the astonished Duncan stared over his shoulder, the lights calmed, finally eased to a steady, familiar glow. "Now," Lasky said grimly, "we have a heart-to-heart talk."

Yelland studied the seas that grew wilder and meaner with every passing minute. Water sprayed with needlelike force against the thick Plexiglas. He turned to Owens.

"Dick, are we all crazy, or did we really have a forecast for severe clear earlier?"

"We did, sir."

"Look at that sea." White foam pounded over growing waves. "Forty knots and increasing. Damn. What was it like when you were coming in?"

"Captain, it was royal blue upstairs. Some high thin cirrus and that was all. Fifty miles out from the flight deck I started feeling some chop in the air. By the time I was set for landing the deck was already into a good roll and pitch. I didn't believe it. It happened so fast it was like going over a falls."

Yelland pursed his lips. "What about the horizon?"

"Strange. Gray haze. Like thick smog that's yellow or orange, only this was gray. I've never seen anything like it. Not even in the Aleutians."

Yelland looked up at Owens. "Get me Black Cloud, *now*," he ordered.

They weren't doing any better in the meteorological office where the mood was frowns, low curses, and questions that had no answers to them. Men clustered about the weather satellite printout and made rude gestures at the equipment. "You know what?" a technician called to the others. "If this thing is right, then every goddamned metsat has either crashed or left earth orbit."

"Get stuffed," came a retort, but they knew he was serious. They all felt the same frustration. Nothing fit.

"Clear weather, right?" snapped another man.

"Shee-yit," came the answering gruff snarl, "yesterday's forecast is always on the button."

Lieutenant Neville Christ, duty officer for the watch, growled at the others. "Cool it," he ordered. "We've still got planes out there and it's getting dark and I wouldn't want to be those guys trying to land on a carrier when the weather people don't even know what's happening *right now*. Let's try to make some sense out of all this." The men about him sobered instantly. Landing a hot jet on a carrier in daylight was a controlled crash. Landing it at night was a controlled crash and a lot of high-level prayers. Adding a wildly pitching deck to the scenario meant a vision of violently exploding fuel and white-hot steel tearing men apart.

In a corner of the room, cut off from the sounds of the rest of the group, a seaman was listening on headphones to a radio broadcast of a heavyweight fight from Las Vegas. His fists clenched and he threw imaginary punches as the ring broadcaster rattled off the details of the battle. A look of confusion came over the seaman's face as the transmission disappeared in a steadily increasing hash of static. He removed the headphones and stared at them in disbelief.

"What the hell?" he complained. "I'm losing the signal." He held the gaze of the others. "Don't you guys understand? It's a comsat broadcast. You know, satellite microwave transmission. It *can't* go out." He shook his head. "But it *did*," he murmured.

Black Cloud stood before the computer teletype printout. His eyes widened, but his expression had nothing to do with a message. The machine operated in erratic fits and starts as though its current input were surging. This had never happened before. Not in the most modern warship ever built with massive nuclear reactors feeding steady current. Impossible. He stared at the machine as paper stuttered its way free. His frown deepened as he read the printout, and the frown became a glare as Lieutenant Christ called to him. "Commander! It's the bridge. The captain wants you and on the double!"

"Tell the bridge I'm on my way," Black Cloud snarled. He tore off the sheet, gathered rolled charts beneath his arm and started out of the room. He stopped for a moment and looked back. "Get every mother on duty status as of *right now*." Then he was gone.

He ran all the way to the bridge, stopped short for

a moment as he looked through the thick windows. Holy Jesus. They were headed straight for a vertical curtain of ugly black clouds. Lightning spit eerily through the darkness. Then he went directly to the captain. No time now for protocol. He spread the teletype printout and the last computer-generated charts before Yelland, Owens, and several other officers. He tapped the papers. "Captain, I don't have any excuses. This isn't a case of my making an error or even being wrong. This weather simply can't exist!"

"But it certainly does," Yelland rebuked him mildly.

"Sir, that's not my point. It's not just *me*. It's the weather satellites, the reports from all across the Pacific, the reports of commercial airliners, the reports from the submarines. You know what we have out there, sir? A violent storm, obviously, but one that's contained in a very small area! And that's as impossible as the rest of it. Look, sir, everything I forecast earlier today was based on hard data and real-time observation and. . . ." He took a deep breath. "It just can't be! All the laws of nature, sir, they're being raped!"

"Very poetic, but useless," Yelland growled. "Explain yourself."

"Sir, please accept that I've interrogated every communications satellite covering this area. That's military and civilian. I'm talking about comsats, not the weather stuff orbiting over us. Captain, nothing shows on a single transmitter and no one is reporting this storm, and—"

"No one?"

"Sir, outside of us no one even seems to know this damned storm exists." Black Cloud gestured in frustration. "We never got so much as a single picture of this storm before we lost all contact with the satellite matrix. And I mean every kind of satellite. The only thing out of the ordinary was that smudge we saw before. Captain, the printout machine is working perfectly. Or it was until it quit a short while ago. But that smudge, well, it wasn't in the machine. It's some sort of electromagnetic interference that screwed up the transmission from the metsat over us at the time. And you know what's crazier, sir? The winds."

"I can see that," Yelland said grumpily.

"No, sir, you can't. What's as crazy as everything else is that we've been holding course, but the wind has gone around more than seven hundred degrees in the last fifteen minutes. The same thing is happening with the ocean currents. The water temperature went through a five-degree drop in just five minutes, as if we'd entered a completely different current. Except that the temperature is still dropping, so it can't be just a current. We've covered too much distance for that."

Dick Owens felt the electricity from the men about him. "Black Cloud's at a disadvantage, Captain. He had his corns removed. It's ruined his career as a weather officer."

Captain Yelland smiled thinly and nodded for Black Cloud to go on. "The sum of it all, sir, is that not only is the weather all screwed up, but we're running into other problems."

"Such as our computers going ape," Yelland said calmly. "What other good news have you for me?"

"I forgot the one about the barometer," Black Cloud answered.

"I know that one. It's going up and that's as impossible as everything else."

"Yes, sir. But we're also encountering severe electrical problems aboard ship, Captain, and our electronic contact outside our area is going to hell in a handbasket."

"Spare me the poetics."

"Sir, the equipment is on. Current flows. But amps, volts, ohms, watts—are all "off normal. We're getting current and resistance surges. It's not from the reactor. I've been in touch with Commander Moss, sir. It's something else affecting us through the entire ship."

Lt. Commander Walt Kaufman stood to the side. Yelland looked at his communications officer. "You confirm, Walt?"

Kaufman's brow was deeply furrowed. "Sir, I'll keep it to the point. *Nimitz* is cut off from all contact of every kind."

Yelland's brows went up. "Go to red alert." That was the open war, reserved for Hell itself, band.

"We did, Captain." Kaufman didn't need to say the effort had been fruitless.

Warren Lasky emerged from the computer control room across the bridge. In the few seconds of his crossing back to Yelland's chair they were treated to a tremendous crash of rain against the bridge, hard enough to be audible through the thick Plexiglas. The lightning was almost steady and the feeling beneath their feet more uncomfortable with every passing moment. The captain studied Lasky carefully, waiting. "To the point, sir, if you please," Yelland instructed.

Lasky stood before him like a stone. "To the point, Captain. The computers have gone bananas. They have literally just instructed this carrier to submerge and to launch an all-out nuclear strike against Bolivia." Lasky let out a long sigh. "All computer contact between *Nimitz* and every other cybernetics system is down. We're—and this is the only way I know to say it—totally isolated from the world."

Yelland looked at him. "Anybody else have anything?"

Black Cloud tapped his papers. "Yes, sir. One item. The only scientific anomaly I can pinpoint is that we are dead center in that smudge we saw earlier on the metsat photos."

"*Let me see that.*" The urgency in Lasky's voice caught them all by surprise. He shouldered his way roughly into their midst and grabbed the photo printouts. "I'll be goddamned," he murmured. He had their attention riveted on him.

"What is it?" Yelland snapped.

"It's the only thing that fits, that's what it is, Captain!" Lasky banged his fist against the paper. "I've seen this same sort of smudge, as you call it, before. From satellite photos. Even hand-held cameras, in fact, from Skylab. This effect, what we call a smudge, is a field. A force field, a matrix; we don't know. All we do know is that they appear. They seem to be an interreaction between the electromagnetic field of the planet and, maybe, just maybe, an interruption in the flow of gravity waves. The waves pulse through the galaxy and we record them about once every three hours, like a very slow breaker on a shore. If the two interreact, well," again his hand hit the paper, "we believe it's possible to get a tremendous electromagnetic effect. Almost a swirling motion." He looked up at Black Cloud. "Have you had any cyclonic wind effects?"

Black Cloud's eyes went wide. "The wind's gone around the compass twice in the last hour."

Lasky nodded. "Captain Yelland, even the Skylab astronauts couldn't figure out this effect. The real-time photos they were taking would show interference like this, well, this smudge, but when they looked down they couldn't see anything unusual in the visual band. Yet there was localized, intense storm activity. Later, the pictures they were taking at this time showed no details—only this same smudge. Even the cosmonauts aboard their Salyuts had the problem."

Dick Owens took one corner of the printout. "Warren, was there any particular geographical area where this was picked up?"

"Ninety percent of all such activity was in the Atlantic, well off the Florida coast."

Silence followed that remark. "Jesus, not that Devil's Triangle crap. Ghosts and goblins. They looked at Commander Dan Thurman; his face confirmed his disgust at even considering anything unusual to do with the area known as the Devil's Triangle or the Bermuda Triangle, as it was also known.

Kaufman motioned for attention. "Commander, we're in the Pacific, not off Florida."

"Stop it," Yelland ordered. "Where we are doesn't matter. What is happening is everything. Mr. Lasky, can you add anything else?"

Lasky shrugged. "The computers will not function because of an overwhelming magnetic field that, for want of a better description, continually short-circuits their magnetic flow. I have never encountered this situation before and I cannot explain it."

Yelland nodded to his met officer. Black Cloud looked as dark as his name. "Sir, whatever is happening is impossible. And I think it's going to get a lot worse before it's over."

"Good point. Mr. Kaufman, is there any contact with or monitoring of those Russian trawlers?"

"No, sir. Not on our wavelengths or theirs. May I add, sir, we have no contact with anyone or anything, anywhere, including our own support vessels. All satellite contact is, well, squeezed out is the best term I have for it."

Dick Owens glanced at Yelland. "Sir, is there a chance this entire effect—the electromagnetic effect, I mean—could be generated *by* the Russians?"

"I don't know. Anybody have anything to offer?"

"Impossible," Lasky said immediately. "The only way to blank out electromagnetic signals is through the detonation of high-yield nuclear or thermonuclear devices at high altitude. You would then get a total sponging effect in the communications band, right on up through UHF, microwave, the works. But the effect would be totally electrical and electromagnetic. It could not possibly produce a physical storm effect like this."

Yelland picked up a red phone by his chair. The simple act of lifting that one particular telephone activated every priority command channel on *Nimitz*. The buzzing and crackling from the phone could be heard by the entire group surrounding the captain.

"It's dead," Yelland said. "Use direct line communications from this point on."

Communications hash stalked the carrier. The last semblance of contact with the outside world came from wide-eyed pilots still in the air trying to reach the safety of *Nimitz*. In carrier air traffic control (CATSEE) men cursed their gear and worked frantically to overcome goblins of static and wavering sounds of their highly advanced equipment. In the electromagnetic sense their world had gone crazy. These were the specialists who handled all traffic to and from *Nimitz* and, electronically, they were being robbed of their senses.

A radio operator kept a microphone close to his lips, talking urgently. "Lightfoot Eighteen, Lightfoot Eighteen, this is Strawboss. Repeat, this is Strawboss. Come in, come in. Over."

A voice crackled weakly in his headphones and from the bulkhead speakers, a great blurring of words and static. "—is Lightfoot—can't—over—"

"Say again, Lightfoot! We're reading you! Repeat your last call! Over!"

Again the distorted voice gabbled at them. "—problems—radio gear—something—vertigo—" Sudden, crashing static. "Fading—over—"

The operator tried valiantly. "Lightfoot Eighteen, this is Strawboss, keep transmitting, keep transmitting so we can get a fix on you. Repeat your last call, repeat your last call, you're garbled. Keep transmitting. Over."

Static hissed at them. Another crewman standing by snatched at a phone.

Lt. Commander Walt Kaufman had left the bridge for the observation complex high above the flight deck, where he would take over as air boss. He surveyed the mad world of the rising storm. Around Kaufman were three walls of unbreakable armored glass and he could see the entire length of the flight deck. Kaufman brought his phone to his ear. "Kaufman here. How goes it in comm?"

"Sir, intermittent, badly broken, mostly hash. Lightfoot Eighteen is trying to get in. He's reported radio problems and he said something about vertigo."

"Jesus," Kaufman swore. "We can't bring him in if we can't talk to him. You getting anything on the transponders? What? You're not painting them? Go to the highest frequencies we've got. Try anything. Yeah, well, hang in there. How'd you like to be the man out there?"

Kaufman was deep in thought for several moments. He had some new pilots out there. If they could hold their headings by using their directional gyros, that didn't depend upon electrical flow; because every fighter had a backup vacuum system, they could get to the carrier in the next few minutes. Kaufman called Dick Owens. CAG would have to make the decision. "Dick? Kaufman here. Look, we've got every light on this barge turned on. Why don't we fire flares every fifteen seconds? The biggest damned things we've got. We can get some good altitude with them and they can be seen almost through a brick wall."

Owens snatched at the slim hope. "Good move, Walt. Okay. Let them go every fifteen seconds and keep them going. And if you do get any clear contact, well, the way things are going, trying to bring them in here could be the worst thing of all. If you read anyone, bingo them."

"You know what you're saying?"

Owens' voice was harsh. "I sure as hell do, mister. *Bingo them*. That's an order. Tell them to head for Pearl. That's in the clear as far as we know, and we've got another carrier between us and the islands. They can transmit mayday on their transponders and they'll have a chance with *Halsey* taking them aboard."

☆ 6 ☆

Dick Owens went directly to Matt Yelland. "Captain, they went to the highest power for transmission we could muster. Six planes out there and five of them acknowledged. They've gone for max altitude on their bingo orders. They'll try to make *Halsey* or go back to Pearl."

Yelland's eyes narrowed. "What about number six? Who and what is he?"

"Bob Stanton. New pilot. He's in an A-7."

"How far out?"

"Sir, we don't know. Encoding altimeter, transponder; none of it reads worth a damn. We've got intermittent voice contact. We're trying to get him down. He's got some kind of problem. Fuel from the sound of it and he's got to come in."

"Take personal charge of the operation," Yelland ordered.

"Yes, sir." As Owens took off, Yelland stared with growing dismay at the bizarre electrical effects of the storm. In all his years in the navy he had never seen a ceaseless barrage of lightning that was the only illumination down what appeared to be an enormous tunnel of utter blackness.

Dick Owens's voice crashed between decks and on the flight deck of the carrier. "This is air boss. All

47

hands, let's get with it. I want a ready deck immediately. Emergency conditions, all hands. Man your huffers and check your wires. Move it, move it. Let's get it together. We've got a Corsair out there trying to get in. Go, go."

Flight deck crews were in frenzied but well-disciplined action. Men in different-colored jackets and helmets moved about purposefully. All crash equipment was at the ready. Dick Owens and the men with him stared gloomily at the violent horizon. Owens couldn't believe that goddamned sky. It was turning from black to a dismal green, seeming to glow from within itself, and turning sallow every face about him.

A seaman tugged at Owens's sleeve. "Excuse me, sir. Would you look at the PPI radarscope? We can't make any sense out of it."

Owens hesitated. What the hell; they wouldn't make an issue out of the PPI unless they had reason enough in the face of all the other crap busting loose about them. Owens moved to the radar seat and peered into the scope presentation. What he saw on the glass was unbelievable. The sweep line pivoted around the face of the scope, showed the normal amount of sea return, picked out the precipitation, indicated the hash of lightning. But within the edge of the storm's ragged limits there had appeared a wavering brilliant line. Owens lifted his head to study the other men.

"You saw that line also? Anybody know what the hell it is?" No one answered; they shook their heads. Owens cursed to himself. He could fight anything he'd ever encountered in his life. But this was beyond all knowledge and all reason. A seaman brought him coffee and he nodded his thanks. Around him men were taking on a new air of readiness, as if everyone could feel some strange sort of hell about to break loose with the weather. Owens looked out across the pitching flight deck. Every man available was securing for the worst. Owens studied the coffee mug in his hand. The mug was vibrating strangely, the coffee almost burbling. Jesus. He glanced up. That green light along the horizon was getting stronger.

A shift-break crew assembled in the mess. CPO Jaime Castillo was worried. Unless everything was completely secured down, the weather could turn his enormous kitchen area into its own kind of devil's broth. But there were men out there who needed food and hot liquids and Castillo rattled off orders to his men. They moved as quickly as the rolling deck would permit. The seated men being served were deep in animated conversation. The atmosphere gripped them all, and the scuttlebutt of freaked-out computers and electronic hash was all over the ship.

Lieutenant John Harris, deck boss for hangar level two, slipped into a seat. He reached for a coffee mug, joining the others in the light-serious conversation about the crazy weather. He never got his coffee; the ship took what felt like an enormous jolt and lurched suddenly. It was like a city heeling over to one side. The only man standing near by was a steward with a full tray that flew from his hands and crashed to the deck with a clatter of metal, breaking glass, and spraying liquids. The steward went down, his hands flailing wildly for balance. No one could move fast enough to help; he screamed as his left arm snapped.

But Harris had no thought for the man. He had an immediate vision of that blow on his hangar deck. "What the hell was that?" he shouted. He jumped to his feet, starting back to the flight deck, when the ship gave another shuddering yaw and that tremendous jolting motion. At the same time the speakers through the carrier clamored with the alarm for Condition Zulu. *Full emergency.* "Oh, shit," Harris swore quietly and struggled to leave the mess. Other men streamed behind him to their stations.

The minute Harris checked onto the flight deck his number one hand told him that everything was under control. "They want you on the bridge, pronto, Lieutenant," he heard. Harris went quickly along a corridor and then turned to a ladder, sprinting upward three steps at a time. He was on the third level, breathing heavily, when the speakers came alive again. My God—they were bringing in a fighter in this weather! Harris ran all the way to the bridge and stopped as if struck a physical blow. For the first time since this weather had hit them he had a true idea of what was happening. He saw the ocean building heavily, and he looked, startled, at the ghastly green glow on the horizon. He heard Owens's voice.

"We've got no choice. We bring him in, no matter what. The poor bastard can't eject into that ocean! His only chance is to land. Yes. Do it, and fast!"

A radar technician grasped Harris's arm. "We got an A-7 out there. Stanton. We were able to bingo the others back to the *Halsey* or to Pearl. Stanton has got a bunch of trouble on his hands."

"Commander Owens!" The voice carried above all other sounds.

"Go!" Owens snapped.

"CATSEE One here, sir. We've got a weak skin track. He's maybe ten miles out. We can't be sure."

"Stay with him!"

"Yes, sir. We got part of his transmission. He cannot get his arrestor hook down."

"Jesus," Owens wore. He hit the comm switch for all channels. Owens's voice boomed through the entire carrier. "We have a Corsair coming in now, about ten miles out on straight final. He can't get his arrestor hook down. All hands full alert. Deck crew, rig the barricade. Rig the barricade. This is no drill. I repeat, this is no drill. Rig the barricade!"

Men moved as swiftly as wing and rolling deck and vicious rain would permit. Owens took another call from radar. "Sir, approach control here. We're still skin-tracking. The pilot . . . well, sir, he's just taken what seems to be mutiple lightning strikes."

Good God. "Is he under control?" Owens snapped.

"Affirmative, sir."

"Stay with him. Keep talking to him. Tell him the barricade is up. Keep him drilling right in, got it?"

"Yes, sir."

Captain Matthew Yelland waited for the right moment. As the deck barricade was being rigged, he knew he had a few precious moments that could be critical for his men. He squeezed his transmit button and his voice carried through *Nimitz.*

"This is the captain speaking. I want all of you to know that we may be running into something different from anything we've ever encountered before. We're in some kind of freak storm, and we've picked up what looks like a pretty mean squall line. That's all the radar can tell us, but whatever it it, it should hit us in the next several minutes. You know this ship can take anything, so every one of you that isn't on immediate duty right now, secure everything within reach. Batten it all down and hang on."

Commander Dan Thurman looked at his captain. "Sir, you know what? You were so calm just then that I think you scared the shit out of this whole ship."

Yelland nodded slowly. "Funny you should say that. Because it's just how I feel."

They secured aircraft and trucks and equipment with cables and chains, they locked cabinet doors, they tied equipment down with ropes and they jammed lockers beneath bunks—everything they could see that might move was secured. Those planes still on deck were triple secured with cables and chains. Every deck hook that was available was raised from its flush position so that a small forest of wires and cables ran to the sturdier warbirds. The last helicopters, much more fragile than the slab-winged jets, had been taken below decks by elevator where the ritual of cables and chains was repeated.

On the flight deck, eyes were turned anxiously to

the sky, looking aft, where the stern of the great carrier made a mockery of the word horizon. Great swells heaved along the ocean surface, and the deck itself, despite computerized stabilization equipment, was like a flat-backed snake crawling over a sand dune. The landing signal officer stood by at the automatic guidance system for approach, knowing the hell Stanton was going through in that A-7; the LSO was ready in case the automatic system went out. He wore a body harness, strapped in four ways to the deck so he wouldn't lose his footing, like a stunt man about to do wing-walking atop a plane. If necessary, he would use the old illuminated hand paddles to bring in Stanton. In the meantime, the automatic light system with mirrors was still working.

The deck crew had completed its emergency rigging of the barricade and the deck was devoid of all personnel. That A-7 was little more than a winged bomb about to impact on an insanely-pitching-rolling deck. A shout went up. "There he is! I can see his lights!"

And they could. The Corsair was still invisible in the blackness but its flashing beacons and strobes and the landing lights were on and unmistakable. In radar approach the operator was jubilant—he could hear Stanton clearly! He began his reply and then his face turned white as Stanton's voice went shrill.

"I've just lost the lights! The approach lights are out!"

The radar controller snapped out his answer. "Use the LSO! Use the LSO! He'll bring you in with the paddles! We're barricaded for you! Just come on in!"

On the deck, six men standing on platforms, braced against the rolling motions, pointed bright battery-powered lights on the landing signal officer. He stood out in brilliant relief.

The LSO's face was starkly white. Not just from the lights. His lips peeled back in a grimace of pain. All through the carrier other men felt the same high frequency sound that was assailing the huge vessel on deck and through its innards. Men ripped off headsets as feedback screeches stabbed wildly into their ears. Several screamed in pain. Those working to bring in the A-7 gasped for breath, suffering terrible agony as the second rose higher and higher. They could barely see the fighter as it bounced and swayed wildly on what was now only a two-mile final to safety. The sound kept rising. In the computer room a man collapsed, unconscious. Lasky jammed his hands to his ears, opening his mouth, trying to equalize pressure. Captain Yelland's eyes bulged as though something alive were within his skull, fighting madly to get out.

Not only were men affected. The sound was both audible and electromagnetic. Electrical equipment sparked and smoked, compasses spun crazily, radar scopes exploded in sprays of fire. Glass shattered everywhere. Vision began to fade, turning white instead of black. Agony raced through the ship, bringing men to their knees or collapsing where they stood. Hundreds of men bled from noses and ears.

Stanton in the A-7 struggled for breath. He knew he was hyperventilating, gasping for air. But he couldn't help it. The fighter was a maddened thing, buffeted and slammed about wildly, and he could barely maintain control. He stared in disbelief as an incredible bolt of lightning leaped off—*away from*—the angled bow of the flight deck. The bolt tore away from the carrier, below the ship, as it ripped along the water and, an instant later, exploded with the force of a string of bombs. Stanton blinked at the retinal afterimage dancing on his optic nerve. He had to keep the LSO and his paddles in sight! Then he saw the carrier's bow going down, plunging, careening, and a mountainous sea lifting to the side like a glo[...] green-black wall. *Nimitz* before him held alon[...] crest of the swell and began her sickening drop.

An icepick jammed into Stanton's ears. He screamed with the pain, squeezed his eyes shut. He forced them open—just in time to see the huge aircraft carrier *disappear*.

☆ 7 ☆

The world fell upward. Impossible, but that was the effect on the men all across the great flight deck who were not tied down or able to grab some immovable object. *U.S.S. Nimitz* came down the slope of the towering swell, tilting at a frightening angle, wallowing in a sickening yaw, and, as she rode the crest of the swell and started to descend, the swell slid away beneath them until there was only empty space beneath the carrier. Men who could see outside the ship, those who were on the flight deck, in the island structure, or peering through portholes, faced the terrifying sight of staring at the green-black water in front of, to the sides, and "above" them as *Nimitz* began her careening drop. All through the great carrier there sounded the groan of metal stressed to its limits and in many places beyond, the singular yet multithroated cry of a living machine being torn asunder through its systems and structure. Men everywhere aboard *Nimitz* heard and felt and sensed the terrible cry as if their ship were the last of a great race of ocean dinosaurs on the brink of final extinction. And over and above all else was that savaging high scream out of nowhere that was everywhere, the knifing blade of sound that tore through their brains. On the bridge, the helmsman fought to retain vision and strength. Yet he felt puny to the point of nonexistence; he was

55

hanging onto the wheel for dear life rather than concentrating on holding course into the seas.

In that terrible, timeless moment the huge carrier had become a small toy, buffeted helplessly, tossed like a wooden chip in the midst of broiling and foaming seas—a toy shoved rudely to the top of a mountain crest, from which it must plunge uncontrolled.

At that moment everyone aboard *Nimitz* heard her scream. No imagined sound here. No mere human empathy for a ship that produced such a keening assault on the ears; this time the sound was the enormous blades of the four giant screws that rammed *Nimitz* through the sea, completely out of the water, free of the turbid friction and cavitation in which they were designed to operate, running free, building to critically dangerous speeds, and shrieking with a gut-twisting whine.

Nimitz fell.

A work crew huddled by a Tomcat fighter stared in utter disbelief as the heavy airplane began to slide sideways across the deck, edging toward the green-black abyss below. The heavy huffer truck was still attached by towbar to the jet, and both were secured by cables and chains. They snapped like fishing line and the Tomcat dragged the truck along with it, the whole assembly making a mockery of the cables and chains. Men fought desperately to anchor new cables and winches to deck tie-downs and hooks, but it was a hopeless struggle as they were forced to fight for their own survival. The carrier continued its yawing tilt to starboard, still careening; and the men, buffeted also by shrieking winds on a slippery surface, found themselves sliding and tumbling toward churning waters mocking their approach.

And only then did the storm strike with its full fury. Men within the ship were hurled away from handholds, battered by furniture and equipment, and from one end of the vessel to another blood sprayed the air. The carrier now swung wildly, her movement violent enough to slam men through the air against bulkheads and equipment, battering them unconscious, breaking limbs, and smashing skulls.

On the bridge, Commander Dick Owens tried to curse. He wanted desperately to throw himself over Matt Yelland, to protect his captain from debris or smashed glass, but the air had been knocked from his lungs. He kept a savage grip on anchored equipment, sucking in air desperately as lights and colors danced before his eyes. He saw Yelland slumping in his chair, strapped in tightly, his hands clamped over his ears. But he was safe. Owens managed finally to drag himself to the edge of the forward window of the bridge. His eyes widened and a low moan escaped his lips as he saw crewmen tumbling over the side of the warship, some by the grace of God into the recovery nets, others to their death in the water beyond those nets. A fighter caught his eye, tipped as it was at a crazy and precarious angle. Owens noticed a crewman inside the cockpit, banging on the emergency release. Then the fighter and a truck were picked up and thrown madly through the air to disappear into the foaming sea.

The bridge was a shambles, with debris everywhere, bodies in all directions and positions, blood running slippery on the deck. If only he could clear his head! He lurched his way to the battle stations alarm, hanging grimly with one hand, banging his fist wildly against the control until he saw that he had torn open the skin of his hand. He stared stupidly at the flayed skin and the blood, realized a hand was gripping his wrist, holding him tightly. Warren Lasky, blood running from a cut on his forehead, face white with pain, but still sufficiently in control of his senses to have helped Owens. Nor did Owens know, even then, that general quarters had been sounding all the time, that he was temporarily deaf from that terrible keening sound that had stabbed through his eyeballs and into his brain.

* * *

Nimitz fell, ponderous, helpless, careening out of control, to the valley of the trough. For long moments no one knew whether the great carrier would ever emerge. Angry green seas boiled across the deck, spray sliced into men with the force of knives, and lightning shattered the heavens and flashed across the ship in an unceasing cannonade. Then the downward motion stopped, the huge warship groaned through every steel plate and beam, and men were tumbled anew as *Nimitz* began to rise along the incredible trough, tilting this time in the opposite direction.

In the combination mess and recreation room, broken chairs and tables and debris from broken dishes and glasses and cutlery pinned a group of men against a bulkhead. Some were unconscious, all were hurt and bleeding. A hulking petty officer fought his way to his feet, by maniacal strength dragged men out from under the battering rams of debris. He roared orders to those who could move, whipped the stunned men about him into meaningful action. They were just starting to get control of the situation when the opposite tilt began, and everyone and everything began the inexorable slide to the oppsite side of the room. A man clutched an overhead pipe, dangling by his arms as the deck fell away beneath him. The others were swept away helplessly, again the targets of debris smashing into them. A door flew open and a lethal barrage of pots and pans hurtled into the wardroom from the galley. The galley itself was a bloodbath. There was a mingling of screams and curses as the mess crew went down beneath violently splashed hot soup and coffee, were burned horribly from grease and fat and slashed by knives and cutlery whipping through the air.

The lights flickered madly. Abruptly battery-powered emergency lights gleamed through the bridge. That terrible keening sound was abating. Captain Yelland looked up, oblivious to the blood running from his ears. He had only one thought, and as the carrier wheeled suddenly in a new terrible yawing motion, he roared orders to the terrified helmsman. "Keep her into the sea, boy!" he shouted. "Into the sea! Don't let her broach or we'll go under!"

Deep in the cavernous belly of the huge carrier the chief engineer felt *Nimitz* straining to stay together. Communications with the bridge were long dead. Even the emergency circuits were out. But Commander Helmut Thompson had been at sea all his life in big warships, and he knew what was happening. Charlie Moss was manning the nuclear console, tending with infinite care to the enormous reactors, secure in his seat with lap and shoulder harness, and he looked across the control center to Thompson, raised a fist in the air, and pumped it up and down. Thompson nodded. They needed no word from the bridge to know what *Nimitz* needed most of all—power to steam straight into those incredible seas just beyond the hull. Thompson went to manual override of the useless electronic controls. There'd been enough hash and screw-ups in the last hour so that he distrusted anything that used current through a cable, and he grasped a large wheel in both hands and turned it with all his strength to go to maximum steam flow. He could feel the deeper thrumming of the screws spinning up, and he knew this could well be the moment that might snatch survival from the murderous waves trying to drag *Nimitz* beneath the surface.

☆ 8 ☆

The night vanished. They tumbled and whirled and plunged and tossed in green-glowing darkness, and when *Nimitz* came down the far side of a swell that heaved almost to heaven itself, the night was gone. Vanished as if it had never been. Where there had been screaming winds and a ceaseless barrage of lightning, rain-drenched skies, unimaginable seas, there was now a presunrise moment on a sea as flat and still as glass, the wake of *Nimitz* showing behind them as a perfect V that stretched to the horizon and beyond. It was a screamingly silent contrast to the nocturnal horror through which they had moved. The sun had yet to break that flat horizon, but dawn had long been with them, and above the quiescent sea floated pink-scalloped clouds.

Matt Yelland and his bridge staff staggered back to reality. They desperately needed time to gather their wits about them but time was still their enemy. Dan Thurman was the first to snap his brain back into geared motion. "The A-7! Where the hell is that fighter!" The exec officer punched the deck speakers. "On the deck! We had a fighter coming in for the barricade! Report! Report! He knew only too well what an unattended deck could mean to a crippled jet without its arrestor hook.

Men turned their eyes to the stern. The background

60

was a cacophony of ringing bells and screeching telephones as *Nimitz* fought off its bruises with reestablished communications. But with Thurman's words everyone looked aft—into a completely clear, calm sky. Yet, and the looks they exchanged said more than any words, no one could block out that final image in darkness of the A-7's strobes and landing lights slicing through green-ebony blackness.

Then it was there. Suddenly, out of nowhere, the A-7 appeared to snap back into existence. The landing signal officer, soaking wet, badly bruised from windwhipped water, looked in disbelief as the fighter roared toward them on its two-mile final, all lights still on. "The tailhook! It's coming down!" shouted an assistant watching the A-7 through binoculars. But the LSO didn't like the way the A-7 slewed from side to side. It had a sickening yaw, as though Stanton's feet were simply moving back and forth on the rudder pedals.

"Check the barricade! Check the barricade! All hands clear the deck! Clear the deck!" Men made a frantic last-moment study of the deck barricade, heard the swelling roar of the approaching fighter, and dove into the safety nets. The LSO waved his paddles carefully, then lowered them to his sides. The approach lights and mirrors were working perfectly! He knew that Stanton was guiding himself in as best he could with the automatic system, and the next instant the jet roar washed over them, then fell as Stanton chopped all power. He would never try for a go-around with the barricade down. He didn't need to. The tailhook grabbed and the A-7 came to a bruising halt.

"Rescue to the aircraft! Rescue to the aircraft!" The teams rushed to the fighter, opened the canopy. The first man on the scene leaned into the cockpit to secure the explosive ejection system. He shut off all power switches and unhooked Stanton, slumped forward against his harness.

"Get that pilot out of there! Medic to the deck.

Medical crew to the deck. I want a report on that pilot immediately. Go, go." They brought Stanton out carefully. He seemed to be unconscious, but there was no damage to his flight suit. The rescue team leader slid back the pilot's visor. He looked up in disbelief at the men with him, then spoke swiftly. "Get him to sick bay. I'll call ahead. Move him out. Carefully now." He thumbed another switch. "Bridge, rescue here."

Thurman's voice came back on the headset line. "Bridge here. Let's have it."

"Sir, we're removing the pilot immediately to sick bay. His face is burned."

A momentary pause. "Did he have a cockpit fire?"

The rescue chief drew a deep breath. "Sir, no sign of a fire anywhere in that cockpit. His suit is untouched. Sir, it sounds crazy, but I've seen that kind of burn before. It's electrical . . . as though he had a lightning strike inside the cockpit."

Dan Thurman exchanged looks with the bridge staff. Then he spoke again to rescue. "Have sick bay notify the bridge at once of his condition. And as soon as the pilot is able to speak with us, I'll be down personally."

"Yes, sir."

Matt Yelland studied his men. For the moment he decided to continue his silence. They were already making the right decisions and implementing them. No sooner had the A-7 been recovered than Dick Owens was barking orders into his mike. The leader of his air group had been under stress moments like this before. "CAG here. All helicopters launch immediately. I repeat, all helicopters launch immediately for sea sweep and rescue of any personnel overboard. Move it, you people!"

Nimitz came back to life, battered, hurt, confused—but still the deadly warship she had been from the moment of birth. As helicopters chopped their way into the air, fanning out to both sides and behind the now-slowing carrier, the angled deck was alive with other activity. Captain Matthew Yelland knew the only way to react to an impossible situation was with a killer punch. No sooner had Owens completed his orders for the helicopters to punch out on their mercy mission than Yelland went to command.

"This is the captain. Launch four F-14's immediately. Launch crews and pilots at once to the emergency. Launch immediately." Matt Yelland turned to Owens. As CAG that was Owens's responsibility, but he had reacted also. Saving any men who might still be alive had been his first blurred reaction. Owens's eyes were still dazed, and Yelland knew his CAG officer wasn't yet back to snuff. My God, who knew how many men were still spinning between their ears from that terrible sound? Only then did Yelland realize both sides of his face and his neck had been soaked in blood. To the devil with that. Yelland had spent eight years in North Vietnam learning how to block out pain. Right now he didn't know what was going on. Two fighters would slam upwards to fifty thousand feet and ride high cover for the carrier. Two more would circle the carrier at a distance of thirty miles in a constant orbit. Four more fighters were on the ready-launch catapult, crews in their aircraft, engines ready to start at a moment's notice. Sixty-four missile launchers were on general quarters, primed to fire on command. Only then did Yelland permit a medical orderly to examine him, and that was on the bridge, which he refused to leave.

The bridge crew looked down onto the flight deck where a big Sikorsky chopper angled to a landing and rocked to a halt. Men with Red Cross armbands ran to the helicopter, assisting crewmen from the machine. Dick Owens studied the scene through binoculars. "Three more," he said without turning. "That makes eleven men we've picked out of the water. The gods have smiled on those people down there." As quickly as the rescued seamen were free of the helicopter, the big rotors of the Sikorsky wound up into a thrumming howl and the chopper swung away from the carrier to resume its search pattern.

Owens lowered the binoculars and studied Matt Yelland. The captain had a knot on his forehead, and a medical corpsman had swabbed his ears clean. He had refused any pain medication. Yelland scanned the horizon slowly. For a moment he was lax as he stared into the sun. He winced and almost at the same moment, as the light intensity kept increasing, the automatic compensators polarized the glass enclosures to accommodate for comfortable vision levels.

The dawn was almost a sacred event for the carrier crew. Every man on deck, or within a porthole or a window, came to a brief pause in whatever he was doing. They all shared the same thought—they knew this was a dawn they had been given as a gift. Several times even the mighty *Nimitz* had come dangerously close to broaching in those violent seas. They took their moment of thanks and bent to their tasks of cleaning up broken equipment and mopping away the bloodstains splattered across bulkheads and decks and gear.

On the bridge, the captain and his immediate staff, determined to remain together to unravel the greater mysteries just becoming apparent, took coffee and doughnuts. The storm had been an enigma; what unfolded steadily in this deceptively peaceful morning began to reveal its promise of equal or even greater mystery.

"I wonder if we'll ever have any idea of what hit us," Owens said, sipping slowly from his coffee mug. "I've been in what I thought was every kind of storm known to man, but the combination of forces that hit us, and then that incredible sound . . . my God." He shuddered with memory of the pain that had rattled his eyesockets. "They haven't written the book on that one yet."

Dan Thurman looked up from notes he scribbled as

he listened to a line from sick bay. "Captain, we have that casualty report. Twenty-three dead, eleven missing. We picked up nineteen men from the water."

"Jesus." The exclamation issued from Lieutenant Artemus Perry. "How many injured, sir?"

"Over three hundred. About fifty will remain confined with fractures, concussions, severe lacerations. The others will return to light or full duty within the next watch."

Yelland listened to the exchange, decided to leave such matters in the hands of his staff. He turned to his master console and punched in CENCOMM for Central Communications. "Kaufman here, sir," came an immediate response.

"Walter, I think you'd better get out a whole batch of special messages," Yelland ordered. "To start with, if I didn't have this bloody headache, it would have occurred to me sooner to issue a warning about the rogue waves that hit us last night. So let's not waste any more time. Get me a report on the location of the destroyers that were with us until that storm. I want a chart layout on all Russian trawlers, and have command at Pearl give us a new location pattern of our subs within three hundred miles of our present position. All contacts on all command channels are to be checked. As the reports come in, have them directed to the bridge. Staff will collate and keep me updated. Get right to it."

"Yes, sir." Kaufman went off the line.

Yelland noticed Warren Lasky standing at the computer command room door. "Mr. Lasky," the captain called, "are the computers back on line?"

Lasky walked across the bridge to him. "Standard processing, Captain. They seem fit, but we're running the programmed internal check to study all elements. It takes about twenty minutes to confirm the electrical surges and other problems have been purged. And we need to do that."

Yelland raised a brow; the entire bridge was listening. "Explain that to me, please," Yelland said.

"Captain, it is physically impossible for a storm of the nature we experienced to end as abruptly as it did," Lasky replied, and he seemed very certain of his words. "The only event even remotely close to this is a neutercane, which is a meteorological event confirmed in what is known as the Devil's Triangle between Bermuda and Florida. And I don't care much of a damn what anyone thinks about triangles. I'm referring to a storm that erupts without warning, that can turn a placid sea in thirty seconds into howling white water. We did *not* experience a neutercane last night. We had a major meteorological event covering tens of thousands of square miles, an unprecedented electromagnetic effect, and it all ended in a period of seconds. Sir, that is unparalleled in the history of weather known to the human race. The computers have rejected such data—if I can translate computereze—as a combination of impossible, insane, and totally rejectable data."

"Mr. Lasky, you might not be so adamant if you had experience with rogue waves," Yelland said a bit tartly.

Lasky gave tartness right back. "Captain Yelland, I have a master's in oceanography." He paused to let that sink in and then went on. "I am familiar to the point of intimacy with such ocean phenomena. Rogue waves come under the heading of tsunamic phenomena and—"

"I don't care what they call it," Yelland retorted. "We both know those things can move of speeds of four to five hundred miles an hour, and that wall of water that hit us wasn't anything that could be called normal, and it certainly can dissipate its immediate-area effects in—"

Lasky broke in. "Tsunamic waves, Captain, are not accompanied with high-atmospheric activity, with electromagnetic disruption on the scale we experienced, they do not disrupt ultrahigh frequency or micro-wave communications, do not put satellites out of commission, and are *not* accompanied by sustained winds—shall I go on?"

Yelland was studying this strange civilian with growing respect. He might be a smart-assed son of a bitch but he knew where he was speaking. "Yes. Go on."

"Tsunamic waves are either long-range tidal forces or the results of such activity as undersea avalanches or earthquakes, and when you're on the high seas, as we have been, you do not even notice such a wave, even when it's directly beneath you. A tsunamic involvement for us is patently absurd and may be dismissed from all consideration."

Yelland rubbed his aching head. "All right," he said finally. "Then what the hell was it?"

"What it was, Captain, was patently, convincingly, historically, realistically impossible."

"That's ridiculous," Yelland snapped.

An unperturbed Lasky stared back without blinking. "I agree."

"Do you have any theories to offer, then?"

"I do."

Damn, the man wouldn't budge an inch. "Tell me, confound it!" Yelland barked.

Lasky had a strange smile on his face. "Give me a little more time, Captain. If I told you right out, I haven't the faintest doubt that you would, to borrow a quaint expression, have me clapped in irons."

Yelland's fuse was burning just a bit brighter. "Mr. Lasky, I have no time for facetious remarks or—damn." He went silent as Walt Kaufman's voice broke in on the priority channel.

"Comm to the bridge. Urgent," came the message.

Yelland opened his lip mike to all channels for his staff. "Bridge here, the captain speaking. What is it, Kaufman?"

The communications officer's words brought the

bridge to dead silence. "Sir, we're down across the board."

"Spell that out." Yelland's voice was rasping and harsh.

"Sir, all equipment functions normally. All antennas are back on line. We have full power and we're transmitting at maximum output. But no matter what we do, we seem to be totally cut off from the outside world. We get no response of any kind. We have interrogated every satellite wavelength and it's a zero response. Nothing on the war alert frequency. Nothing to other ships and nothing for aircraft, as well. We've even sounded sonar and long-range underwater masers; plenty of echo response but nothing directly answering." There was a brief pause. "Sir, we're receiving mostly hash. We've scanned every band possible. What has us puzzled, sir, is that we picked up some code transmissions in the 200-meter band. Otherwise, as of this moment, we're as dead as a doornail."

Yelland saw the strange smile, almost a grimace, on Lasky's face. He put aside questioning that man for a few moments. "Keep me posted," Yelland said crisply. He tapped into another line. In the navigation command center the emergency call flashed. Commander Leo Slattery snatched up the phone. "NavCenter, Slattery."

"Leo, this is the captain. Flat out—what's our position?"

"Uh, Captain, a few hours ago we were holding course two six two and two hundred four miles west of Pearl."

"What the hell do you mean a few hours ago!"

"Captain Yelland, as far as I know we're still in that same position. But the sun has moved. I mean, uh, it's moved, well, sir, it's crazy. If we had maintained our course and heading, based on the same scale as solar movement, we should be two hundred and thirty miles farther west than we are. But according to all checks, we're right where we were eleven hours ago, as though we hadn't moved an inch."

"That's impossible!"

"Yes, sir."

"Is that all you've got to say, Kaufman!"

"Yes, sir."

Yelland snapped off the line. He looked again at Lasky and was disturbed by that sad, terrible smile. He pushed his gaze away from that tremendously disturbing look. Why the hell didn't Lasky say what he was thinking!

"Owens, Thurman, Lasky," he said swiftly. "Come with me. We're going to talk to Kaufman. He sounded as if he was ready to lie down and cry."

Lasky nodded. "Captain Yelland, he was. He *is*."

Yelland walked from the bridge, the others following behind. They pushed into the communications center. Commander Walter Kaufman was trembling visibly. That shook Yelland. Kaufman was unflappable and he looked as if he'd seen a ghost.

"All right," Yelland said. "Spare me all poetics and nuances. Has anything changed from your last conversation with me?"

Kaufman's face was now stone. "No, sir."

"You said you had something in the 200-meter band. So there's something intruding into that vacuum of yours."

"Yes, sir, but that's all we're getting."

"No question about your equipment?" Yelland's eyes narrowed as he took the measure of the man. Kaufman was stricken but still with it.

"No, sir. We're smack on."

"How strong is that 200-meter band?"

"On a scale of ten, sir, about three for signal strength."

"What are you getting?"

Kaufman took a very deep breath. "Morse code, sir. Most of it in five-letter groups. It's ridiculous."

"Why?"

"It sounds like someone is putting us on, sir."

"Explain that!"

"Well, sir, these codes . . . I studied them a long time ago as a student at Great Lakes. These are old codes for the Royal Navy."

"The *what?*"

"British, sir. But archaic. It hasn't been used for years."

"How long is that, mister?"

"Sir, at least forty years."

Yelland looked about him, his patience scraped thin. "Jesus, has everybody gone mad around here?"

The others were blank-faced. Warren Lasky smiled. He knew, damn him! Yelland turned back to his staff. "Get a recon Vigilante into the air immediately with orders for an extreme-altitude photosweep of Pearl and the islands. It is to avoid all contact at all costs. And I mean at *all* costs, including running from anything that even shows up in the same sky. It is to exercise full capability; long-range radar, full-scan optical and laser photography, and a full ferret electronic sweep. I want real-time data return to this carrier, right into the war room, and then I want everything brought back here processed and delivered to the meeting we're about to have." Yelland motioned for the others to follow him and continued as he talked. "Dan," he said to his executive officer, "you know what I want. Set it up. Full staff." He glanced at Lasky. "And you, sir, well, I would appreciate your remaining with me. Have you had any further news on your computers?"

Lasky nodded slowly.

Yelland stopped in mid-stride. He lowered his voice. "Sir, you have the damnedest smile on your face. I'm not sure if it's the Cheshire cat or if those are canary feathers floating about your mouth. Would you care to enlighten me?"

Lasky sighed. "It is a smile, Captain, because I am terrified."

Yelland was astonished and showed it. "Of *what*, for God's sake?"

"Yesterday, Captain, yesterday. You see, it's caught us." That strange smile returned. "But you're not ready to hear what I mean, because even I'm not ready to accept what I believe is the truth." He turned away from the captain and walked on alone, strangely, utterly alone.

☆ 9 ☆

A feeling of intense but subdued motion marked the
deck as the launch crews prepared the rakish Vigilante for its reconaissance mission. Lieutenant Paul
Pearson, the pilot in the front of the tandem cockpit,
and Mike McCready, the electronics officer in the
rear, went through their final checklists. Hand and
voice signals told them the launch crew was now at
the ready. The Vigilante was fully alive in the sense of
the aircraft, and its complex innards as well as the machine were ready to swing into full service. Usually
there was an élan at such moments, but now all
through *Nimitz* the sense of the unknown, the inescapable fact of the sun shifting in the sky, had per-
vaded the thoughts of every man, and they had
substituted a cautious expectancy for other feelings. It
was difficult, if not impossible, to ignore the dead and
the injured and within the aura of the unsolved it was
difficult to get back into the hard swing of operations.
What saved sanity in many cases was the inescapable
reality that they were here, right now, steaming under
power at sea with all systems returned to normal. Yet
suspicion and fear and distrust roamed through every
mind. Every gun position on the carrier was manned
with live rounds. Missile systems for use against aircraft, ships, and submarines were kept at the ready.
Fighters were on the line for instant launch in full

numbers, and three big antisubmarine helicopters were on station, one ahead of *Nimitz* and the others to each side, antisubmarine warfare (ASW) equipment probing for any submarines that might be in the area.

In CCI—Combat Control Center, or more commonly, the war room—Captain Yelland had assembled his key staff to watch the plotting boards and to listen to any word from either the Vigilante or any other aircraft and systems. Large banks of Lucite display boards glowed from the liquid crystals that were sandwiched between the transparent sheets, ready to come alive at the touch of controls by technicians plotting the Vigilante and other flights. To the rear of the war room sat Yelland and his staff and Warren Lasky, commanding a full view of any activity that might be displayed. The room was set up for direct aural signal from the Vigilante, so that any two-way conversation with the airplane on UHF (ultra high frequency) could be heard as the pilot talked back and forth with the controlling teams.

The main plotting center glowed with life. In the middle of the panel appeared a small representation of the *Nimitz*, and from the carrier there stretched an arcing dotted line that represented the flight path of the Vigilante. Digital numbers flickered steadily to show the course, heading, altitude, and speed of the airplane. The glowing lines representing the Hawaiian Islands moved steadily closer to the Vigilante.

They heard Pearson's call sign over the speakers. "Victor Fox Trot, this is One Zero Niner, radio check."

Air control answered at once. "One Zero Niner, you're five by five. Over."

"Roger that," came the answer. "Loud and clear."

They knew what the moment was like in the long cockpit of the Vigilante, both crewmen wearing pressure suits and bulbous helmets, sealed into their pressurized compartment, the second man, to the rear of Pearson, literally surrounded by banks of equipment. Pearson normally would be flying this kind of mission with his autopilot controlling the swift jet, but not now. He was on his own ragged edge, and, like the others, he wanted to be capable of instant response to any situation. In the muffled quiet of the cockpit, Pearson studied the readout of his onboard computer. Before him on the windscreen there appeared a grid pattern with thin glowing yellow lines. A red dot moved across the grid toward Pearl Harbor and the coasts of the islands. Pearson tapped several command buttons, and numbers glowed on the screen. He nodded to himself. Everything was on the line. In a few minutes he would have visual contact with the islands themselves. Damn—heavy cloud cover was coming up. It looked like it would be broken clouds over the islands. He nodded to himself and spoke into his helmet mike; no need to transmit any button because he was staying on "open line" to the air controllers and the war room itself.

"One Zero Niner commencing search pattern of the northwest quadrant."

Air control answered at once. "Confirm and continue."

Pearson worked the computer before him until the grid pattern winked out; it was replaced by a series of green circles radiating outward from a center point. He studied the pattern and spoke to the electronics officer behind him. "Mike, I'm clean on the board. You got anything?"

"Negative. We—oops, got something. Nothing in the visual range, but radar sweep is picking up something airborne beneath those clouds."

Pearson called in directly. "Control, you read?"

"Go, One Zero Niner."

"We've got a solid cloud deck now beneath us at about twenty-eight thousand feet. No results on visual, but radar picks up what we confirm as several aircraft in the vicinity of Pearl at altitudes of less than seven thousand. I'm about to start an infrared sweep."

"Confirm."

"Ah, roger that, Control. Okay, we're picking up some heat patterns. Definite aircraft, very slow moving. Also, we seem to be getting thermal high points on the surface. Nothing we can really tell from here. We're rolling all tapes for analysis. Over."

"Very good, One Zero Niner. Proceed."

The war room had been taking on an air of quietly growing excitement. At least they had their teeth into something. The softly pulsating line that represented the flight path of the Vigilante had begun a new curve, and now it intersected and crossed the irregular shape of a coastline. They studied the digital curve of the reconnaissance plane holding at forty thousand feet just below supersonic speed. The pilot's voice came across the speakers. "One Zero Niner now at the end of the scheduled first run. We're starting Leg Two now. Over."

"Roger that, One Zero Niner. Be sure you have comparative radar scans of that coastline below you. Confirm, please."

"Got it."

"Any visual contact yet?"

Pearson's voice reflected his own puzzlement. "It's an empty sky out there. Not only that, but not a single sign of a contrail at our altitude or below, and that's strange, with all the airliner traffic between the island and the mainland."

"We agree, Paul. Just keep on trucking."

"That's a big ten-four from One Zero Niner."

No one thought Captain Yelland would mind the joshing. Indeed, he found it an excellent sign that his men were emerging from their blue funk.

The only man in the war room who didn't respond with some sort of smile or laugh at the radio exchange was Warren Lasky. He had spent every spare moment communicating with the great computers in the carrier. Thoughts swirled in his head, making him dizzy. The realization that his hunches seemed to be correct disturbed him even more.

Jesus freaking Khee-rhist, he murmured to himself.

Captain Yelland tapped the control console before him for attention. "Control, turn off the speakers in the war room. Break in on open line only if something unusual comes up."

"Yes, sir," answered a disembodied voice. There would be no unnecessary interruptions from this point on. Yelland looked about him and stopped his gaze on Lasky. "We've been going at our problem for some time now. What we're working out is a general consensus by which we can set our course to try to find a way out of this mess. I would appreciate it if you would listen to what we have to say, and if you find it pertinent, please interrupt at any time. You've kept a real-time profile with the computers?"

Lasky nodded. "Yes, sir, I have."

Yelland nodded and glanced at the rest of the men. He held up a sheaf of papers in his hand. "Gentlemen, this represents the findings, conclusions, ideas, and recommendations of every responsible control officer of this carrier. And there's an overwhelming conclusion that's been drawn by at least ninety percent of everyone involved."

Men stirred in their seats. This was more like it. They were finally coming to grips with this thing that had been nipping at their mental heels. Lasky well understood the feeling. Whatever you do, it's best to make a decision and commit to it. Sink your teeth in, that sort of thing.

"It's the general feeling," continued Yelland, "that the odd effects, even those incredible effects, the enormous lightning discharges, and most of all, the weird electromagnetic effects and communications blackouts are the result of a massive nuclear weapons exchange." He paused, looked around the room of frozen faces, and went on. "Somehow, we were in an extraordinarily fortunate location at sea where we experienced the violent disruption of the atmosphere and the sea, but consider these to be, no matter how severe they were, the periphereal outpouring of the direct association of what may well have been. . . ." His voice trailed off as he began to comprehend the enormity of what he was saying; he picked up slowly. "As I was saying, what may well have been the detonation of thousands of fission and fusion warheads. In short—all-out nuclear war."

For at least a minute there was no sound in the war room. Yelland shook off the blanket about them all. "High-altitude bursts of megaton-yield thermonukes could produce the overwhelming electromagnetic pulse effect we're run into. It would wipe out all communications with any satellite systems. A sheath effect is created in the upper atmosphere. We've known that from our own bomb tests. The storm we went through is a bit tougher to handle in terms of experience, but when you combine a natural storm with hydrogen bombs that may have detonated in the sea, well, it makes things a lot more likely. In fact, the nature of the storm that nearly destroyed us may well have been our saving grace. Our nuclear warfare people have explained how the storm could have screened off the immediate radiative effects, visible light and infrared, of any fireballs. We had sufficient density of cloud and rain acting as a thoroughly effective shield against any immediate radiative effects."

Dan Thurman gestured and Yelland nodded for him to speak. "Sir, on this point of radiation, have we picked up anything in any way of an increase in background count from the sensors we carry on *Nimitz*?"

"No. Not yet. But we've got everything out. So far the .Vigilante, or even the Tomcats as high cover, haven't picked up any drifting radiation, but that situation could change at any moment. We'll examine the screen traps when the aircraft returns. Any comments?"

He looked directly at Lasky but the computer scientist remained silent. Yelland couldn't figure out the strained look on his face. Nerves; he had good reason. Yelland returned to his papers. "The fact that we're not receiving radio transmissions from anywhere—the States, Asia, Europe—I repeat, anywhere, speaks for itself. There are no satellite relay contacts. MF, VHF, UHF, omega, loran, sideband; even the FM and microwave channels are silent. That's as much a mystery as anything else but our comm officer, Commander Kaufman—and he's offering a supposition rather than a hard conclusion—feels that the EMP, the electromagnetic pulse, of weapons designed to blank out all radiative traffic could be responsible. After all, we've never dealt with a massive release on such a scale of these weapons."

"There's something else, sir," an officer broke in. He received Yelland's gesture to continue. "It's like Pearson reported from the Vigilante, sir. And the same from the Tomcats, as well as what we have been able to see from here ourselves. Not a single sighting of a contrail from anything, and the Tomcats are showing a contrail right now."

"A very good point," Yelland acknowledged. "Nothing is flying at altitude anywhere within visual reach and the only air traffic reported by the Vigilante, if what they detected beneath that cloud cover is air traffic, is very low indeed. That's another unknown, this not seeing anything in the air. Our radar is just as blank as our eyeballs."

There was silence in the room as everyone considered what had been said. For a while they had wondered if they were absolutely alone in the world. But that Vigilante had detected something, and right now an unknown that was moving was a hell of a sight more welcome than a complete absence of any movement. Yet they could not escape the specter of what a gigantic nuclear confrontation meant to them personally. Were they among the few survivors left in the world? Were their families wiped out? Was it possible that the ultimate nuclear cataclysm had destroyed entire civilizations and left them behind to face a living hell?

Another officer stood up slowly. "There are two points I'd like to make, sir."

"Go ahead."

"I believe there's no question every ship with us went down. Our destroyers . . . even the Russian trawlers. We know people in the sea even during the worst of the storm could survive, because we rescued our own. So what took those ships down had to be violent wave action, not just . . . well, just some overwhelming radiation."

"Very good," Yelland acknowledged. "You have more?"

"Yes, sir. It took a while, but sonar has finally picked up some signals. The range is extreme and we're not getting any kind of target we can identify. What I mean, sir, is that the targets seem too small to be submersibles, and yet we're picking up a beat of screws. It doesn't fit into anything with which we're familiar."

"Go on, go on," Yelland urged.

"Sir, we have the equipment to home in on the ocean-bottom grid pattern for our nuclear boats. Like I said, we've picked up some underwater echoes of screws, but the entire worldwide grid pattern for our nuclear subs has gone silent. It's as if someone had set up its destruction for a specific time as a deliberate act."

Yelland absorbed what he had heard and finally sighed. "Thank you. It provides yet another confirmation. And there's still more mystery than answers. The only radio we've picked up has been some activity far down in the 200-meter band, and that's been in Morse. I don't understand it. We're also getting some pretty heavy hash in the AM band, and by hash I mean without any patterns with which our equipment is familiar. Archaic would be a good word for it. Mr. Thurman, would you provide a summary, please?"

Nimitz's executive officer was pale and drawn, but Dan Thurman somehow got a good grip on himself. "Yes, sir. The more we look at it the clearer it seems that we're now involved in that war we always feared. What we're seeing seems more and more to be evidence of the big wipeout. We must have just missed catching it because of an extraordinary set of circumstances. We can go into the details later, but what counts now is just that—what happens *now*?" He took a deep breath. "We're a major combat arm of the United States Navy. As soon as whatever hostiles are operating become aware that *Nimitz* has survived virtually intact, that we're a powerful fighting force with aircraft choppers, missiles, and hundreds of nuclear warheads well into the high-megaton range, well, I don't think anyone needs to question that we'll become a subject of intense interest. Another way to spell that is *target*. However, it would be unwise to keep a large screen of fighters in the air at all times. We can expect severe problems in supply for some time to come. But I recommend that we stay, if not on general quarters, just below combat alert. That way we're prepared for any contingency and we can be on full attack capability within minutes' notice. We must contact our own high command, assess the situation, coordinate what we do, put all our strength at the disposal of our nation. We must—"

Dick Owens waved an arm urgently for attention. "You're rushing things!" he said with a half shout. He turned directly to face his captain. "Sir, you're ignoring everything before that storm! Not a single twitch from the warning boards. Not a single communication from Washington or Pearl or Pacific command. Nothing on the news. No unusual air, radio or any other kind of traffic or activity from anywhere in the Soviet sectors. Did every one of our intelligence services go deaf, dumb and blind? I—"

"You're trading suppositions with us, Commander," Yelland said heavily.

Warren Lasky moved into the sudden breach. "No, he's not, Captain," Lasky said, his voice heard clearly through the war room. "He's the first man I've heard here who has managed to step back far enough not to draw conclusions based on—even if overwhelming—circumstantial evidence."

Yelland was amazed. "You call everything we've reviewed to be circumstantial?"

"On the basis of everything I've heard as being solid enough to draw the conclusion of the detonation of thousands of nuclear devices, Captain Yelland, there isn't a single shred of evidence to support anything at all." Lasky turned to Walt Kaufman. "You're comm officer. You have nothing on normal bands, is that correct?"

"Yes, it is."

"You're familiar with the electromagnetic pulse effect?"

Kaufman flushed. "Of course I am!"

"Then you should know that while this could knock out the low-level array of defense comsats, it does not affect the synchronous orbit satellites at just over twenty-two thousand miles. Nor does it have any effect on the monitoring satellites at orbits of sixty thousand miles. Have you tried to interrogate those satellites?"

Kaufman stammered. "Why, n-no. There's no reason, I mean, we don't use those for communications or weather data—" He turned white with Yelland's sudden command. "Commander, follow through on what Mr. Lasky has just detailed—*immediately!*"

Kaufman was gone from the war room like a shot. Yelland turned back to Lasky. "All right, let's hear the rest of it," he demanded.

Lasky wasn't bothered by the intense stare of Yelland's icy blue eyes. "Captain, I don't have all of it, but I have one word to describe my reaction to what

I've heard here in this room. And that word is nonsense. It's all just so much rubbish."

Yelland was on his feet, his disbelief stark in his expression.

"You can't be serious!"

"I am absolutely serious. Except for Owens, here, everything else has been completely hypothetical, and it is still nonsense. The truth, which is hiding behind the corners of your own minds, is too much of a shock to face outright. And if you all weren't in such shock you'd see it more clearly yourselves. As soon as Commander Kaufman interrogates those satellites we described, he will literally be in serious shock, and I recommend immediate medical attention."

"Why do you say that?" This time Thurman raised the question.

"Because he won't receive a word from any satellites—not Ferret or Big Bird or any of them. Do we have laser aboard? Of course; I forgot. We interrogate navigation satellites. They won't respond either." Lasky looked around the room. "Does anyone here believe the electromagnetic impulse of nuclear strikes would wipe out our bases on the moon?"

"You're crazy!" Thurman snapped. "We don't have bases on the goddamned moon!"

Lasky showed a tolerant smile. "Of course we do, Commander. Unmanned, but they're still there. They were left by the Apollo crews that landed on the moon. They're still powered with isotope reactors. More to the point, they have passive laser array receivers that will pick up an earth-transmitted signal and beam back a bounce response. The computers on this ship have the exact location and can fire a laser interrogation quite accurately to the lunar sites." Lasky looked at Yelland. "I suggest you try that as well, sir."

Yelland was measuring Lasky. "You're making a slow and tedious point, Mr. Lasky."

"Yes, sir. The only way. I'm facing a huge wall of

circumstantial evidence I've got to destroy effectively enough to let the truth sink in."

"Lasky, what happens when we laser beam those Apollo sites on the moon?" Owens shot at him.

Lasky smiled again. "Absolutely nothing."

"And why the hell not?" demanded another officer.

The enigmatic smile knifed through him. "Because," Lasky said slowly, "They're not there."

"But you said—!"

Lasky was holding up his hand. "Never mind what I said. You all know historical fact. It's in the records, the books. You know about the Apollo missions, what was left on those landing sites. What I'm telling you, now, is that the laser interrogation will be quite useless, and that the lunar site equipment is not there."

Yelland felt his mind was reeling. "You're being contradictory, Mr. Lasky."

"No, sir. I was never more serious in my life. It will become clear soon enough."

"Then what in the hell has happened?"

"Captain, it's not what has happened. It's—"

The wall speaker interrupted him. Commander Walt Kaufman's voice came in, high-strung, excited. "Captain! We're picking up signals!"

"Spell them out, Mr. Kaufman, and be quick about it."

"Yes, sir. It's mainly low-band transmissions. Strictly manual stuff, Captain, and very low wattage."

"Can you communicate with the source?"

"Sir, not right way. We'd have to rewire our equipment to transmit in that range."

"Well, do it, damnit! Hold one, Walter. What about those satellites Lasky spoke about?"

The pause was unmistakable. "Nothing, sir."

"Not even the early-warning satellites at sixty thousand miles?"

"Nothing, sir." Kaufman's voice sounded hollow.

"All right. Get busy on modifying your transmitters." Yelland hesitated. "And, Walter. The instant you can pick up something somebody can understand, feed it into this line."

"Sir, I can do that right now. I said those signals were, well, weird. What I'm getting sounds a lot like Armed Forces Radio, but the signal strength is, well, Captain, it's so weak it sounds like an amateur station. It's on the entertainment circuit, and—"

"Put it on!" Yelland was close to shouting.

Kaufman's voice went off the line, and the assembled officers in the war room stared at the speakers as the signal, rising and falling in strength, hissed and crackled at them in strange voices.

"Boss . . . boss . . . I'm back!"

"Rochester!"

A hissing roar. It was—they looked at one another—the sound of applause, then the familiar voice continued.

"At last! When I gave you your annual vacation I didn't expect it to last a week!"

Dan Thurman stared at his captain. "Sir, that's Jack Benny. And that other voice, his sidekick, he said Rochester, didn't he?"

Yelland stabbed a button. "Kaufman, turn that damn dial of yours and let's hear what you've got on it."

Static, signals warbling, rising and falling, hissed and crackled from the speakers. Thurman wiped sweat from his forehead. "Captain, it sounds like they're running some nostalgia programs." Belief was missing from his words; confusion was obviously paramount.

"Kaufman, anything else?" Yelland asked.

"No, sir."

"Stay with it. Record everything we pick up. And keep working on modifying your transmitters."

"Yes, sir."

Matthew Yelland leaned back in his seat and his eyes moved about the room. No doubt that he'd come to a meaningful decision. "All right, gentlemen, this is how we do it. Stand down, as we agreed, for general quarters to the next level of readiness. I want ferrets out for a meticulous search of anything in the air, on the surface, or beneath the surface for two hundred miles in every direction from this vessel, and not one mile beyond that." Yelland turned to Commander Bill Damon, his operations officer. "Bill, you get together with Thurman and Owens. I want tankers and a scale three strike force, mixed fighters and attack aircraft, on ten-minute alert. If you have no questions, get with it as of right now."

"No questions, sir."

"Take off, then."

Yelland rose to his feet and looked at Warren Lasky. "Mr. Lasky, I want to go into your computer control room off the bridge. You, and me, and nobody else. I want to see what's going on behind that strange smile of yours and I don't want anyone to interrupt us except in event of an emergency. Lieutenant Perry," he said to his officer of the deck.

"Yes, sir."

"You heard where I'll be and with whom, and you will break into our conversation only if there is urgent reason to do so." Yelland didn't wait for a response. He nodded to Lasky. "Let's go."

They reached the bridge quickly and Yelland took a long moment to study the flight deck. Hangar deck crews scurried purposefully along the enormous flat expanse, huffer trucks moving fighters, bombers, and air-refueling tankers into position for immediate launch. The operations speakers boomed. "Secure from general quarters and stand by Condition Three. Secure from general quarters and stand by Condition Three." Other trucks came into sight with small trains of bombs, rockets, and missiles. Yelland's attention turned to the stern as the speakers called out for recovery teams on the double. In the far distance they saw sunlight glinting off the canopy of the Vigilante returning from its reconnaissance run over the Hawaiian Islands.

Yelland started for the computer control cubicle, Lasky only a step behind. Off to his right, standing by the bridge Lucite plotting chart, a seaman made his first mark on an otherwise spotless chart. Lieutenant Perry's voice rang out sharply.

"Captain! CIC reports surface contact, bearing three five zero degrees at one three zero miles."

"Identify!" Yelland snapped.

"No joy, sir. Contact only at this time," Perry replied.

Yelland swung back to his control console and hit several buttons simultaneously. "Launch the ready alert. Launch the ready alert. I want surveillance and visual on that report surface contact."

Speakers confirmed immediate response. The flight deck was alive with crews bringing in the Vigilante on one deck and preparing to catapult two Tomcat fighters on the mission to find the surface contact.

Yelland turned to Lasky. "Mister, it seems we're going to have to delay our little talk. I'd rather have been alone with you for five minutes. Somehow I'm convinced you have answers to a lot of this you're just not telling me."

Again that infuriating smile. "Captain, I could tell you right now."

"Then do it, man!"

Lasky shook his head. "No need to, sir. You'll start getting your answers just as soon as those fighters make contact."

Yelland glared at Lasky, but the civilian was already walking to his computer room.

☆ 10 ☆

The only clouds were on the distant horizon, and the steel-hulled yacht moved steadily and comfortably through the sea of slow-moving swells, its motions in roll and pitch so gentle as to bring on a desire to lapse into sleep. A beautiful day, a beautiful ship, a chef who had been bribed away from one of the finer hotels in Washington, D.C., a good crew. A great bar, time to spare. Even a dog having the time of his life, chasing hovering gulls that followed their deliberate course back toward Honolulu.

Two men watched the dog, both with the same thought. He's going to chase one gull just a bit too damned far and go sliding off into the water. But Charlie was a four-footed expert with the changing angle of a deck, and he managed always to stop just in time. Senator Samuel S. Chapman exchanged a smile with his close friend, Arthur Bellman, who also owned the yacht. And a steel mill, and an aircraft factory, and two lumber mills, and a shipyard, and God knew what else. Chapman was one of the grand old wizards of Capitol Hill, a veteran of the senate floor, and a man with determined high aspirations to keep ascending the political ladder. Bellman took the moment to study his old friend and associate. Damn, but Chappy looked the part he had cast for himself. Silvery hair, a face of wisdom, and that marvelous leonine head atop a body of splendid conditioning. Smooth, bright, even brilliant; above all, skilled in political maneuvering and industrial manipulation. A damned good politician, and one who knew also that more deals were made and closed in back rooms and on yacht decks, like right here and now, than ever took place on any floor where the powerful men of the nation met before the naked view of the press.

Arthur Bellman lacked the polish of the senator, but as a man whose wealth could literally be counted well above a billion dollars, he didn't give a damn about urbanity or the social graces, and neither did anyone else who curried his favor or made the mistake of risking his wrath. The right people in the right places in Washington meant continued favoritism not only for the industrial machinery owned by Bellman, but for his close professional associates as well, and if this crowd that looked down on Wall Street knew how to do anything, it was to maneuver together and keep their differences from interfering with their mutual welfare. Bellman stood a hulking six feet three inches, had a permanent five-o'clock shadow, and a musculature from working up the ranks as a steelworker that not even years of power on top had diminished. He worked, played, loved, and fought with a sheer delight in the struggle. Yet he knew that there was only a certain point he could reach without the added touch of political clout. Thus this private "pleasure cruise." You scratch my back and I'll scratch yours; that was the routine with himself and Chappy. It had been good enough for the times of the Roman senate and it was good enough for today. They had much to offer one another. Sam Chapman wanted to keep ascending the political staircase and Art Bellman wanted all the industrial muscle he could gather. They made a good team. They'd known one another from the early days of their respective lives and by whatever special touch there is in two people they had remained faithful—and scrupulously honest—with one another. Now it was time to forge another rung in their parallel ladders.

They watched the antics of the dog, but their ears were on a different wavelength. The shortwave radio of the yacht, powerful enough to pick up broadcasts from around the world, carried the hypnotizing tone of the master politician of them all, the one and only Franklin Delano Roosevelt, exhorting the American public to ever more and newer new deals and in almost the same breath issuing stern warnings to the Japanese to slack off on their murderous forays through the Far East.

Sam Chapman gestured lazily. "Think the emperor is listening to old Franklin?"

Bellman snorted. "Wouldn't matter if he did. He don't count for diddly-shit, anyway. Wanders around in those stupid robes and carrying that sword, and the cabinet meets with Mitsubishi and the shipyards, and they decide everything. Why should they care what Roosevelt says? He talks out of both sides of his mouth. We send aid to the Chinese, charging them through the nose for it, and we also sell raw goods and machinery to the Japanese at the same time."

"And you charge them through the nose for it," Chapman said.

"Is that a surprise?" Bellman responded. "We sell and we buy all over the world and we're all in the same business."

Chapman's eyes narrowed. "How much interference are your people getting from the White House? You know what I mean, Art. With the really big business. Not the tourist crap."

"Nothing to bother with," Bellman said, a shrug dismissing the issue. "Lots of noise but little else. Don't worry, Senator, I'll be pounding on your door when the government starts screwing with the bankroll."

"Be sure you do," Chapman said easily. He sat erect, looking for the steward. "Harvey! Make it a fresh round, will you?"

The steward's white coat gleamed in the sun. "Right away, Senator. The same for you, Mr. Bellman?"

"Yeah. All around, son."

The steward poured drinks and Bellman tapped his arm. "Fix one for the lady, Harve."

They watched her approach, a stunning body in a one-piece bathing suit, long blond hair caught by the wind. She was as lithe and graceful as a cheetah, and the only item disturbing the touch of total femininity was the package of typed paper in one hand. Sam Chapman leaned to his left and turned down the radio volume. "Finished so soon?" he asked Laurel.

"A pleasure cruise is not made where there are typewriters present," she said lightly. "Yes. Finished in what I consider final draft. There are a few rough spots. Why don't you read them while I do damage to this long-delayed and deserved drink?"

He waved aside her suggestion. "Drink, then you read," he instructed.

She drank quietly for several moments, then put aside the glass as she scanned the papers. "Um. You've already approved most of it. Here it is."

"Go ahead, honey," Chapman said.

Laurel read slowly the words that Arthur Bellman would be speaking before a meeting of the most powerful labor union leaders and industrialists in the country. No one, aside from those present on the yacht, would ever be aware that Laurel Scott, under the direction of Senator Chapman, had them written for Bellman.

"So if he does choose to support my program," Laurel read carefully, "then let Senator Chapman be assured now, because of his impeccable and brilliant record in sustaining the industrial strength and military might of our great country, that we will bring all our resources to bear upon the president of the United States, that the qualifications of Senator Chapman are those which are most needed for the cabinet. There is a need that is imperative, a need that is overwhelming, in the White House. There is needed a voice, a conscience, between our labor and industrial family and the office of the president. That voice and that conscience, so clearly established through selfless service, are found in Senator Samuel S. Chapman. I urge all of you to—" She stopped as Chapman gestured.

"I don't think we could improve on what Laurel writes if we wanted to," he told Bellman.

"And there's no need to," Bellman said. "Laurel, that's perfect. I begin to get the idea that we should retire Sam and run you for the Senate."

"She's too beautiful, Art," Chapman laughed.

"Then let's make her a diplomat, for Christ's sake."

Laurel smiled at them. "I rather thought I was," she said in a low voice. She sipped from her drink. Sunlight reflecting wetly from her lips, Bellman thought, could turn a man to jelly.

Arthur Bellman sighed. "Well, let me tell you something, Laurel. We've had to tread a very fine line right now, and your words are the—well, I didn't expect middle-ground perfection. You know what you've done? You've cooked up a broth of a compromise that could very well make your boss the next vice president of the United States."

Laurel smiled her thanks and rose to her feet. "Then, Mr. Bellman, I believe it's urgent that I do the final typing on these papers right now. I don't want you two talking it over and trying to improve on what the best diplomat in this crowd has already done."

"Ouch," Chapman said, wincing visibly. "I'd fire her except that she's right."

"And stunning," Bellman added as Laurel disappeared below decks to her office. He gazed longingly after her. Which was surprising, since Arthur Bellman could buy just about any woman he wanted. But, he knew, not this one. The price tag here didn't come in dollar signs. Laurel Scott had her own qualifications. She was never hired. She allowed Sam Chapman to hire her, as if it were the woman and not the senator who controlled the moment.

Chapman watched Bellman and chuckled. "Arthur, at least let the girl keep her suit on, will you? The way you're undressing her with your eyes she's liable to catch her death of a cold. And she's much too valuable to us now for the sniffles."

Bellman turned his gaze back to Chapman. "You had her in bed yet?"

The senator chuckled. "That's no question to ask a married man, Art."

"You didn't answer me."

Chapman shrugged, as if to dismiss any further talk on the matter. "Well, you know how these things are—"

"Chappy, you son of a bitch. If ever I've seen prime, that girl is it."

Chapman pushed himself to his feet. "Conversation is pleasant with you, Art, but those papers are critical to both our futures. I'd better check with Laurel and see how things are coming."

"Sure, sure. Business first. Right, right."

Chapman laughed at him. "Oh, come on, Arthur. Have yourself another drink and stop being concerned about how much everybody is getting. You know you can fill this goddamned boat of yours with beautiful belles."

"Thanks, but no thanks," Bellman said tartly. "A man who mixes broads with business ends up with bruises somewhere down the line."

Chapman gestured his goodbye and took the ladder below decks to Laurel's stateroom-office. He heard typing as he opened the door and he peered over her shoulder, his hand touching her arm lightly. He tried to keep his voice calm but the jubilation within him spilled over.

"We swung it, Laurel! By all the holies, we really

swung it, thanks to you. Art is going to throw everything into the campaign. If he needs to, he'll buy the goddamned cabinet position."

Laurel had a half smile on her face. She stopped typing but didn't turn around. "Did you tell him you were sleeping with me?"

Chapman was caught off balance with the question he had never even dreamed would be tossed at him. "What?"

Laurel's voice remained as deadpan as the back of her head. "Sniggering together like a couple of kids," she intoned. "You offer any sordid details?"

Chapman grasped her shoulder; firmly but, as always, gently. "Laurel, for God's sake! Please, turn around."

Hazel eyes bored into his. "Look, I won't lie. I haven't yet to you or about you. By God, I wish I were sleeping with you. I'd give up even my seat in the Senate to—"

"That's stupid, Chappy."

"I *mean* it, damnit!"

And then, in one of those easy but deft motions of hers, she took control of the situation and eased it aside. "It really doesn't matter, Chappy. People assume you and I are shacking up. You know that, don't you? Sometimes you let them believe that, in fact. It doesn't matter. We know. I guess I can live with what people think. It never mattered before and it doesn't matter now. So there's no real difference."

Hope lit in his eyes like a candle. "You mean you'd—"

"I mean, Chappy, that I'm going to put you into the White House—*not* into my bed."

He walked slowly around the table and eased himself to a couch, never taking his eyes from her. She was so beautiful it took his breath away. "You're a strange girl, Laurel."

"I've thought for a long time the word was woman."

"Oh, shit, you know what I mean!"

"Senator, your own rule is never to assume."

"Jesus! You give me more lip and sass and backtalk than any female on Capitol Hill! I don't know why I just don't up and fire you!"

"Because the White House is out there, Chappy. That, and because I'm the best speechwriter you'll ever find, and I know political infighting, and because I'm a woman and beautiful men would never believe all that, and so they let me know things that's pointing you straight to that same seat where Roosevelt sits right now. And strange as it seems to you, if not the rest of the world, I'm more interested in your political career than your erections. I—"

She stopped short with a strange sound from her dog, Charlie. The animal had followed Chapman below decks, and now the dog was on all fours, looking up toward the ladderway, hair bristling, and trying to snarl and whine plaintively at the same time. "Charlie, what's the matter?" Laurel spoke to the dog, trying to soothe the obviously disturbed animal.

The snarls gave way to the whines as if the dog were in pain. "He hears something," Chapman said. "Something we can't hear yet. Whatever it is, it's tearing the hell out of his ears." They watched as the dog suddenly emitted a series of painful yelps and tore out of the compartment to scramble up the ladder.

"Charlie!" Laurel shouted, running after the fleeing dog. Chapman was right behind her. They ran to the deck, watched the dog tear past the astonished Bellman, growling and yelping until he stood on a higher part of the deck. His head pointed in a fixed direction, and he laid back his ears, crouching down as if he could see or hear some terrible overwhelming enemy. "Laurel, what's the matter with him?" Chapman called to the woman.

She stared in dismay at the dog now more than ever in pain. "Sam, I—I don't know. I've never seen him like this."

"He sees or hears something we don't. I—*There!*" His hand shot out to two small specks on the horizon.

"Planes," Bellman said as he came up behind them.

"What kind?" Chapman queried.

"Damned if I know. Too far out to tell yet." Bellman's brow furrowed in creases. "Goddamn, but they're fast. Look at them coming at us."

A low thunder carried across the water. They looked at one another, confused. They couldn't believe the speed at which the two strange machines plunged toward them. They had a head-on view of a thick and squarish body on each machine. "Where the hell are their wings?" Bellman said aloud, talking as much to himself as the others. "They look like they have only stubs for—"

That was all he had time to say before the two aircraft were upon them, faster than they could believe. They couldn't really *see* the planes as they screamed over the water at better than 700 miles per hour. Gray-and-white shapes ripped by, just above the water, and the sound crashed upon them in a terrifying crescendo of pain. There was that first distant thunder rumble and then a shattering *CRAAAACK!* that brought a scream of pain from Laurel and gasps from the men. In that instant the two shapes were gone, stabbing into the sky like two insane arrowheads.

"My God!" Chapman said, wincing as he spoke. "It sounds like a volcano going off!"

A canine shriek followed his words as the dog ran madly for the ladder to take him below deck.

Bellman pointed. "They're coming back! Hang on!"

The two Tomcat fighters came over on their backs, rounding out in an enormous curving loop, and then they fell wildly toward the ocean, pulling out at the last moment, and again there came that incredible blowtorch explosion and scream of thunder. The air about them seemed to boil with maddened sound and they felt pain all through their bodies. They blinked several times and the impossible craft had already diminished to tiny shapes climbing upward until they disappeared in the bright sun.

Chapman rushed to Laurel's side. She had collapsed on the deck, her hands held tightly to her ears, her face screwed up in pain. "It's all right, hon. They're gone." He helped her to her feet. "This time it's you who needs the drink."

"Goddamnit, so do I," Bellman said, his voice strangely hoarse.

They were silent for several moments as they drank deeply. "Art, what the hell were those things?" Chapman asked.

"I have no idea." Bellman polished off the drink, poured another.

"For Christ's sake, Art, you own an airplane factory! Surely you know something about them. You—"

"Shit, Sam, they're impossible. Will that do for an answer?" Bellman was angry and confused. "You saw what I saw! They didn't have any goddamn propellers! No props, so how the hell are they flying! Not only that, they didn't have enough wings to stay in the air. And you saw how they climbed. Holy Jesus, we don't have a thing in the air that can dive that fast, even going straight down!"

Chapman took control of himself. "I swear those were American markings."

Laurel added quick agreement. "I saw that much. A star, but it had strange bars—"

"Not like any other. Our planes have a star with a red ball in the center," Bellman corrected. "Those markings were not what we paint on our planes."

Chapman looked off into the distance where there was only open sky to be seen. "Well, I'll tell you one thing," he said grimly. "I'm on the Senate War Appropriations Committee, and I know every goddamned thing this country is building or even testing, and if those things are ours, they've kept them the best secret in the world."

"And if they're not ours," Bellman murmured, "then God help us."

Laurel put her drink aside. "You two keep right on talking. I'm going to send a radio message to our fleet headquarters at Pearl Harbor. Maybe they'll know something, and if they don't," she added, "we'd damned well better tell them."

☆ 11 ☆

The polished tones, perfect in every reflection, played for every emotional value, carried from the speakers. Not much attention was being paid to the speech, even if the speaker was President Franklin D. Roosevelt. The bridge of *Nimitz* was occupied with far more pressing matters. Dan Thurman and Warren Lasky stood near Captain Yelland as he listened to the voice of Commander Bill Damon from the Combat Information Center. Finally, at a sudden annoyed gesture from Yelland, the officer of the deck switched off the radio background of the speech. Damon's voice came in clearly.

"Captain, close-in visual contact by the fighters of that radar contact."

"Patch me in immediately," Yelland ordered.

There was a momentary pause, then Damon's voice came back in. "Sir, patch complete. Command eleven, if you please."

Yelland's finger stabbed a button marked with the number eleven; he now had direct contact with the flight of two Tomcat fighters.

"Alert One, this is Old Salt. What have you got out there? Over."

"Old Salt from Alert One. Sir, we've overflown the vessel. It's by itself. A private motor yacht, estimated

98

eighty feet. Looks pretty old to be this far out to sea. It—"

"What flag?" Yelland interrupted.

"Star and stripes, sir."

Yelland mulled that over. "Okay, that's fine. Alert One, we'll keep a Hawkeye up at altitude for down-look radar. They'll take over monitoring. Return to your departure point, and take up a CAP station. You'll hold angels fifty. Over and out."

Yelland turned to Thurman and Lasky. "We'll keep them as carrier air patrol at fifty thousand feet, and they can relieve the aircraft now airborne." He touched his lip mike. "Mr. Damon, did you monitor?"

"Yes, sir," Damon's voice came across the speaker.

"Launch a tanker immediately. Modify the CAP orders to take on a full fuel load, then take up their high station."

"Aye, aye, sir."

Within sixty seconds they saw a deck elevator raising a big twin-engine tanker to the deck, crews waiting to move it immediately to its catapult position. The speaker came alive again.

"Captain, COMM here."

"Go ahead," Yelland said.

"Sir, this is Kaufman. We've been monitoring all channels as you ordered. Captain, I really don't understand what's going on. It sounds like, well, sir, it's as if every station has gone bananas on the nostalgia scene. We've had that old broadcast of President Roosevelt, and the music we're hearing is out of an old collection of records. One more thing, sir. We're still picking up the broadcasts in the AM range, and it's all mono. No stereo like we'd get from FM."

"You consider that significant, Mr. Kaufman?"

"Very much so, sir."

"Bring me a report on one page as soon as you can, mister. Bridge out."

Yelland turned to look at the two men with him. He

knew he was still up against that mysterious wall
Lasky continued to present to him, as if he were
trying to shield deep inner thoughts. To the devil with
that, Yelland mused. He'd go around the man. He
turned his gaze to Thurman.

"Well, Dan, you heard Kaufman. What do you make
of it?"

"Sir, I'm a bit confused. We've had plenty of nostalgia programs, but I don't understand the wavelengths
on which they're broadcasting. Besides—"

"Besides," Yelland said dryly, "what the devil would
Armed Forces Radio be doing broadcasting nostalgia
on an AM band after a nuclear war was under way?"
He snorted his own disbelief. "It doesn't tie. It just
doesn't tie."

"Maybe it does, sir," Thurman said. "If we really do
have a nuclear exchange, they could go to AM instead
of the regular channels. It would show we were still
operating and the enemy wouldn't know just how
badly we'd been hurt, or even if we had taken damage at Pearl."

Lasky spoke so quietly they had to strain to hear.
"There's always the chance that all this is a surprise
war games test, I suppose."

To his astonishment, Thurman didn't pick up the
sarcasm in the remark.

"There are always people who'd like to see how we
would react under just this kind of pressure," he said
in agreement.

"Commander," Lasky sighed, "I withdraw the remark. Not even the best stunt men in Hollywood
could have cooked up that storm for a war game."

Thurman turned red. And defensive. "I'm not so
sure about everything you're saying, Mr. Lasky. It appears a strange coincidence that you show up on this
carrier, without notice of your identity until you're on
board, replacing someone else assigned to this vessel,
and then all hell breaks loose. Maybe you were sent
here to watch a lot more than we gave you credit for."

Yelland showed the trace of a smile. "A neat possibility, Mr. Lasky. Care to comment?"

"Sure. I arranged that storm, and the electromagnetic pulse effect, and from my bag of magic tricks I blanked out the satellites, and those lunar stations, and—"

"We get your point, Mr. Lasky," the captain interrupted.

Lasky stayed in there. "Do you, really? How in the name of hell can you even entertain such nonsense in your minds? Doesn't anyone remember that storm was seen long before I ever got here—even if there was the astonishing, impossible, and totally insane possibility of any other consequences of my presence? You're all befuddled and you're not thinking. You're reacting. Don't take this as a personal criticism or a challenge. I've watched you pick up the pieces and operate instantly as a beautifully oiled machine. I daresay I doubt if I could have done the same."

"Is that a backhanded compliment, Mr. Lasky?"

"No, Captain, it's just the truth."

"Tell me more, then," Yelland said in an exchange that he and Lasky only could understand. But Lasky stood firm. "You've *got* to find out for yourself, Captain. It's the only way."

"I could order you to—"

Lasky flared. "No disrespect intended, Captain; you can't order a damned thing from inside my head."

Thurman started an angry protest, but Yelland brushed it aside. "Stand easy, Mr. Thurman. We're having our own private chess game."

"COMM to the bridge. Urgent."

Yelland pressed his mike transmit button. "Bridge. Let's have it."

"Kaufman here, sir. I know it's, ah, a bit strange, but we're getting a news broadcast and I feel you should hear it directly."

Yelland reacted with an angry gesture. There were so damned many parts and pieces to this damned puzzle! "All right, Mr. Kaufman, switch it to Plot. I'll listen in there." He turned to the two men with him. "Come with me."

They left the bridge for Captain's Plot. Several men were working feverishly on electronics equipment. Wires were strung in all directions, but the men stiffened to attention as Yelland entered. He gestured easily. "Stand easy. Stay at your work," he ordered. Yelland went to a master communications console and flipped a switch. A strange voice came from the console speaker.

". . . the headlines. For the first time the Germans appear to have suffered some reverses in their Russian campaign. Soviet resistance has stiffened unexpectedly with the onslaught of freezing weather and sharp counterattacks have thrown the Nazi blitzkrieg off balance. In North Africa, Tobruk is still holding out gallantly against the armored froces of Field Marshal Rommel, but supply lines to the Allied bastion remain cut and its collapse is now considered only a matter of days. On the other side of the world, Japanese troops continue to slice deep into China with major gains on all fighting fronts. In the meantime, the Japanese peace envoys to the United States are now. . . ."

"Turn it off."

Kaufman's face reflected his bewilderment at the sudden interruption of Yelland. "I said to turn the damned thing off!" the captain snarled. Silence followed, and Yelland looked slowly about the room. Everyone was as baffled as he was—except that damned Lasky—and they were a hell of a lot more frightened. That's what comes with living so long with death, Yelland mused to himself. It helps you fight off what scares you more—the unknown. And there it was, he knew. He was some ancient Don Quixote rushing with his giant carrier at an enormous windmill flapping in the fog and he could never quite come to grips with that haunting shape.

The door opened suddenly and they turned to see Commander Bill Damon standing still, making absolutely certain Yelland was here. Then the operations officer blinked several times, as if snapping back from somewhere else in his mind. He handed an envelope to Yelland. "Captain, sorry to break in like this, but—" He pointed to the envelope. "You've got to see these immediately."

The more the stress, Lasky noticed from the side, the better Matt Yelland handles it. The captain took the envelope but made no move to open it. Keeping Bill Damon cool was equally important to him at this moment. "What's in it?" he asked his operations officer.

"The reconnaissance photographs from the Vigilante of Pearl Harbor, sir."

Yelland's expression froze. He turned to the technicians working about them. "Everybody outside," he said quietly. "Stand by in the corridor to resume work when we finish here."

With the room cleared, Yelland opened the envelope, withdrew large glossy photographs, and placed them in a table beneath a bright light. They watched in silence until, without removing his eyes from the pictures, Yelland gestured Thurman and Lasky closer. "Look at these, gentlemen, if you would," he said calmly.

The pictures were in sequences of three—three pictures of each particular scene. The first had been taken in visible light, and few of these revealed much detail, obscured as they were by the heavy cloud cover. A second picture, computer enhanced for clearer readout, had been taken in ultraviolet to penetrate much of the cloud. But the third picture of each sequence was the most effective; this was a radar scan of the subject under search. Computers enhanced the radar image, then translated the return into the equivalent of visible-light photography.

"Tell me again, Bill," Yelland said. "What area is this?"

Damon looked at the photographs of Pearl Harbor, showing the 1941 United States Pacific Fleet at anchor, most of the heavy warships clustered about Ford Island.

"Sir, it's Pearl, like I said."

Dan Thurman tapped the pictures. "The hell it is. I know Pearl and I know this area and it is *not* Pearl Harbor. It may look like Pearl Harbor, but—"

"It's Pearl," Yelland said heavily. He pointed to a row of huge warships, then selected one in particular, secured to its dock. "Do you know what that is?" Yelland continued.

Damon leaned forward between them. "It's a battlewagon, all right. But it looks ancient, and—" He looked at the others. "The only battleships we have are national monuments. Or maybe some in mothballs."

"That ship is active," Yelland said. "Now, look at the raked afterdeck."

Thurman's voice was hollow. "It can't be," he said, dragging out each word. He picked up the photograph, studied it through a powerful magnifying glass. "My God," Thurman said.

"Something like that," sighed Yelland. "It's what it looks like. It's the *Arizona.*"

Thurman forgot himself. "Goddamnit, Captain, she's *intact!*" he shouted.

Yelland ignored the outburst and turned to his side, eyes locked on Warren Lasky. "You don't seem very interested in these photos," he observed, a bit too easily. They held heavy eye contact for several moments, their message known only to themselves and not shared by the others about them.

"I—shall we say, anticipated them?" Lasky countered.

"You know what they show without looking." It was

a statement from Yelland and, significantly, not a question.

"Yes, Captain," Lasky said quietly.

"And that's *all* you're going to say?"

"Yes."

"The same reasons?"

"Yes."

"I have come to respect your thinking, Lasky, but there is one question I demand to have answered. And I want it out straight and honest."

"Ask."

"Did you know any of this before you came aboard *Nimitz*?"

"My God, Captain—no."

Yelland smiled. "You improve my emotional well-being, Mr. Lasky. Seeing you frightened reduces the issue to something I do believe we can fight."

"The word, Captain Yelland, is adapt."

The smile on Yelland's face vanished. Then he studied Lasky with new interest, for the scientist's face suggested a sudden absorption, as if he were just now remembering something seen before, vital to this moment, but remembered anew. There was a memory, a connection. Lasky snapped his fingers. "Captain!" He spoke as if he'd just come awake with a shout.

Yelland again found cause to smile. "I'm wide open to whatever suggestion you're brewing, Mr. Lasky."

"Sir, ask Commander Owens to bring to us the photographs he's using to illustrate that historical work he's writing. I think we can get to grips." He looked at the others. "But when we do, Captain, I want it alone. You and me, nobody else."

"You have it," Yelland snapped. He turned to Thurman. "Get Owens to bring that material here immediately."

Dick Owens came into the room precisely six minutes later, carrying a thick folder with him. He was puzzled, but had a good enough grip on himself to hold his questions. He handed the folder to Yelland, and the captain immediately spread them on the table beneath the bright light. He studied them for a while and then looked up at his air wing commander. "Dick, where did you get these?"

Owens was openly puzzled. "Sir? These pictures? From the archives, Captain. Some from Anacostia and the others from the Smithsonian. A few from the air force, as well. I even got some from the private collections of Japanese pilots." Owens stared at the glistening photographs moved to one side of the table. "But I haven't got a thing as clear as these!" he said with sudden excitement.

"Your photos are not like these," Yelland said. He was making a determined effort to keep his face straight, to show no emotional reaction.

"May I look at them, sir?" Owens asked. Yelland nodded and Owens studied the pictures. "They're magnificent. I would never have believed they could do high-altitude photography like this back in the early forties."

"They didn't, Commander Owens." The CAG officer looked up. "These pictures, Dick," Yelland said softly, "were taken by the Vigilante recce mission no more than two hours ago."

Owens's answer was instant. "Sir, I don't believe you. It's some kind of joke."

"No joke."

"But that's impossible!"

"Yes, it is."

"Damnit, sir, these are pictures of the fleet that was clobbered by the Japanese on December seventh and. . . ." His voice trailed away. "With all due respect, Captain Yelland, I do not understand why this hoax is going on."

The "hotline" speaker came alive in the room. "CIC to the captain. CIC to the captain. Priority One, repeat, Priority—"

Yelland hit the contact button. "Yelland here. Let's have it."

"Lieutenant Perry, sir. The high radar patrol reports two bogies, angels fifteen, course zero nine zero, very slow moving, current distance one hundred twenty-five miles. Over."

Yelland acted as if he'd had a shot of adrenalin. "Very good, Mr. Perry. Notify CAP to move out for an extreme altitude lookdown over the bogies. They are to make every effort to avoid even visual contact. Out."

Nimitz's first pair of Tomcats had descended in a swooping curve from fifty thousand feet to rendezvous with the turboprop air-refueling tanker at thirty thousand. One fighter was already tanked, holding off to one side as the second Tomcat took on a fast and heavy fuel load. In both cockpits the pilots received the same message.

"Alert One, this is Old Salt. Condition Red, Condition Red. Vector Two One Zero at angels five zero for overfly two bogies low and slow. Respond to call sign Buster. Avoid visual contact if at all possible. Read back your orders. Over."

Moments later the Tomcat still hooked to the tanker fell back to disengage lines. The two fighters eased into formation and swung to a heading of 210 degrees, climbing swiftly to fifty thousand feet and leveling off.

Yelland pulled the lip mike to touch closer to his face. He had returned to the bridge after swearing to strict secrecy the men who had studied the Vigilante reconnaissance photos, the subject not to be even mentioned without his direct order. Warren Lasky went with Yelland and was requested to remain by his side. "Right now, Mr. Lasky, I don't believe your computers need you. Or should I say, our computers. Our people will tend to whatever's needed. I want you by my side at all times, because I have the definite feeling you may just develop a hole in the side of your brain and all those thoughts you've been clutching so tightly may spill out before me." Despite himself, Lasky grinned. No wonder they'd put Yelland where he was at the command of the mighty *Nimitz*. What they faced now with the great carrier was enough to chew apart a man's mind, even more so than danger to life itself.

At the moment, Lasky's interest matched that of the captain's. The captain had assumed direct contact with the two Tomcat fighters on their intercept vector of the two unidentified aircraft. "Buster, this is Old Salt One. You copy? Over."

The radio speakers crackled with the sharp transmission. "Ah, roger that, Old Salt One. Buster One here."

"Very good. What have you got, Buster? Over."

"Buster flight at angels fifty. I've got binoculars out now. Radar confirmation two bogies, holding close together just above the cloud deck. Estimate six to nine thousand, and doing about two hundred knots. They— man, I don't believe this."

"Say again, Buster."

"Uh, sorry, sir. It just took me by surprise. Those planes, the ones below us. I swear they're Zero fighters. You know, the old Mitsubishi Zeros out of the Second World War. Over."

Lasky tapped Yelland's arm. "The mike. May I?"

Yelland pushed a headset and microphone to him and Lasky spoke immediately. "Uh, Buster One from Old Salt One. Can you get a good look at the bogies? They might not be Zero fighters. There are a bunch of old SNJ trainers rebuilt to look like Zeros for Hollywood. Can you be certain of your identification?"

Yelland looked with open admiration at Lasky. Why the hell hadn't he thought of that? There were a bunch of pilots who rebuilt and flew World War II fighters and bombers and trainers. That outfit in

Florida; the Valiant Air Command. And the Confederate Air Force down in Texas. There were others. They flew every old warplane on which they could get their hands. My God, maybe all this wasn't so crazy after all. The bubble burst.

"Old Salt One, we can't see that kind of detail from up here, but there's no way they could be the modified trainers. We've got radar track over the surface of those two aircraft and they're cruising at 200 knots, which is faster than the old SNJ could ever do. Maybe it's an air show of some kind. I heard they had a couple of Zero fighters flying, and it could be a kind of special ceremony for the Pearl Harbor anniversary. Over."

Lasky shook his head slowly at Yelland, who nodded his own agreement. Yelland spoke into his mike. "Have you been spotted, Buster?"

"Negative on that, sir. We're too high. We've got our wings swept forward and we're making S-turns to stay well behind them. We can pretty much hold six o'clock high on those old crates. Over."

"Very good, Buster. Continue as you are. Try to keep them in visual contact at all times and maintain your position out of their visual. Take no action without direct clearance from Old Salt One. Do you copy? Over."

"Copy five by five, sir."

Yelland removed his headset. "Mr. Damon, you will assume the con, if you please. I will be in my cabin with Mr. Lasky."

"Aye, aye, sir."

☆ 12 ☆

They ate lunch quietly, by unspoken agreement holding off from the conversation Matthew Yelland and
Warren Lasky knew they must finally broach. The
mess attendant cleared away the dishes, left a full pot
of coffee, and at Yelland's orders closed the door behind him, leaving the two men alone. The captain
opened a humidor and offered Lasky a slim dark cigar. As he lit up, Yelland spoke easily. "I used to
smoke these before 'nam. One of the things that
helped pull me through in two years of solitary, in a
cage not big enough so I could stand, was to smoke
three imaginary cigars every day. I suppose I actually
mesmerized myself. I could smell them and taste them
and it became a ritual. Now," he sighed, "I'm keeping
a promise I made to the me that used to be in the cell.
Three a day. The flight surgeon," Yelland said with an
easy laugh, "gives me hell. He tells me smoking isn't
good for my lungs after all the damage they took.
What the hell does he know? These are the things that
saved my sanity and my life." Yelland let smoke drift
from his nostrils. He looked at the smoke as he spoke
to Lasky.

"Warren, you ever wear the uniform?"

Lasky didn't miss the first name from the other
man. He twirled the cigar in his fingers and nodded.
"Surprisingly, yes. Would you believe coast guard?

Four years and one of them at sea and in the Antarctic. Scientist type. Oceanography."

Yelland swung his gaze to him. "That's right. You chewed on me pretty good when we were talking about tsunamis."

"Sorry about that, Captain."

"Never be sorry for being right. Especially," Yelland emphasized, "when your right keeps someone like me from being wrong. I suppose I was grasping pretty desperately for straws."

"You were," Lasky said bluntly. "Now you're doing your best to avoid the reality that's shaken you to the depths of your soul."

"It's time to cut the mustard, Warren."

"I know."

"I just don't understand it. All that radio crap with Jack Benny and Franklin Roosevelt and then that wartime newscast—"

"The satellites and lunar stations that winked out of existence," Lasky added.

"Those Vigilante photos shook me up," Yelland said, continuing the slow sparring.

"The Zero fighters didn't help, either," Lasky continued, driving in yet another nail.

"Goddamnit, Warren, *somebody*, for *some* reason, *wants* us to believe we're back in 1941!"

"Captain, you can quit now. You can face the absolutely impossible. You're lying to yourself. Those straws again. You don't believe for a moment that someone wants to believe we're back in 1941."

Yelland snorted with disdain. "Either that or I have to accept that I've gone off the deep end. And don't give me that mysterious knowing smile again, damn you!"

"You're not crazy and we both know it. That eliminates two possibilities." Lasky locked eyes with Yelland. "There's the third."

The words came out slowly, distinctly, each a separate utterance. *"I—don't—believe—it."*

"You'd better, Captain. Because it's the only reality we have. Is it that difficult to say it out loud?"

"You want me to believe that all this, everything that's happened, is *real?*"

"I know it and you know it," Lasky said with open irritation, "and all we're doing here is sparring. I'll spit it out. Somehow, in a way we don't understand and may never understand fully, the *Nimitz* and its entire crew was warped back in time from 1980 to December 6th in 1941. *There*, goddamnit, it's out in the open now!"

"But it's completely crazy!"

"It's not crazy and above all, for the reason that it happened. It happened, it is happening right now. That was no ordinary storm. I said before there can be a confluence of a massive electromagnetic effect and a stumbling gravity wave. If that happens, it can twist space into a knot. It did happen. Space is the same thing as time, just as you can't exist unless you have a lifetime. There was this storm beyond all our knowledge, and it ripped up space one side and down the other, and we were caught right in the middle of it, like a web that's pulled and distorted, and when everything snapped back into place—we're here, forty years ago."

They settled on another period of silence. Their cigars went out. Lighting up again was their agreement to renew the utter, stark impossible.

"That is one hell of a pill to swallow, Warren."

"I don't argue the point. I just face the reality."

"What do your computers have to say about all this?"

"I think they tried to throw up."

They laughed together. It made things easier. Lasky swallowed a cup of coffee, chewed on his cigar, and leaned forward with both elbows on the table. "Captain, do you mind if I lay something on you?"

Yelland waved aside all objections. "Jesus Christ, man, the name is Matt. Go on."

"All right, Matt. Think about this. If I had a time machine, and for some reason I decided I had a score to settle with, oh, let's say my grandfather, and I got in that little fancy gadget of mine and went back through the years with a revolver—"

"I'm with you and ahead of you," Yelland broke in. "You spend a lot of time with paradoxes when you live in a cage as long as I did. So you go back in time, right? And you find your grandfather and you fill him full of neat holes, and that spells finis for the old boy right then and there. The next question comes of itself. What happens if you shoot your grandfather before he bedded down with your grandmother, and your own parent never happened?"

"Very good," Lasky said. "I'll take it another step down the line. It's the old paradox that's confounded physicists for decades. Or at least it was more of a paradox before we confirmed the existence of black holes. You know, a collapsed star that begins its collapse with a mass at least three times or more than that of our own sun."

"I'm up with the subject. Go ahead."

"Well, in that kind of situation, the inward acceleration of gravity of a black hole is so great that not even light can escape the gravitational field."

"Agreed."

"My point is, Matt, that such a situation is absolutely impossible. Do you understand what I'm saying? I am postulating a literal condition that is impossible—at the same time that it's acceptable. Presto; we have an understandable paradox, which in itself, at least in the philosophical sense, is impossible. Now, let me take the next step. In our universe—call it our physical space-time—we know that the velocity of light is an absolute. The speed of light is a finite reality. If you accelerate a mass to the velocity of light, what happens? That object reaches infinite mass, time comes to an absolute standstill, and since you're out of moving time, you can't accelerate something that's reached infinity."

Yelland made a sour face. "So they taught me in school."

"But when you went to school they didn't know about black holes. Hell, they weren't confirmed until 1968 or so. Do you understand my point, Matt? We know, we absolutely know, it is impossible to travel faster than light. That means you cannot have anything, mass or energy, that exceeds light velocity. You still agree with me?"

Yelland eyed him suspiciously. "I still agree."

"Well, you're wrong and what you were taught was wrong and what almost everybody believes is wrong. Because when you enter the situation created by a black hole, inward gravitational acceleration is so great that not even light can escape. Something exists that breaks all the rules. It's a gravitational acceleration that exceeds light velocity."

"That's impossible. Or else it's permissible to violate the laws of actuality. Is that your paradox?"

Lasky nodded. "It is. We are face-to-face with a situation that is impossible. But it exists. And that's the real brain twister. It's so impossible it can't exist. It absolutely cannot. But it does. What happens when you hold the impossible in your hand—or the impossible has grabbed you? Ah. It is at this point that nature steps in and says, it's not nice to screw with nature, and the black hole winks out of existence. The inward acceleration is infinite, so a human body entering a black hole would be subjected to infinite, or greater than infinite acceleration. It would be nasty beyond all comprehension."

"In what way, Warren?"

"If you were going down into a black hole feet first, your feet would likely be accelerating a million or a billion or a trillion times faster than your head was moving."

"That sounds like a very special brand of nasty," Yelland agreed through a cloud of smoke. "And it's both paradox and theory—"

"And reality," Lasky insisted.

"All right, it's paradox and theory and reality all wrapped in one because you can't prove it, right?"

"Proof is a relative thing," Lasky snorted. "You can't prove the sun will rise tomorrow. If I make an X on the back of my hand and present the unmarked side to you, you can't prove the X is there."

"Sure I can. I just turn over your hand."

"And until you do that," Lasky countered, "what? You have no proof. You've got a hell of a supposition but you can't prove a damn thing."

Yelland tightened his grip on the cigar. "Go on."

"We know, and I'm not playing theory handball with you, Matt, that black holes exist because we still judge and measure their effect. *That's* the key. It's like dealing with a neutrino. It moves with the speed of light, has no discernible mass, can pass through an average of fifty light years of solid lead before it's even affected by that medium. We've never seen a neutrino but I'm as certain that it exists as I know I'm in this room with you. Back to the black hole. It twists space and you can't do that without twisting time because they're the same package. Something happened to this ship, Matt, that could well have involved, and indeed seems to have involved, a tremendous twisting of space-time."

"Are those gravity waves you spoke of real?"

"As real as waves breaking on a seashore," Lasky said. "That's why I'm convinced that everything that's happened to us, even if we understand only a fraction of the cause and must live with the effect, meets these newly confirmed laws of astrophysics. Only," Lasky said with careful emphasis, "we have more than theory with which to work."

"I'm dying to hear *that* one," Yelland sighed.

"For Christ's sake, Matt, *we're here*. We're not in our familiar time anymore. You know that. We're in yesteryear."

"So it seems," Yelland said dryly. "Now tell me something else. How does all this fit in with your going back in time to do the dastardly deed to your grandfather?"

"Neatly done," Lasky said with a grin. "You've brought me full circle, haven't you?"

"Don't be evasive or cute, Warren."

"I'm not trying to do either. I can't shake the headache all this is giving me. I feel like the scientist who spent all his life proving a rocket can't work in space because it doesn't have any air against which to push, and then I discover that the damned thing works very well in a vacuum because it pushes against itself. It's a bootstrap effect that is very real, very physical, and makes instant common sense once you learn to understand the mechanism of action, reaction, and acceleration. Right now we face something of the same situation. We have to step through some cerebral diaphragm and throw away all the common sense on which we've based our lives. It's not easy." Lasky took a deep breath. "So we'll do as you ask and we'll consider the grandfather paradox. If I do the old gent in before he meets my grandmother, they simply do not meet. They produce no children, and so on down the line. I am never born. But I exist—therefore, I could never have gone back in time to kill my grandfather, because I'm here. So how could I have been born and have come to invent the time machine, and—"

"You're giving me your bloody headache, you know," Yelland growled. "You're also carrying on what seems to be a splendid exercise in futility."

"Captain, very soon you may put that exercise to it's ultimate test."

Yelland came fully alert. "How do you mean that?"

"What if someone, today, kills your grandfather out there in this world where we find ourselves? Or my grandfather? Or kills the man who invented the jet engine when he did? What happens to the time stream?"

"The answer serves itself, Warren. The answer is that no matter what else happens or has happened or is going to happen, the dominant and pervading reality is that *we are here*. We exist. You can't deny that."

Welcome to my den, Captain," Lasky said with a smile. "Yes, we do exist, and the denial is a verbal muttering with no value. But I have another question for you."

Yelland groaned. "Go ahead."

"We both agree we exist, right?"

"Yes."

"My question, then, is not whether we exist, *but when?*"

Try as he might, Matt Yelland had no answer.

☆ 13 ☆

Laurel stretched out on the stern deck, soaking in the high sun. Shorts and a thin blouse knotted to support her full breasts, her flowing hair spread behind her, created a sensuality that brought murmured compliments from the passengers and crew alike. Sprawled near by, calm after the hysteria of the strange aircraft with their shattering thunder, was her dog, Charlie. To her other side, his head aching from trying to settle too many questions at one time, Senator Sam Chapman lay inert, hat over his face to shade his eyes, dozing. It was almost as if they had all declared some form of emotional truce aboard the yacht. The sight of those impossible machines, their bulletlike speed, had jangled them all far more severely than they were aware. Instinct had taken over direct thought, guiding them to relax, to give the whole thing a respite. Art Bellman was the only one in the group who had rejected the euphoria of hiding behind a mental wall. That wasn't his way. He'd gone to the radio shack to make contact with the navy at Pearl Harbor. He described the two machines to a bored radioman to whom, obviously, the voice of Bellman was a crank, a drunk, or a weirdo. The radioman had promised to take down the information and to pass it on to the proper authorities, and as Bellman demanded his name, the radio went dead.

Frustrated, Bellman whipped the headset from him and smashed it to the table. He took a deep breath. Well, scratch one headset. But goddamn that fool operator, they had something that couldn't exist, *but did*, and they had several expert witnesses for the navy, and Bellman couldn't get some son of a bitch off his ass because it was a weekend, and the sailor was probably pissed because he had duty instead of being free to chase broads on the beach. Well, when he got back he'd have them go through every duty roster and he'd track down that son of a bitch and put his feet to the fire.

Art Bellman forced himself to calm down, then climbed up the ladder to the stern deck. For several moments he stood quietly, looking down in frank admiration at Laurel. He shook his head slowly. That was the most sensual, desirable woman he'd ever known in his life. And the smartest. Bellman made up his mind right on the spot that Chappy was a lying son of a bitch. He'd never bedded down this woman. No way in the world. He just dropped little hints and innuendos that he might be sleeping with her, but—

Bellman lifted his head at a familiar sound, a deep-throated but still low growl in the distance. He knew that sound. Aircraft engines. And from the sound, they had to be radial engines. Probably a navy flying boat on patrol. The Japanese had been kicking up a shitfit in recent weeks and Roosevelt had ordered increased patrols in all directions from vital American bases. But . . . he listened more carefully. Damnit, he knew engines. He'd listened to enough of them on the flight line and in the air over his own plant. He knew Wrights and Pratt & Whitneys and these weren't any of those engines. The back of his neck tingled. The buzzing-hornet sound was louder. He could tell there was more than one plane out there. And they were low and coming in their direction. Not the planes he'd heard and seen before. This sound came from a radial, no question.

Laurel was looking up at him. "What is it, Art? You look like something's wrong."

He nodded, still scanning the horizon. "Listen . . . you hear them?"

She raised to one elbow. "Planes. I guess. It could be a boat."

He shook his head. "No. They're planes. And they're low. Too low. Chappy! Get the hell up!"

The senator pushed the hat from his face. "What is it?"

Bellman didn't have to answer. Now they could all hear the deep-throated rumble of engines coming closer. "Art, those crazy planes again?" he asked.

"Uh uh. Those are radials. I was just telling Laurel there's no reason for them to be this low. Except maybe someone's in trouble."

"Look!" They turned to Laurel's cry, looked where she pointed. Two small dots on the horizon moving toward them, slowly. "What are they, Art?" Chapman asked again.

Bellman shrugged. "Dunno, Chappy. Scouts or fighters, by the size of them. Can't tell yet. Too far away. We'll know in a few moments when they're closer."

"I'll be in my cabin," Laurel announced, leaving for the ladderway. Chapman nodded to her, and he joined Bellman standing by the stern rail. The steward had come to the deck from below and stood by the ladder. When the senator roused from a nap he almost always wanted a drink. Harvey would stand by until the request came. But at the moment the senator and Mr. Bellman were preoccupied with those aircraft coming closer to them.

Aircraft approaching head-on always surprised you. They were tiny dots way out, then you could see the wings and the round shape of the fuselage, and abruptly, faster than a man realized, they were upon you. The hornet sounds turned into a swelling roar and then an overwhelming rush of thunder as they passed directly overhead. The three men on the stern ducked instinctively as the two planes flashed over them and continued beyond, beginning a slow turn.

Chapman gripped Bellman's arm. "Did you ever see anything like those before? I swear they had Japanese markings!"

Bellman's face reflected his own suspicions. "Red ball insignias. Japanese, if they're anything. But—"

"But what? What were they?" pressed Chapman.

"Chappy, I don't know," Bellman said candidly. "When I first saw them I thought they were P-36 fighters. Curtiss jobs. Radial engines, single-seat, low wing. But there's something different about these. I don't know. And those Japanese markings. . . ." His voice trailed off as he searched his memory.

"From everything I've ever heard about Japanese planes," Chapman said with open disdain, "they're made of bamboo and rice paper. Those planes were sleek, Art. They didn't look like they were made by people with buck teeth and rotten eyesight."

"No, no," Bellman said thoughtfully, "they didn't. But I swear those markings are Japanese." He looked across the bright ocean as the two dots continued in their turn. "I think they're coming back."

"Well, we'll know soon enough," Chapman said easily. "Besides, how could they be Japanese, anyway, this far out in the ocean from Japan? They wouldn't have the range."

"Could be carrier based," Bellman murmured.

"You don't sound as if you believe that," Chapman laughed. "A Japanese carrier this close to the Hawaiian Islands? They'd never take that kind of chance of getting Roosevelt pissed at them. Lose their trade advantages with us? No way, Art, no way." Chapman turned. "Harvey! Make it a tall, cool one."

"Yes, sir, Senator."

Petty Officer Jiro Simura looked up rfom the cockpit of his sleek Zero fighter. Hiroyu Togawa held perfect formation off his wing, the two planes flying as one. They had maintained the flight percision for which they were so well-known among the other carrier pilots. A perfect team, leader and wingman, picked especially for this long-range patrol well ahead of their task force. And now Simura was disturbed. They were under the strictest orders to maintain radio silence. He could understand why. So far as anyone knew the task force might never have existed. It moved across the Pacific expanse without knowledge of its presence or its purpose. Radio silence was absolutely critical, Simura and the other pilots had been told.

And now there was that American ship, by its flag. A yacht of some kind, and worst of all, it had a tall aerial mast. That meant it could reach American navy installations in Hawaii. If it reported sighting two Japanese fighters, their whole mission would be revealed. Simura waved to Togawa. The other pilot looked back and Simura held up a clenched fist and downpointed thumb. Togawa nodded at the prearranged signal. Attack the unknown vessel immediately. Try to sink it. They had no bombs, but each fighter was equipped with two machine guns and two 20-mm cannon, and that was a thin-hulled and vulnerable target. Simura signaled Togawa to ease slightly away from his own fighter so that they would have a better field of fire. They rolled out of their turns and dove for the yacht.

Art Bellman followed the two aircraft through powerful binoculars. "I don't believe it," he said quietly.

"What is it?" Chapman questioned.

"Chappy, I don't give a damn about buck teeth or bamboo, but those markings are Japanese, that means there *is* a Japanese carrier somewhere in this area. We'd better notify the navy at once."

Chapman snorted. "We tried that before, remember? All we got was a lot of crap about notifying the proper authorities or something, and that means probably Monday morning at the earliest."

"I don't give a damn about before," Bellman snapped. "This time you say they're Japanese planes and that—shit, Chappy, call in a mayday, for Christ's sake! Get their attention somehow."

"Mayday? That's an emergency, Art, and we don't have—"

His mouth remained moving and he tried to talk but no words came forth. A stuttering sound rolled across the water from the planes now rushing directly at them in a steady dive, but preceding the sound was the white froth of ocean boiling in spouting rows that kept moving toward the yacht. The noses and wings of the Japanese planes were ablaze from the firing guns and cannon.

"My God, they're shooting at—!"

A cannon shell exploded in his chest. Chapman had no time to even cry out in horror as Bellman's torso erupted in a huge gout of spraying blood, bones, and flesh. At the same moment the impact hurled his body wildly through the air like a rag doll. Blood splashed on Chapman and instinct brought him flat to the deck. Immediately over his head came an ear-splitting roar of glass shattering, wood being torn apart, the heavy cough and explosions of cannon shells going off. Chapman hugged the deck. He looked up as their engineer came rushing up the ladder. "Durrell! Go back down! Get down, for God's sake!"

Machine gun bullets pounded the ship from its bow back to the stern, cannon shells intermixing and exploding steadily. Four holes appeared magically in Durrell's head, and as he stood motionless, his head came flying apart as if a grenade had gone off inside an overripe melon. Chapman vomited, choking and gasping. Above the tumultuous roar he heard Laurel scream. Smoke billowed from the entranceway to the below-deck cabins. "My God," Chapman moaned. He started to his feet when cannon shells exploded across the yacht again and he hugged the deck, his face slippery from the blood all about him.

Commander Bill Damon's face showed shock, then amazement as he listened to his headset. "Captain!" he called, at the same moment punching in the bulkhead speakers. "It's Alert One, sir!" he said to identify the voice on the speakers.

". . . coming around for a second run. Jesus, they're firing everything they've got against that yacht. We've got smoke and some flames visible. You copy, Old Salt?"

Captain Yelland let his war room continue controlling the two Tomcat fighters shadowing the Zeros. He turned to his operations officer. "Mr. Damon, I assume this was their second firing run?"

"Yes, sir."

Dick Owens looked at them, confused. "Is that the same yacht radar picked up before?" He knew by the answering looks he was right. "What's this about Japanese fighters? And they're shooting up the yacht? What the hell is going on here?" He asked the question at the group. He received no direct answer.

Instead, Yelland turned to the civilian, and instantly Dick Owens was aware that these two had had some heavy conversations with no one else present. There was too clearly a deep understanding between them.

"Are we thinking the same thing?" Yelland was saying to Lasky.

The civilian scientist nodded. "It's got to be, Captain. Advance patrol has to be the answer. They find a ship, they can see the aerials and that means—"

"Of course," Yelland said quietly. "Knock them out before they can get off a message about the presence of Japanese fighters."

"For Christ's sake!" Owens shouted. "What's going—"

"*Commander Owens,*" Yelland said icily. It was enough to snap Owens out of it.

"Yes, sir," he said with instant control.

"A question. You're the historian here. Where was the Japanese fleet, the task force that struck at Pearl Harbor, at this same time, on the sixth of December in 1941? Better yet, show us on the plot table. Now."

They moved to the plotting board and Owens's finger circled a small area. "The northwest sector of Pearl Harbor, Captain. Round about here."

Yelland nodded, looked sideways at Owens. "Dick, have the recce plane check out that area. I want maximum altitude, everything they can get. If they sight any surface craft, they're to remain as far distant as possible. Get oblique radar coverage and whatever the cameras can pick up. Avoid visual contact if at all possible. Get on it right away."

"At once, sir," Owens replied.

Behind them the speakers crackled into life again and they turned with the urgency of the Tomcat pilot's voice. "They're making another run! Old Salt from Alert One, they're shooting that ship to pieces down there! Request permission to break up the attack. Repeat, request permission to open fire. Over!"

The men on the bridge watched Captain Yelland, shrouded in some mysterious agony of indecision. Thurman's voice broke into his thoughts.

"For God's sake, Skipper! You heard them! We've got to—"

Yelland's finger stabbed the transmit button. "Old Salt One to Alert One. Hold your fire. I repeat, *hold your fire*. That is an order. Confirm. Over."

The men on the bridge—with the exception of Warren Lasky—stared in dismay at their captain.

"Get these life jackets on!" Chapman shouted to Laurel and the steward. "Get them on right now, goddamnit! Our only chance is to get the hell off this tub. Jesus, will you two move it? They're coming in again!"

Laurel and Harvey slipped into the life jackets,

moving at the same time to the deck opposite to that of the diving fighters. Laurel stopped suddenly, wide-eyed, staring at Chapman. "Charlie!" she cried out suddenly. "Where's Charlie?"

Chapman grabbed in desperation at her arm. "Laurel! For God's sake, *not now*! They're coming at us again!"

She jerked away, started for the entryway to below decks. Chapman lunged at her, shouting to Harvey. "Get her!"

They grasped her arms, fought off her frenzied attempts to reach the ladderway. "Over the side!" Chapman yelled. "Damnit, they're almost on us! Throw her over the side!"

Laurel screamed, but the two men were as desperate and much stronger. They picked her up physically and threw her over the rail into the sea, jumping after her. Chapman spit out water as he came up to the surface, looking wildly for Laurel. "Swim, damn you!" he railed at her. "Get away from this thing!" He started swimming furiously. Harvey was already paddling for his life, and after a final agonized look behind her, Laurel followed.

Behind them they heard the stuttering of the machine guns and then the heavier coughing bark of cannon firing. Almost at the same instant a wave of heat passed over them. "Down!" Chapman screamed. "Get under!"

Three heads ducked under the water as the yacht exploded in a great sheet of flame and erupting debris. Laurel had a split-second image of blood appearing on Chapman's head, and then he flopped still and his face fell into the water. She screamed his name, swimming wildly to reach him. She lunged across his body and jerked back on his hair to bring his face out of the water. He coughed water and gasped for air and she held him upright. "I—I'm okay now," he said. "Hit . . . I think I was hit."

"It's your head."

"Never mind that. I'll be okay. Where's Harvey? Did he—there; he's okay. Good God—the ship." Flames enveloped the yacht and they swam steadily away from the heat washing over them.

"Alert One, this is Old Salt One. How is it down there? Over."

"Old Salt One, there's been a pretty bad explosion. The entire yacht is covered in flames. Looks like they hit the fuel tanks. The ship's a goner. Over."

Yelland nodded to himself. He looked at the men with him on the bridge as he continued talking directly to the fighters. "Report on any survivors."

"Uh, hard to see. Lots of smoke and we're using binoculars and— Yes, sir, I can see three Mae Wests! Bright yellow, in the water. Uh, Old Salt One, those bastards are going in for another run! They're going to strafe them in the water. *Request permission to fire.* Over."

Yelland felt he must walk the thin razor line of action. He made a sudden decision. "Alert One, start your descent immediately. Do whatever you can to pull their fire, but do not open fire with any weapons. Do you understand? Pull their fire, but do not use any ordnance. Confirm; Over."

"Yes, sir!" The voice cracked hard from the speakers. "No shooting, but we'll get 'em! Over." Then they heard the first Tomcat pilot calling his wingman. "Fold 'em back, Mickey. Full AB's and let's go."

"Roger, One. Wings coming back now."

On the bridge they could picture the scene. The Tomcats had been holding high-altitude formation with their wings swept forward for maximum lift at slow speed. Now the wings swept full back, turning each Tomcat into a giant arrowhead shape. Afterburners spat flame from the jet engines now screaming at full power, and in brief seconds, noses pointed down steeply, the Tomcats ripped through the speed of sound and plunged earthward in a steep curving supersonic rush.

Chapman and Laurel struggled to remain concealed by debris hurled about them by the explosion. They floated in a sputum of deck chairs, screens, cushions, sections of paneling, and other wreckage. "That's it," Chapman gasped, struggling to assist Laurel. "We've got to get out of these life jackets. Those pilots are aiming at the yellow color. Get it off, girl! When I tell you, dive under the water. It's our only chance."

He slipped out of his own jacket. "Be ready, now." He looked for Harvey, who was still wearing his life jacket. Goddamn! In that white jacket and bright yellow vest he was a brilliant target. "Harvey! Get the hell out of your vest! Get under the water when they come at us again!"

He heard engines winding up in another dive as the Zeros rolled from their turns. Harvey's voice was the rattle of death. "Can't . . . I can't, sir. I can't swim. I—"

"Get under!" Chapman shouted to Laurel. "They're firing again!" He swam desperately to reach the steward, but at the same moment the sea boiled as bullets and cannon shells ripped up a line of boiling foam. Chapman took a deep breath and went under. He heard bullets smacking the water and the cannon shells exploding. Then the blows stopped and he broke the surface, gasping, looking for Harvey. He was as helpless as a toy duck in a shooting gallery, and—

"Oh, Jesus." The top half of Harvey's head was gone. Chapman turned to swim towards Laurel, who looked in wide-eyed horror at the corpse bobbing up and down in the water.

Jiro Simura broke sharp left after the firing run, just high enough for his wingtip to clear the water. He knew Togawa had plenty of room to ride the high side of the turn, and both men had the chance from minimum altitude to search for the survivors. That at least three of the Americans had escaped the ship just before the explosion was evident. The life jackets and moving arms told them that. One now was dead, the corpse slumped bloodily amidst the debris. But the other two *must* be killed. Simura rolled out into a steady climbing turn to five hundred feet and came about sharply once more. His face remained devoid of expression, neither triumph nor sadness. This was his duty. His orders were clear. If they encountered any American craft that might signal the enemy, they must dispose of them before any radio signals might be sent on to their main base. He was convinced they had destroyed the yacht before a radio signal could be dispatched. Now they must continue their duty—be certain that there remained no survivors to compromise the secrecy of the great task force. Simura saw signs of splashing. Ah; the Americans would not fool him. Two people in the water. They had shed their life vests so as not to be clear targets. But he had them in sight. Without taking his eyes from the two people swimming below he gave the hand signal to Hiroyu Togawa to commence another strafing run. This must be their final attack; fuel was running low.

A flash to his left startled him. He looked up and his eyes widened in surprise and disbelief. What could that be! Two silver shapes and they had no wings, rushing at terrible speed straight toward himself and Togawa! He was an experienced aviator and a single glance told him a great deal. He saw no place for a propeller, only a great wedge-shape, another flying immediately behind and close to the leader. But their speed—it was not possible! He stamped hard right rudder and slammed the stick over to the right in a punishing corkscrew roll out of the left turn, knowing Togawa would stay with him. The Zero could outmaneuver anything the Americans could put in the air, but these machines could not be, and—

He had no time for further thought as the great arrow shapes exploded into being, so fast was their speed. The strange machines had rushed at them from the very waves and now they pulled up to whip directly before the rolling Zeros. Simura's world filled with a blurred streak as the machine tore past him. He knew what would happen next and frantically he jerked back on the throttle to kill power and speed, but it was too late. A tremendous blow smashed the Zero, whipping the stick painfully against his thighs. Never before had he ever heard the sound of another plane in flight over the roar of his own engine. It simply was too loud, but for the first time he heard a thunder, a deep howling cry, and then another explosive wave hurled the Zero fighter wildly from his control. His ears rang and his vision blurred. He tried to comprehend what was happening, but all he could do was fight desperately for control before his fighter struck the water. To one side he saw Togawa recover barely in time, pulling up sharply from the same terrible blow that had struck his own Zero. Simura tried to understand. There had been no flashes of machine guns or cannon. He knew the severe turbulence that could come from another machine's wake as you flew into it, but this was more, a fierce explosive blast that—

No matter. That was not a Japanese machine out there, and he must do his duty. He signaled Togawa to take up position off his wing, and he watched carefully as the devil airplanes swung high above them in an incredible zoom he did not believe possible. Then they were coming back, curving earthward and rolling. Simura watched the moves, knew the acceleration curves they must follow, and he worked his controls swiftly, surely so that his nose would be in such a position that the devil airplanes must cross before him. *Now!* The arrow shapes hurtled at them and Simura opened fire with all his guns and cannon. Flashes to his right told him Togawa was doing the same. But they had no way to anticipate that terrible speed and their firing was as if nothing. The swift shapes flashed by and again there was that tremendous explosion of sound. The Zeros rocked wildly; instinct brought Simura's hands and feet to swing him to the left. He knew Togawa would be doing the same in the opposite direction. The Zero staggered from a violent blow. When his vision cleared, Simura tasted blood in his mouth where his teeth had slashed his lips. For this moment on he would ignore those survivors in the sea. The fleet must know of those terrible machines! The high command knew nothing of them. At all costs they must get back to their carrier. Togawa had slid back into formation, and Simura pointed toward their carrier and gestured for the fly-home signal. Togawa nodded. He had come to the same conclusion. They went down to wavetop level. At least they could keep their new enemy from getting beneath them. It was their best chance.

Yelland had left the bridge to the war room, his staff with him. He paced intently in a small place, listening to his pilots talking as they whipped by the Zero fighters, their sonic booms as dangerous as weapons. Then the speaker crackled again.

"Old Salt, Alert One here. We convinced them to break off the attack on the survivors. I don't know how they kept control. Those pilots are good. Right now they're on the deck, holding tight formation, heading one seven five. What are your orders? Over."

Dan Thurman looked up at Yelland. "Sir . . . look at the plot. Those Japanese pilots are screwed up. They're headed right for us, and . . . and we've got a fully loaded strike force on deck. If they think we're enemy and they decide to dive into us—"

"I get the picture, Mr. Thurman." Yelland thought another moment, then went with the only decision he could make.

"Alert One, this is the captain. Do you copy? Over."

"Alert One here, sir. Go ahead."

"Alert One, attack and destroy the enemy immediately. I repeat, attack and destroy the enemy with all weapons at your disposal. Splash the bandits. They're all yours. Over."

"Yes, *sir!*" In the war room they listened to the two pilots talking. "Two from One, you copy Old Salt?"

"Loud and clear, One, loud and clear. I'll take the boy on the right. Over."

"He's all yours. Check all ordnance live."

"Hot to trot, One."

"Let's get 'em."

The Tomcats howled upward in a high, looping arc, rolling at the top so that they sliced the peak of their curve along a vertical angle, wings pointing at ocean and sky. Far below them they watched the Zero fighters hugging the waves, knowing the Japanese were using their on-the-deck position to prevent a belly attack. That also meant the Japanese would neither turn left nor right from a stern attack, but would use the only real maneuver left to them—a sharp pullup at the last instant.

It meant nothing to the two navy pilots pursuing them. Simura looked behind him, judged the tremendous speed of his pursuer, and at what he judged the precise moment Simura jerked back on the stick. Instantly the agile Zero leaped upward into the beginning of a tight loop intended to bring him on his back and diving seaward as the strange craft passed beneath him.

It was over before Simura knew what was happening. The Zero lunged upward and was still climbing vertically when Alert One opened fire at maximum range. The Vulcan cannon in the belly of the Tomcat, a modern Gatling gun spewing out cannon shells with a rate of 4,000 rounds per minute, erupted in a terrible sawing burst. A small avalanche of exploding shells smashed into the right wing of the Zero and severed it instantly. The wing flipped crazily over and over, and ahead of it, sailing like an erratic leaf, the Zero spun flatly to pancake into the water.

"Scratch one," came the laconic comment over the war room speakers.

Togawa abandoned any hope of an upward lunge. Perhaps the other way would work— He tramped right rudder as he banged the stick full over to the right, sucking it back to his belly, and jamming the throttle forward. The Zero clawed about in an incredibly tight turn. But Alert Two had anticipated the maneuver, had already slowed his Tomcat. The moment he was clear, Alert Two fired a Sparrow missile. Flame streaked beneath the Tomcat and shot ahead with blinding speed. The startled Togawa saw a thin white shape leading a blossom of flame rushing at him. Desperately he reversed his controls in a corkscrew turn back to the left. The Sparrow plunged into the engine and exploded. A huge ball of flame erupted in the air. Blazing debris splashed into the ocean.

"Scratch two," came over the speakers. "Ah, Old Salt One from Alert One, that first Zero pancaked into the water. I think we got one survivor down there. Over."

Yelland nodded to Owens, who took over the transmission. "Alert One, return to cover position. We'll have your replacements up shortly. Over."

"Roger that, Old Salt. Alert One and Two coming home."

☆ 14 ☆

Dan Thurman turned to Captain Yelland. "Sir, I've been on open line with the Hawkeye. They're coming up on Point Charlie on the board."

Yelland studied the plotting board. The Hawkeye reconnaissance plane was at maximum altitude, cruising above nine-tenths cloud. It was a perfect position. They would be invisible from the ocean surface for anything but a glimpse of a tiny dot in the sky, and their electronic systems would pinpoint and detail anything on the surface. Yelland nodded. "Put them on the speakers and tie me in for direct comm if I want to talk to them."

Thurman punched several buttons. "You're on the line, sir."

Yelland nodded again and took his seat, leaning back with his eyes closed, completing a mental transfer into the Hawkeye.

The fuselage of the big reconnaissance plane was a miniature combat information center, configured so that its systems functioned as an airborne version of the *Nimitz*'s CIC. Three electronic warfare officers sat before complex panels, packed with monitoring and communications equipment. The officer in the center position studied a digital readout radar scope. As fast as the radar picked out its targets on the sea, it presented in digital form the numbers of vessels, gave a computer-calculated impression of size, laid out the formation of surface vessels, and presented navigational position, course, and speed. The officer spoke in a calm tone.

"We confirm multiple radar contacts. Definite on four—belay that—six heavies. Possible battleships but more likely we've got six carriers down there. Twenty-four other vessels. Ten screening the heavies, the others trailing in typical support formation. We are negative on all radar scans. Repeat negative radar. We are also negative on all radio frequencies. Repeat negative radio frequencies. Request further instructions, please. Over."

One of the officers released his restraint harness and went forward to the cockpit. He had a glimpse of white wakes seen through a cloud break. "Damn, if we got just one hole, we could get some direct television pickup and beam back to the carrier." He tapped the pilot's arm. "How high is that cloud deck?"

"Thirty-two thousand. Flat as a board."

"Okay. Sit tight. I'm going to request permission to drop just below that cloud deck, you know, skim the very bottom of it. We'd still be high enough for a line-of-sight TV picture." He returned several minutes later. "CIC's okayed the pass. Take her down to where we break through the clouds, hold course for no more than thirty seconds. We're all set with the cameras. Set up your heading so we fly parallel to that target down there."

"Got it. Here we go."

They eased down into grayness, watching carefully ahead of them. At 31,000 feet the clouds began to break; just a bit lower than they'd expected. At 30,000 feet they were in the clear, the television cameras sending back an incredible real-time picture of the Japanese assault carrier force steaming to its attack point off Pearl Harbor.

They looked at the television monitor for thirty seconds without speaking. No one felt able to talk. Then the screen went gray as the Hawkeye pulled back into the clouds and started its climb to 42,000 feet. Thurman punched in COMM. "Give us a rerun on that last transmission. Run it in three minutes from now."

"Aye, aye, sir."

Matt Yelland sighed and looked at Warren Lasky. "No doubts?"

"None before, none now," Lasky said.

Yelland climbed tiredly to his feet. "We'll return to the bridge." He started from the war room, several men following him. Thurman stared in dismay, then found his voice. He was to stay here in the war room, but he felt a sense of choking frustration. "Captain?"

Yelland turned. "Yes?"

"Sir, that fleet. What the devil is it?"

Yelland spoke slowly. "Dan, you'd better sit down. That is the carrier attack force under the command of Admiral Chuichi Nagumo on its way to attack Pearl Harbor. You will remain here in the war room and stay on open line to me on the bridge. Those are your orders. Understood?"

"*Nagumo!* But he's . . ." Thurman's voice was a hoarse rattle. "*Captain, he's been dead since. . . .*"

"I know. That was in the Second World War."

On the bridge Yelland was all business again. He turned to Bill Damon, his operations officer. "Attend to the details. Get four more fighters for cover at altitude immediately. Keep the Hawkeye well clear of any visual reach of that Japanese force, but I want continuous radar sweep and immediate word on any change in their course. Get to it."

Yelland turned to Owens. "Dick, this isn't your job, but I'd appreciate it if you would take personal charge of a rescue helo team. Take four choppers, two for rescue and two for heavy gun cover. I don't want anyone hurt. If you can pick up any survivors from that yacht, bring them aboard and *keep them isolated*. Understood? Very good. The same goes for that Zero fighter. If our people really did see that pilot swimming we may be able to get to him. I hope he's in shock. You remember what it was like when we tried to pick up their people. They'd rather die than surrender."

"I've got it, Captain." Owens left the bridge on the double.

The men about them were in a state of shock from what they'd heard. The words *Japanese* and *survivors* were spreading like wildfire through the ship, but anyone within hearing range of Captain Yelland was maintaining silence, no matter how badly they wanted to ask questions.

Lasky stood by Yelland, looking out across the sea shining in the afternoon sun. "You know something, Matt? How I wish to God I'd been wrong. Because when I wake up tomorrow morning, all this," he gestured, "is still going to be real. The only thing I know that's worse than a nightmare is reality."

Yelland nodded. "Amen."

The big Sikorsky grew slowly in size, four hundred feet above the water, its huge rotors pulsating the air. Immediately behind, in line-abreast formation, were three more helicopters. Treading water, exhausted, hanging on to a piece of floating wood, Sam Chapman tried to point to the approaching strange machine. "I see it, Sam," Laurel told him. She was a better swimmer and in far better shape than the senator, who was also weak from loss of blood and his head injury. "I don't know what it is but I'm goddamned glad to see it." She moved her hand to comfort her dog. He'd been swimming in panic at her side after the last strafing run by the Zero fighters. She'd pushed and shoved until Charlie was on the impromptu raft, shivering and frightened.

"Sam, it hasn't got any wings!" she exclaimed. "And

it's slowing down . . . over us. . . ." She couldn't say any more as the full blast of the rotor blades walloped into the sea, hurling wind and spray over them. She looked up, her eyes stinging, as two men in dark suits dropped away from the hovering giant into the water near by. Voices called out to them. "Hang on! We'll be right with you!"

She turned in wonder to Chapman. "Sam . . . they're Americans!"

She turned back as a navy frogman reached her side. Laurel shook her head. "The senator . . . get him first. He's hurt. He can't hang on any more."

"Yes, ma'am." In a moment he was gone, and Laurel saw the two men reach the senator. They rigged a vest about him and moments later Sam was safe, buoyed up, held by the men. She looked up in wonder as a cable with a sling at its bottom lowered steadily toward the group. The men rigged a line about Sam's exhausted body, and one of them swung his arm over his head. She couldn't believe the sight as Sam ascended into the sky. Other hands pulled him into the yawning door and he disappeared from view.

Aboard the helicopter, Dick Owens shouted. "Hey! The girl! What the hell is she doing!"

He saw her swimming away from the rescue team, then understood why. The downblast from the chopper had blown the drifting wood with the dog huddling aboard away from them, and she was trying desperately to save the animal. From the looks of it she didn't have much strength left. Owens went overboard without hesitating. He was a powerful swimmer, and he was afraid the other men might miss her as she stroked steadily, her arms weakening with every moment. He swam strongly and called anxiously to her. "Hey, wait! Don't swim anymore! I'll get the dog!"

She stopped as he approached her. He needed only one look at her glazed eyes to recognize nearly complete exhaustion. He slipped out of his life vest.

"Here. Now hang onto this, okay?" She rested her torso over the inflated Mae West. "Just stay here. I'll be right back."

She watched Owens reach the wooden wreckage, then push it back to her. The helicopter drifted sideways above her. She was too worn out even to wonder about all the impossible things happening. "Those men in the water . . . they'll put the harness around you and winch you up. Just let them take care of you!"

"My dog . . . Charlie! I've got to save my dog!" She struck out wildly. He knew she was losing control, she was swimming and fighting purely on instinct. She reached over him and grabbed the animal, dragging it off the wood into the water with her. Owens cursed as he and the frogmen fought to get the harness around the woman and she in turn fought desperately to keep her grip on the terrified dog, coming close to drowning the hapless animal in the attempt. Owens shoved her away, grasped the dog, and held his head above water. "Get the harness on her!" he shouted. She still fought, but only weakly, as the frogmen slipped the rescue harness about her body and signaled the chopper to start winching. The sudden lifted force brought her to panic. Her eyes widened and she started to scream, even as her strength gave out. She slumped and hung unconscious in the harness.

Several minutes later, wrapped in a blanket, she looked in wonder as the winch turned, and the head of Owens came into view at the bottom of the open hatchway. He continued to rise and she cried out in wonder and relief as a frightened but ecstatic animal licked his face avidly. The winch operator couldn't help it; he burst into laughter, then choked back the sound to swing Owens and the dog into the cabin.

Owens slapped him on the shoulder. "Carry on, sailor. I'd like to have had a picture of that scene myself." He released the harness, which dropped immediately to pick up the men still in the water. Owens called to flight engineer. "As soon as we pick them up, head straight for home plate."

"Yes, sir."

Owens looked down at the girl, clutching the dog tightly. "Just rest easy. My men will attend to you. I'll be right back." He went to a rear compartment and changed quickly into a dry flight suit, rubbed his wet hair with a towel, and returned to the forward cabin. Two medical corpsmen were busy with the two survivors. As Owens took a seat on the side of the cabin, the second of the two frogmen was winched aboard, the sliding door slammed shut, and they began the run back to the carrier.

"How do you feel?" he asked gently.

She was shivering, but swiftly regaining control. A corpsman held hot broth to her lips and she sipped gratefully. She looked up at Owens. "I—I'm okay." She glanced to her side. "Sam. How is he? He was hurt and—"

The corpsman glanced up, anticipating the questions. "Miss, he'll be fine. He took a pretty good scalp wound but I don't believe it hurt the bone. He's worn out and weak from loss of blood." As he spoke the corpsman completed his work. They remained quiet for several moments until an intravenous hookup was completed. "That'll bring him out of it soon, miss."

Chapman rested back. He had remained silent through the exchange. Knowing he was safe seemed to infuse strength through his system. The broth had helped, and medical attention by swift and competent people is a great tonic.

Owens gestured to the bandage being applied about Chapman's head. "You made out lucky, mister. I'm pleased for you."

Chapman was still trying furiously to sort out this madness about him. "You're navy?" he asked suddenly. Owens nodded. "*Our* navy?" Chapman insisted.

Owens showed a thin smile. "If you mean the United States, yes."

"I mean just that."

Crusty old bastard, Owens thought. And then he also realized that was the best sign. The man would be all right. The man's eyes moved back and forth to take in the incredible sights about him. First those wild arrow shapes. Then the Japanese planes, shooting the hell out of them. And now *this*—huge machines with no wings and a boilermaker's nightmare of noise, hovering like a blimp in the sky, plucking people from the ocean and now rushing through the air like an airplane. My God, for a while he felt he must be going mad. But all this was real, all too real. Chapman looked up at Owens.

"I know authority. You seem to be the one in charge here. What the hell kind of machine is this thing, anyway?"

"Sikorsky," Owens said with a half smile.

"What the hell are you talking about! Sikorsky . . . they're in Connecticut. They build flying boats, that sort of stuff. They never built anything like this!"

Owens hesitated. "It will all be a lot clearer when we're back aboard ship, sir."

"Neat sidestepping, mister—?"

"Commander Richard Owens, sir."

"Commander, huh? And what's your ship?"

"Aircraft carrier, sir. I'm CAG."

"What the hell is CAG?"

"Ah, sorry about that. Air wing commander."

Chapman stuck out his hand. "I didn't mean to be so damned gruff." He winced as he pulled against the IV needle in his arm. "It's been a bit wild. I apologize for my bad manners. The name is Sam Chapman."

His eyes narrowed as there came no response to shake his offered hand. The commander had frozen in place, was staring at him, suddenly white-faced. "Did you say Sam Chapman?"

"Yes, yes. What's wrong?"

"*Senator* Sam Chapman?"

Chapman looked at Laurel. "I'll be goddamned! I'm not crazy, after all, not if someone knows *who* and *what* I am! Commander, I'm getting more delighted with your presence with every passing moment. Shake hands, man!"

They clasped in silence, Chapman beaming, Owens still acting as if he'd been struck a terrible blow.

Jiro Simura wanted no part of rescue. Instinct, and curiosity, had kept him alive until now. The Japanese pilots flew from their carriers with cork-style life preservers wrapped about their bodies. When the spinning fighter cartwheeled into the sea, the remaining wing absorbed most of the blow. Simura was thrown about in the cockpit but aside from a few bruises he emerged relatively unhurt from the slow impact with the water. Without thinking he pulled back his canopy hatch and climbed onto the wing. Moments later the Zero sank beneath the surface, leaving a still stupefied pilot floating in a vast ocean. Simura tried desperately to think clearly. He had failed in his mission, for he and Togawa had left survivors in the water. And then they had been swatted from the skies like helpless flies before those terrible, strange shapes. He knew he should die, because he was still alive with no way to return to his carrier, and the idea of becoming a prisoner—in a war that hadn't even started!—was beyond his wildest imagination. Yet he could not bring his mind to function properly and—

He turned, paddling furiously, at the strange sounds in the sky rapidly becoming louder. He looked up in astonishment, calling on all his ancestral gods for help, as two hulking shapes *without wings* and emitting a terrible broken thunder fell toward him. A screaming wind roared across the waters, blowing him about helplessly. One of the machines came to a stop in mid-air directly above him. It could not be! Then he saw

moving bodies, the faces of men, and several of the
men leaped from the floating, roaring machine into
the sea and swam toward him. Simura tried to swim
away but his cumbersome vest impeded his movement. The vest! He must rid himself of it so he could
drown his worthless self!

He was still trying when two frogmen reached him.
Simura lashed out wildly with his fists, screaming
curses in Japanese. One of the strange men grabbed a
wrist and pulled. Simura was momentarily helpless as
a powerful fist smashed against his jaw, once, twice,
and a third time before blackness washed over him.
He was still unconscious when the winch operator
brought him aboard the helicopter. "Get his gun, and
look for any knives. Don't waste any time. Get that
cable over there and tie the son of a bitch hand and
foot. I don't want him able to twitch a finger. And
while you're at it, gag him."

The sun burned a copper streak across the water as
the first helicopter turned into the wind and settled
easily to *Nimitz*'s deck. Anchor cables were snapped
to the gear and the crew shut down the howling jet
engines. Medical teams rushed forward, and moments
later Chapman and Laurel were carried on stretchers
across the deck and through a wide entryway into the
carrier island. Chapman stared, almost hypnotized by
the furious activity and the strange shapes about him.
"Commander Owens!" he called. "What in the name of
God is—"

Owens gripped his arm. "Senator, do me a favor. Let
it wait. Please. Just let it wait. We'll get you to sick
bay, and then we'll let you catch up on what's happening. I promise we'll clear away all the questions."

Chapman studied the officer before him. "All right,
Commander. You've already saved our lives. I guess I
can be patient for a while."

Owens smiled. "Thank you, Senator." He stepped
aside as the medical team went off on the double to

sick bay. Right behind him came another team with Laurel strapped to the stretcher. Her eyes were glassy and she was again close to hysteria. She looked up at him, eyes imploring. "Please! My dog . . . what will happen with Charlie?"

"Rest easy, miss," Owens said. He leaned over the stretcher and smiled. "I promise you he'll be all right. The crew will take care of him."

A doctor loomed by his side. "Commander, we've got to get her to sick bay. If you would?"

Owens stepped aside. "Of course. Sorry, doc."

Owens turned to watch two helicopters approaching, one carrying the Japanese pilot, the other the heavily armed escort. Owens ran to the fist chopper as it was anchored to the deck. "Keep this hatch closed until I tell you otherwise, got it? And let no one aboard!"

They showed their surprise but said only, "Yes, sir." Owens turned to the marine guard detail. "Clear the deck between here and that hatch over there. I want no one to interfere with us. We're going to remove someone from that chopper. He's to speak with no one and he's not to be spoken to. Keep him under tight security. Take him to the brig. I'll have a doctor meet you there. And whatever you do, keep him under your surveillance at all times. Got it?"

"Aye, aye, sir."

Owens returned to the helicopter cabin. A terrified pilot looked at him. "Untie his feet," Owens directed. "But keep his hands tied behind him until you reach the brig. I want a marine hanging on to each arm, and tightly. Don't stop. The detail outside will take you down. All right, now, move it."

They released Simura's feet. Two husky marines grasped his arms and led him from the helicopter, moving quickly across the deck. They almost stumbled as Simura stopped moving, his head snapping to one side. A Tomcat fighter howled to the deck with its terrifying roar and scream of jet engines, crashed

into its arrestor hook, bobbing up and down on the
nose gear. Immediately the cables were released and
the fighter taxied forward. Another crash of thunder
as the second Tomcat slammed with bone-jarring impact to the deck. Simura's mouth was held open by
the gag, but his eyes were bulging as if all that he saw
confirmed he was truly mad. Then the marines
dragged him forward and he stumbled, trying to
match their pace. A moment later he was gone inside
the ship.

The world was dark, the ocean a fog of blackness
beneath the high cloud deck. In Captain's Plot several
men sat with Matt Yelland, who held a damp photo in
his hand. "Lovely thing," he murmured, and passed
the picture of the pretty Japanese girl in a flowered
kimono to the others. Personal effects had been laid
out carefully on the plotting board. A slim wallet, a
crushed cigarette pack, a small penknife. And a leather
bound pocket diary. The pages were still damp and
in places the ink had run. Japanese characters had
been written in painstaking detail on each page. Yelland tapped the diary and looked at his operations
officer. "Commander, I want this translated immediately."

Dan Thurman took the diary. "Yes, sir. I'll get Lieutenant Jose Kajima to do it."

Lasky looked up, surprised. "Jose Kajima? What the
hell kind of name is that?"

Thurman grinned. "He's a Filipino, but his father is
Japanese, and he lived in Japan for several years. He's
fluent in the language."

"How long will it take?" Yelland asked.

"I don't know, sir. I imagine a while, with all these
pages here, and—"

Lasky reached for the diary. "Captain, I can get it
done a lot faster." He saw the unspoken question in
Yelland's expression. "The computers, Captain. They'll
take a photo impression of each page and we'll have a

complete translation, printed out, in just about fifteen minutes or so. One of the technicians can handle it."

Yelland nodded. "Very good. Get it going, Warren, and then join me on the bridge."

They took hot soup and bread on the bridge. Exhaustion dogged their steps but none of them could sleep. Or wanted to. Every moment was unspeakably precious to them. They feared that if they even turned away from every succeeding event, they'd never catch up with what was happening about them. Yelland had his immediate staff surrounding him: Dan Thurman, Dick Owens, Bill Damon, Artemus Perry, and John Arthur—Black Cloud. By now they had all accepted Warren Lasky as a member of their most intimate team. Indeed, slowly but surely they had come to accept that Captain Yelland's own composure about all that had befallen them had been provided by Lasky's knowledge of mighty forces still beyond their own understanding. They didn't know if the captain, or Lasky himself, truly understood what had happened to them, had caused this mighty rupture of time, but at least they knew how to handle it, and that was good enough for them.

"Gentlemen," Yelland said slowly, "I won't go into all the detailed aspects of what's happened. The results are enough for this moment. You are all aware of what's happened to us?"

They nodded or murmured their assent. "In short, somehow, we've been thrown by that storm back to December 6, 1941. Tomorrow, by local time, that Japanese fleet we spotted earlier will launch its attack against Pearl Harbor. We know the events, we know the sequences, we know the results. What we don't know, and I'm sure the question has haunted all of you, is what we do about it."

Thurman gestured. "Sir, how can there be any question? You said we know the consequences of their attack. We *all* do! They'll tear Pearl to pieces and . . .

well, everything else. There's only one thing to do, sir, and that's blow that Japanese task force to hell and gone."

Yelland let the others absorb Thurman's words. Only then did he speak, carefully, slowly. He didn't want emotion running out of hand and too many men on this ship were already as taut as bowstrings. "In other words, then," Yelland spoke, "you are recommending that this ship, *U.S.S. Nimitz*, launch an all-out assault against the Nagumo force, with the express purpose of destroying that force?"

"Yes, sir, that is exactly what I'm saying," Thurman said with undisguised heat.

"You are recommending that we open undeclared war against the Japanese Empire?"

Thurman's jaw dropped. *"Undeclared—I"* He took a deep breath. "Sir, they bombed the hell out of Pearl!"

Yelland's face was a stone mask, his eyes unblinking. "No, they haven't," he said quietly. *"Not yet."*

"But . . ."

"It hasn't happened yet. We know from the past that it is supposed to happen, that if history unravels itself along the same paths, it will happen. But it has *not* happened. This is the sixth and not the seventh of December."

Thurman looked about him, saw no one else stepping into the breach. "Captain, I'm not trying to play with words, but it's in the history books, in our records. The Japanese tomorrow morning are going to launch their air strike against Hawaii, and we'll be at war, and—"

Bill Damon gestured and Yelland nodded. The operations officer turned to Thurman. "We can't count too much on those books, Dan."

"And why not!"

"Because we're here, right now, and there is absolutely no record anywhere of the nuclear-powered *U.S.S. Nimitz* in these waters on the sixth of December in 1941."

"You must consider that, Dan," Yelland said gently.

"Then why don't we consider what happened today?" Thurman demanded. "Those Zero fighters, remember? They attacked an American vessel on the high seas and shot it up and sank it and they killed everyone aboard with the exception of two survivors. Isn't that an act of war? My God, what more do we need?"

Yelland shook his head. "No, it's not an act of war. It comes under the heading of isolated incident."

Lasky moved closer to the others. "It does open up, um, shall we say, amazing possibilities? The awesome firepower of *Nimitz* back in 1941. Jet fighters, guided missiles, radar . . . and all those nuclear warheads." He paused, and the suddenly alarmed Yelland became aware that Lasky was playing a role as devil's advocate. "Just think," Lasky went on, "we don't even need an all-out strike such as you're calling for, Commander Thurman. Why bother? Just one hydrogen bomb in the water under that Japanese fleet. Just one, and it's all over. No survivors, no ships, no question that we can accomplish total extinction with just one warhead. And the attack on Pearl Harbor, if indeed it is going to take place tomorrow, will never be."

"Holy Jesus," someone murmured.

"Of course," Lasky went on smoothly, "it has other possibilities. What we might regard as a review of the next forty years of history."

Dick Owens took a verbal swing at the scientist. "I suspect, Mr. Lasky, that history might just be a touch more difficult to beat than even you imagine."

Lasky studied the CAG officer. Warning suspicions sounded in his mind. Owens was a brilliant man, but he'd just overplayed his hand. There was something hidden within his last remark, but it would have to be extracted slowly. "Look, we're talking about the classic time paradox." He paused and moved his gaze along the others present. "I don't want to go into a long song and dance on the subject, because Captain

Yelland and I have already worn ourselves hoarse on this matter." He paused again to let the news sink in. *Captain Yelland had been into a deep discussion of the classic time paradox. . . . That would affect how every one of them would think and react. The old man is being regarded in a different light. He's their hero. Now suddenly he's a deep thinker. Good.*

"The gist of it," Lasky continued, "is where I go back in time and meet my own grandfather before he sires my own parent. I kill him. That means since he doesn't father children, then on down the line my own parent fails to come into existence. But if I'm never born, how can I go back in time to meet my own grandfather?"

Owens gestured angrily. "Lasky, I'm not the theorist you are. I don't know those computers of yours and I haven't delved into the philosophical aspects of astrophysics or topology or whatever you need to understand what you call warps in space and time. But I have a damned good gut instinct that tells me that things happen only once. Time isn't a revolving door—"

"Very good," Lasky murmured, and he meant it.

Owens swept right on. "If something has happened, then there's nothing we can do to change it. And we shouldn't even try to change it," he added with sudden emphasis.

"There are two flaws to that remark," Lasky said quietly. "Not to try, as an avenue in life, is to accept the doctrine that if God wanted man to fly, he would have created us with wings." Pause. "The second flaw won't go away, either. How can we avoid not only what's happened in the past if we can't avoid the present? *We're here*, Commander. We're a part of what's happening right *now*."

Dan Thurman's interruption was an emotional explosion. "For Christ's sake!" he shouted. "What the hell is this! Some half-assed Princeton debating society? We're in a war situation here! We've had a ship shot to pieces. Our own fighters have shot down two planes that carried out a war attack. We know that task force out there intends to bomb Pearl Harbor tomorrow morning. And we are a warship of the United States of America. Or at least, we used to be. Or will be . . . or whatever the hell! Goddamnit, this stuff will drive us all crazy if we don't hang on to the only reality that counts—ourselves. We're here, we *are*, and if that's not true, then what the hell are we doing affecting things around us by shooting down Japanese planes!"

Yelland coughed quietly to draw their attention. "All right, everybody cool it. As Lasky told you, we've been through this rat maze a couple of times. I'm getting tired of this house of mirrors where you see reflections of yourself from every corner. We don't need theory as much as we need a good grip on ourselves. Everybody got that signal loud and clear? Good. Now, we do it one step at a time. And if we don't know what's coming down on us, gentlemen, then we look to see if the book is real. I assure you it is. The good old book of regulations and rules. *We* go by the book. We function as what we are in the best way we know how and to the devil with the theoretical implications. To put it bluntly, gentlemen, we simply grasp Old Father Time by the short hairs and I guarantee you he'll come right along in the same direction we're traveling. If, no matter what else is going on, tomorrow morning the United States comes under military attack, then our job is to defend her—whether it's in the past, right now, or in the future."

"Jesus, but I am glad to hear that," Artemus Perry said in a hoarse whisper.

Lasky looked at him. Yelland had made the only right move. His badly shaken men were reaching into their emotional reserves and coming back stronger than ever. It was a great lesson in how to put Humpty Dumpty back together again. Lasky turned to the captain.

"Sir, and after that—" He knew Yelland would interrupt him. They both knew it. They might almost have rehearsed it.

"And after that," came the interruption, "we *still* go by the book. We take our orders from the commander in chief of the armed forces of this country."

Lasky's smile this time was of amusement rather than tolerance. "Franklin Delano Roosevelt. I've always wanted to meet the old boy."

☆ 15 ☆

"He won't eat a thing and he won't drink." The burly marine guard glanced through the cell bars at the Japanese pilot, who sat rigidly almost as if he were at attention, on a hard wooden bench bolted into the steel decking. The lieutenant with the guard nodded. "He's afraid we'll poison him."

"Those people are nuts, sir," the guard snorted. "If we was going to poison him, why'd we go to all that trouble to rescue him in the first place?"

"Ordinarily, that would be the logical way to go," mused the lieutenant. "But something's crazy here. Why would a Japanese be afraid of us? The war ended thirty-five years ago, and our countries have been friendly ever since I was a kid. It doesn't fit, mister, it just doesn't fit."

The guard looked at him almost regretfully. "I'm sorry to hear you say that, sir, because I was hoping maybe you could explain a couple of things to me."

"Like what, private?"

"Well, look at him. It's like we've all got horns or something. Besides, where the hell did he get a Zero fighter in the middle of the—"

"A *Zero fighter?*"

"Yes, sir. Oh, I forgot. You just come on duty, Lieutenant. I guess you didn't hear the scuttlebutt around the ship."

The lieutenant's eyes drilled into the guard. "Lay it on me, mister."

"Yes, sir. I don't know too much, but this guy and his friend were out in Zero fighters, and they shot up a yacht, an American one, and there were only two survivors, and then our patrol went after them. They shot him down and they blew up his partner with a Sparrow missile, and then one of our helos picked him up from the water."

The lieutenant's eyes glazed. "Private, if you're pulling a trick on me, I'll—"

"Lieutenant, you ask for it, I give it to you, straight. Far as I know, sir, what I told you is the facts."

The lieutenant shook his head. "I don't get it. A Zero fighter. The only place that could come from—and you said they shot up a ship?—would be a carrier. And the Japanese don't have any carriers!"

"They ain't got no Zeros either, Lieutenant. I spoke to one of the fighter jocks topside about it."

"And what did he say?"

"He was gonna' get drunk, sir. He looked pretty upset by it all."

The lieutenant held up both hands. "Okay, okay; let it ride for now. They're bringing some people down to interrogate this man. Sergeant Cunningham will be in charge of the detail. You remain right here, but be sure that if anybody is inside that cell, there is always a guard present. Any questions, you tell them it's a direct order from me."

"Yes, sir."

Commander Charles G. Barton, USN, chief medical officer of *Nimitz*, followed by a medical orderly and two marine guards, knocked on the door to Number Four Isolation Ward. An inside guard studied his face, studied his ID tag, then nodded. The door opened into a small room. The marine locked the outer door, turned on a brief flood of ultraviolet light, and a green light appeared by another door. "Clear, sir," the marine said.

Barton went through into the small but elaborately equipped isolation room. He saw Laurel sitting tensely on her bunk, eyes much too wide for the doctor's pleasure. Standing by the other bunk, in the same shapeless hospital robe, stood an older man with a bandage about his head. By the looks of him, judged Barton, he's angry enough to have his blood pressure coming right out of the glass. A medical orderly had apparently just completed a basic check of the two patients.

"I'm Commander Charles Barton. Medical officer of this vessel. I've come to check you out, be certain you're both all right, and then get you out of this rather confining isolation room."

Laurel looked up hesitantly. "You're not the . . . man in charge of this, uh, ship?"

"No, Ma'am. I'm your doctor. The captain of this ship is Matthew Yelland, and I understand you'll be meeting shortly with him. In fact, he asked me to apologize for the long delay in arranging your meeting. I'm sure he'll see you as soon as possible."

"I should damned well hope so," Chapman said unhappily.

Barton studied their charts. "I'm really quite pleased with your preliminary examination," he said, smoothly changing the subject. "Despite some initial overexposure to the sea, you're both healthy and your recovery is excellent."

Chapman's snort of contempt was a language unto itself. "You call what happened to us a *mishap?* You call being shot to pieces and having everyone else on our ship *killed* a mishap? Being blown into the sea and machine gunned by some crazy Japanese pilots— all this is a goddamned mishap to you? What do you need to have a flesh wound, doctor? A decapitation?"

"Doctor, are we at war or something?" Laurel broke in. "I mean, those Japanese planes, and all those strange machines, and where we are—it's all so confusing, and it's frightening. What's happened?"

Barton shifted his position uncomfortably. "I'm sorry," he said with a long sigh. "I know those questions can be very frustrating without answers. But I must ask you, please, to hold off on any—"

A knock interrupted him. Gratefully, he motioned for the medical orderly to open the door. Laurel's sudden shriek of joy was the best sound he could have heard. "*Charlie!* Come here, boy, come here to me!" The animal let out a canine yelp of total pleasure and leaped into her arms. She hugged her pet closely.

The sailor who'd brought Charlie down beamed at her. "Ma'am, he's been examined and he's okay. We also fed him and he's been groomed and he's just like new. I got one like him at home."

Laurel looked up with bright eyes. "Thank you," she said, smiling.

The sailor left. Chapman had been sizing up the doctor and had come to a sudden decision. "Doctor, if you would?"

"Yes?"

"Clear everyone out of here except us and yourself. What I have to say is to you alone. Please do it now."

Commander Barton hesitated. He knew a voice of authority when he heard it, and this man obviously wielded just that sort of power. He turned to the medical orderly and nodded for him to leave the room. The door closed and they were alone. "Now, what can I do for you?" Barton asked.

"Doctor, I would appreciate your informing the captain of this vessel that Senator Samuel Chapman, who is the co-chairman of the Senate Defense Committee, would like to see him, *and at once.*"

Commander Barton swallowed that one slowly, considered what this man had been through. He nodded. "Of course, Senator." While he spoke he prepared a syringe for injection.

Chapman's voice was taking on a tone of steel.

"Doctor, you have a problem with your hearing. I said *at once.*"

"Of course, sir, in just a moment. First, Senator, you need a vitamin booster. You've had severe exposure, along with some trauma. If you'd roll up your sleeve?"

"Take your goddamned needles, and your vitamins, doctor," Chapman roared, "and get the hell out of here. *Now!* You stupid son of a bitch, you need to learn how to listen instead of practicing patronage! Get out of here!"

Taken aback by the explosive tirade, nibbled by the suspicion that there could be a lot more here than he had been told, Barton replaced his materials in his bag and went to the door. He knocked twice and it opened at once. A marine corporal looked at him. "I'm leaving, Corporal. Maintain security here as ordered."

"Yes, sir." Barton went past the marine and the door locked after him.

Sam Chapman and Laurel stared at one another in mixed disbelief and confusion.

Warren Lasky rapped on the door to Owens's cabin. No response. He knew he was treading on very thin ice but he felt he had to ignore the protocol of privacy at any cost. He went directly to the manuscript on the desk, fast-scanning the pages. He seemed to freeze at one page. Slowly, still reading as he moved, he selected the page from the stack of paper, reading with intense interest. *Good sweet Mary*, he said to himself. He went into his own cabin and leaned back on his bunk, waiting.

Ten minutes went by before he heard the corridor door to Owens's cabin open. Owens, with Lasky watching from his bunk, went directly to a desk drawer, then paused. He studied his desk, his eyes moving back and forth. Lasky walked silently from his cabin to the small corridor between the two cabins, watching, unnoticed by Owens. The commander confirmed what had bothered him—his manuscript had been moved in his absence. Owens sat before his desk, checking the pages. A muffled oath escaped him, and he spun about almost violently at the sound of Lasky's voice.

"It's right here, Commander." Owens stared at the missing page in Lasky's hand. Lasky walked slowly into the cabin. "I should have listened to you a bit more closely," he told Owens. "I almost remember it word for word. History may be tougher to beat than I imagine, right?"

"Damnit, Lasky, for a man of your intelligence you take some stupid risks," Owens snapped.

"Stupid? Hardly," Lasky said to dismiss even the thought of a threat. "What the hell would you do? Kill me? And why?" Lasky stabbed a finger at Owens. "Because all of a sudden *you*, Mister Owens, got the cockamamie idea that because you know something the rest of us don't know, or," he gestured with the paper, "didn't know, then you just might be able to do a little time-twisting on your own."

"Look, you don't understand—"

"The hell I don't," Lasky said to dismiss the protest before it even got off the ground. "Let me refresh your own memory from your own words." He tapped the paper and read aloud. " 'The attack on Pearl Harbor was not even remotely a surprise to many people who were aware of international machinations in the struggle for power maneuvering—among them the prominent and coldly ambitious Senator Samuel S. Chapman, who only two weeks before the slashing Japanese carrier assault against Pearl Harbor, had publicly taken up the anvil for a massive increase in our military strength across the entire Pacific. What is particularly ironic in this issue is that Senator Chapman was among the missing, and presumed dead, following the attack he had foreseen so clearly. Had he lived, and this is no moot point, there was every possibility that Chapman would have been thrust into the position of Roosevelt's running mate in the victorious and precedent-setting third-term election of 1944, and upon the death of Roosevelt, would have assumed the presidency of the nation.'"

Lasky lowered the paper. "Aside from everything else, Owens, my congratulations on this. That was neatly and incisively said. I now add the observation, more germane to this moment, that if that doesn't come under the heading of beating the drumroll of history, you'd better dream up a new title, and quickly."

Owens shook his head. "I don't know whether to say thanks or give you a mouthful of knuckles."

"For Christ's sake, will you stop this overgrown macho shit and come back to reality?"

Owens sighed. "Okay, okay. You move too fast between the ears, Lasky. And I guess I just don't have your appetite for playing God with the world. I realized who Chapman was when we fished him out of the water. I was so startled I almost didn't shake hands with him when he made the move."

"And what comes next, Commander? Do you propose throwing him back into the ocean when no one's looking? That way, in this one particular context you'll preserve the natural course of history, just as you've put it down on paper: Chapman doesn't survive the attack on Pearl Harbor tomorrow morning."

"You can go straight to hell, Lasky."

Lasky grinned. He tapped the paper. "No rose gardens in here either, right?"

Laurel sat on her bunk, legs tucked beneath her, idly petting her dog. Before her Sam paced the floor like a caged animal. He had been building to a fine white heat ever since the doctor, bland and unresponsive to his words, left the room with an unmistakable click of the lock behind him. He stopped and looked at Laurel, his eyes narrowed to angry slits.

"Goddamnit, if this wasn't happening to me I wouldn't believe this whole crazy thing was possible! Who in the hell *are* these people?"

Laurel nodded her agreement with his mood. "Sam, this has all been so crazy. I mean, we've seen a strange insignia that *may* be American, and there are the words United States everywhere, but it all seems so—so *alien*. Do you think that perhaps they're not our navy? I mean, really not part of the American fleet?"

He waved his hand to dismiss the bizarre notion. "Oh, no, sweetheart, they're good old stars and stripes, all right. U.S. Navy from bow to stern. That's not what's driving me mad. What part of our navy is this? That's the sixty-four dollar question. I've never seen machines like they've got on this thing. Airplanes without propellers that *fly*? And they fly so fast you can hardly see them. And that . . . whatever it was that picked us up out of the water. It hovered in mid-air! And then it flew away at well over a hundred miles an hour and sets down as lightly as a feather on an aircraft carrier that's so goddamned big it makes the Queen Mary look like a bathroom toy. When the hell did we start developing aircraft and ships like these? There's no way, Laurel! The navy's fiscal requisitions, every last damned one of them, have to pass through my committee, and I swear to you I've never heard the first whisper for. . . ." He struggled for words he didn't have. "Well, for airplanes that can't fly and big machines that hover like blimps and, Jesus, this whole thing gives me a headache. And why in the hell are they keeping us prisoner? They took care of us. Good care, but it's still all wrong."

She chewed her lower lip. "Sam, sometimes there are secret programs. We both know about things like that. Is it possible that there's a secret navy of some kind? I know it's incredible, but after what's happened today—"

"Sure. Today. One hell of a day," he grimaced. "You know something? We've been so blinded by all this unbelievable hardware we lost sight of something else. This ship is named after Chester Nimitz."

"I don't understand. Is that significant?"

"It sure is. Nimitz is an admiral on active duty. The navy doesn't name its line ships after people who are living. That's an honor for the dead."

"Sam?"

Her voice was so plaintive he stopped where he was. "Yes, honey, what is it?" he asked gently.

"Sam, there's another possibility." She took a deep breath. "What if all this is part of a military takeover?"

"My God. . . ." He breathed the words hoarsely, groped for his bunk, and sat slowly. He thought over what she had said, but shook his head. "I can't buy that, Laurel. Roosevelt's too strong with the military. He's supported them to the full. In fact, he *owns* the military, and everyone knows it."

"But surely the president—"

Chapman leaped to his feet as if he'd been stung by a wasp. "That's it!" he shouted. "By damn, I think you've got it, Laurel! That's who's behind all this. . . . Of course, of course!" He slammed a fist into his palm. "Who else? F.D.R. has wanted the United States in this war ever since it really got going. But he knows the people and he knows the isolationist force in the country. The whole mood is to keep us out of the war. So the next step is to arrange for the enemy to attack us. . . ." Chapman smashed his hand against his forehead. "I must be blind! Those Japanese planes that shot us up today—the Japanese don't have anything like that in the air! They're not that good, Laurel. Their airplanes are antiquated, made of fabric. A couple of good mechanics could take the P-36 and round out the wingtips and modify the tail and build a new canopy on it, and then all you have to do is paint those Japanese meatballs on for insignia—and just like that, you've got yourself an act of war. They shot us up. Who knows how many planes were out there doing the same thing to other boats? You know what, Laurel? I talked about this with Art just before he was killed. Fighters don't have the range to operate anywhere in this area unless they're flying off a carrier or from land, and we know there aren't any Japanese carriers around here, which means. . . ."

His voice trailed away and she picked it up. "There's only a land base left, then, isn't there?"

"Land only," he repeated. "The Hawaiian Islands. You could hide a hundred airstrips in the hill country and no one would ever know about it. There's another way. There could be an American carrier out there flying the Japanese flag. Who'd know? We haven't got any carriers in Pearl right now. No one is absolutely certain where they are. If Roosevelt wanted one in the right place at the right time he could do what he wanted and in full secrecy. No one could ever prove it wasn't the Japanese, because they're been a growing pain in the ass for months. We all know they'll get into it with us sooner or later, and this just moves up the timetable."

"No one has been more consistent than you in warning about Japanese aggression," Laurel said aloud, voicing what they both knew. "My job is to make sure everyone keeps hearing you say those words."

"Uh huh. Those words are about to come true, it looks like, and here I am sitting out in the middle of the goddamned ocean with no press, no way to reach the newspapers or the wire services, neatly cut off from everything—while the White House takes all the credit for raising the alarm—and being ready to hit back! It's a bitch, all right."

She looked at him steadily. "I think you're forgetting something, Sam. Something you'd better think over very seriously."

"What's that?"

"Washington knew what yacht we were on, where we were, and when we'd be there. Everybody on that ship was killed today except us—and we were only lucky. I think they had you, and me, Sam, set up."

He turned white.

Owens and Lasky walked rapidly along the corridor, followed closely by Lasky's assigned aide, Corporal Kullman. "Have they found out anything yet?" Lasky asked Owens.

The commander shook his head. "Apparently he speaks only Japanese. No way he's faking it. His name is Simura. Jiro Simura. He's repeated it carefully and slowly a number of times, but that's all we have going for us. Our favorite Filipino, Jose Kajima, should be with him now. We'll see what he gets." He pointed ahead of them to where four powerful marines guarded a doorway. "That's it. Let's find out for ourselves."

They went through the cordon of guards into the main ward of sick bay, itself isolated from the rest of the medical area. Kajima was just rising to his feet, a sheaf of notes in one hand and a pen in the other. He nodded to Owens and Lasky. They studied the Japanese prisoner who wore ill-fitting fatigues to replace his flight gear stripped from him. Simura's eyes were never still, moving constantly about the room, seeking a means of escape, always seeming to dull when he saw the husky marines standing guard in the ward.

Owens turned back to Kajima. "Anything?"

"Not much, sir." Kajima tapped his notes. "His name, as you probably know by now, is Jiro Simura. I went over his flight gear, and he's a chief petty officer. I learned a couple of other things. He's one of their best, part of a group selected for a special mission. He won't say anything about where he's from or what mission they're on. I don't know if he's too well briefed to maintain his silence or if he's just too scared to talk."

"Look at his eyes, lieutenant. He's not *that* scared."

"Yes, sir. Will you excuse me, Commander? I'm to

report to the captain personally on anything I found out from the prisoner."

"One last question. You think about using drugs on him?"

"Yes, sir, I've thought about it. But that's not my decision, Commander."

"No, it isn't. Thanks. Go on topside."

"Thank you, sir."

They waited until Kajima was gone, and Owens turned to the guard leader. "Where are the other people, the man and woman, being held?"

"Sir, that door to your right. It's a small isolation ward."

"All right, let us in."

"Yes, sir." The door opened and a wild flurry erupted in the form of a dog wanting to play. Charlie shot out between the legs of Owens, yapping wildly. Lasky made a desperate lunge for the animal and tripped over the marine guard. Laurel came running after her dog and knocked Owens off balance, and the guards swung their attention to the hysterical scene—and gave Simura the opportunity he sought so desperately. The Japanese pilot leaped from his seat at the marine to his left and a powerful hand chopped into the marine's throat. He stiffened, paralyzed. The automatic rifle was jerked from his hand, the butt came around to crack the marine across the side of the head, and the marine fell unconscious. A second guard threw himself at Simura but the desperate Japanese proved as agile on his feet as he had been in his airplane. He sidestepped the lunge, smashed the butt against the forehead of the guard. Another marine was already bringing his own weapon up to fire, but Simura had already found the safety catch of the weapon in his hands. The firing gun exploded with terrific sound in the closed-off room, and a short burst shredded the marine to bloody froth and physically hurled his body against a bulkhead. He crashed to the deck, dead before he stopped moving.

Kullman, unarmed, threw himself against the door leading out to the corridor. Sirmura fired wildly after him. At least one round caught Kullman in the shoulder, spinning him about helplessly. His bid to escape had failed. The partly-opened door beckoned to him mockingly.

Simura shouted in Japanese. They couldn't understand his words but no one escaped his meaning. They froze in position as the gun barrel moved slowly from side to side. Laurel bit her knuckles to keep from crying out and panicking the Japanese pilot. Chapman stood by her, not moving. The Japanese was trembling, which meant he was probably more frightened than anyone else—and that made him all the more dangerous.

The wild chain of events was not yet ended. The blast of gunfire had terrified the dog, all this time cowering beneath the table. Now Charlie sensed the fear in Laurel, identified the source as the Japanese, and burst from under the table, barking and snarling. Simura whipped around, bringing the rifle to bear. Laurel's scream jerked his aim off and the single shot fired at the dog missed. The newly-terrified Charlie let out a high-pitched yelp and scrambled through the still-open door. Simura cursed and kicked the door closed. He spun around, the rifle now very ready. He motioned his prisoners to back up against the opposite bulkhead. Under the menacing stare of the gun were Owens, Lasky, Laurel, Chapman, and one marine. One dead guard lay on the floor and Kullman lay prone in a slowly spreading pool of blood. Another marine groaned, just returning to consciousness from the blow dealt him before by Simura. The Japanese motioned for the marine guard still on his feet to drag the other marine across the room with him. He barked out orders in Japanese, ever more frustrated.

"Nobody do anything but slow," Owens said, spreading his arms from his body. "Do what I'm doing and show him the palms of your hands. Do it slow and easy, slow and easy. Don't panic him, let him ease off. That's it, arms wide, palms up."

They stared back and forth at one another, all of them frightened, confused, and not knowing what to do.

Standoff.

☆ 16 ☆

Dan Thurman picked up the call on the bridge. He listened with his eyes wider, then narrowing. "Stand by," he said into the phone and looked up at Captain Yelland. "Sir, they've got themselves a situation down in sick bay. The Japanese prisoner got his hands on a weapon and—"

"I'll take the call here," Yelland broke in. "Who's on?"

"Major Stevens, sir."

Yelland switched lines on his control panel. "Stevens, the captain here. Spell it out short and sweet."

"Sir, all hell's broken out in sick bay. I'm not sure how it happened but that Japanese pilot grabbed an M-16. He's killed one of my men and hurt a couple more. He's holding Owens, Lasky, and the two civilians we picked up prisoner, as well as several marines. At least two of them are wounded. We've sealed off the area, so he can't go anywhere."

"What about the people he has with him?"

"He hasn't hurt them, sir. I think it's clear he's using them to reach us, but no one in the room speaks Japanese, and—"

Yelland looked up at Thurman. "Get Kajima down there as fast as you can," he ordered. Then, back into his mike. "Major, we've got an interpreter on the way down. Lieutenant Kajima. He's already spoken with the Japanese pilot, so they can pick up again." Thurman was signaling frantically. "Hold one, Major," Yelland said and looked up at his executive officer.

"Captain, it's Owens. In that room with the Japanese. He's on the phone."

"Patch it onto my console."

"You're patched, Captain."

"Owens, Yelland here. What's the situation?"

"The Japanese got me to understand he wanted me to use this phone. To get to someone in authority. It's sticky, sir. We need someone who can talk to him."

"Kajima's on the way. He just left the bridge."

"Captain, it's better if Kajima stays the hell out of this room and talks on the phone."

"All right, I'll get him back here." Yelland motioned to Thurman, who nodded and immediately went to the carrier's speaker system, recalling Kajima to the bridge. "He'll be here in a few moments, Dick," Yelland said to Owens. "Can you keep that man calm for a while?"

"Yes, sir, but I'd better not talk too long or he's liable to panic on us."

Yelland heard feet pounding. "Kajima's coming in now. Stand by. Thurman, put all this on the box. And Owens, you listening?"

"Yes, sir."

"Do it slow, boy, do it slow. Point to the squawk box switch in your room and tap the phone. That'll tell him the two are connected. When he hears voices, he'll understand."

"Hold one. . . ."

Owens held up the phone as Simura held the rifle unerringly on him. With one hand Owens pointed to a speaker box and a switch underneath, nodding to the box and tapping the phone. Then he waited. Simura grasped his message and nodded. Moving carefully, Owens activated the speaker. They heard Yelland's voice from the box.

". . . and try to find out what he wants. Owens, that box alive yet?"

"Yes, sir, but get Kajima on fast, sir. We need Japanese here and now."

"You've got it," Yelland said. A moment later Kajima's voice came over the box in Japanese.

Relief swept Simura's face. He listened for a moment, then looked at Owens and touched his lips. Owens nodded. Simura had wanted to know if his voice would be picked up by the speaker system; it could, and that would help. Simura shouted a question.

Immediately Kajima's voice responded. The prisoners relaxed a touch more. So long as those two were talking there was hope. Simura rattled off a long sentence, harsh and demanding.

Yelland's voice came over the speaker. "What is it, Lieutenant?"

"He wants access to a radio, sir," Kajima responded. In the sick bay they could hear both sides of the conversation.

"Does he say why?" Yelland asked.

Kajima and Simura talked rapidly and then Kajima spoke again to Yelland. "He won't explain, sir. He just demands the radio."

The silence on the bridge carried into sick bay. Simura's expression left no doubt he would settle only for what he wanted. Lasky motioned to the Japanese pilot, touched his lips, and pointed to the speaker box on the bulkhead. Simura nodded.

Lasky raised his voice so it would carry to the microphone on the bulkhead set. "This is Lasky!" His voice carried both anger and sarcasm. "Have you all lost your minds up there on the bridge? He wants that damn radio so he can warn his superior officers about us!"

Chapman took it all in with mixed emotions. So that Japanese couldn't be a fake. . . . But whoever he was, why would he have to warn his superiors about this insane ship, unless his superiors also knew nothing about it? Chapman groaned inwardly. It was too much for his aching head. But he felt a smile tug at his lips. It was too ironic. That Japanese wanted to warn his superiors about this ship—which was exactly what he, Chapman, also wanted desperately to do.

Simura shouted again to the speaker box, and Kajima's voice answered in Japanese and then he used English as he spoke with Yelland. "Captain, he says if we don't let him get to a radio so he can talk to his superior, he'll kill everyone in that room with him."

The silence almost drove Lasky mad as the men on the bridge tried to come to a decision. Lasky turned to Owens. "Jesus, I wish they'd make up their minds. Letting him have that radio could be the best way out of this mess. It just might stop the Japanese attack before it ever gets started."

They heard him on the bridge. Dan Thurman looked at the captain. "Sir, is there a chance they'd believe him?"

"There's no chance at all if things remain the way they are," Yelland replied. "Mister Kajima, tell our friend down there we agree to his demands."

Kajima spoke carefully into the microphone. In sick bay, they were already coming down from the edge of imminent death. They understood Yelland before Simura had the chance to hear Kajima.

They heard Yelland's voice on the box talking to the marine commander in the corridor. "Major Stevens, do you hear me?"

"Yes, sir."

"Clear that corridor at once. No one is to interfere with the Japanese pilot. No one. Those are my orders, understand?"

"Yes, sir."

"All right. Kajima, tell the Japanese we're clearing the way for him to get to a radio. In the meantime, have Kaufman set up one of those radios he modified to talk on the wavelengths they're using now. We want to be certain that pilot talks to someone who can hear him."

In sick bay, Lasky smiled at Owens. "Here's your chance to twist time, commander. Just be careful the tail of that tiger you're holding isn't too much to handle."

Owens didn't reply. He turned his gaze back to Simura. The Japanese pilot motioned with the rifle for the hostages to precede him. Then he stopped, shouted into the speaker box. Kajima's voice came back at once.

"He wants you all to walk forward, in pairs, just ahead of him. You're to walk side by side and link arms. At the first sign of trying to overpower him, he'll kill everyone he can."

Owens glanced up at the box. "Tell him we understand and we'll do exactly as he wants."

It went slowly, carefully, until Chapman's self-control snapped. He was a proud man and if he knew any enemy in his life it would be called humiliation. He had been shot up by a Japanese fighter plane, forced to dive into the ocean to save his life, watched his best friend die, had been yanked from the sea, pushed and prodded and patronized and held prisoner first by these Americans, and now by this Japanese pilot, and it was all too much. The frustration of not knowing what was happening to him, of being totally baffled by events that prodded and poked at him, had brought him to search his soul for a way out. Whatever was his emotional conflict, it finally rejected the logical thinking that had so long dictated every action, and with a sudden howl of rage, Chapman hurled himself bodily at the Japanese pilot.

The marine major waiting outside heard and judged the moment and burst through the door into the room. He was too late. Jiro Simura was tough, wiry, young, fast, and explosively tense. He sensed Chapman's move and in what was almost a gesture of contempt, slammed the rifle butt into the senator's ribs, bringing forth a howl of pain and a body crumpled on the deck. In a single swift movement Simura acknowledged the danger of holding so many hostages. One hand shot out to grip fiercely the long hair of Laurel, and the other brought the muzzle of the M-16 directly behind her ear. He shouted loudly at the speaker box on the wall, then waited, his finger tensed on the trigger.

On the bridge, Kajima turned to Captain Yelland. "Someone made a grab for the Japanese. He knocked him down and now he's got his rifle up against the woman's head. He says, he'll kill her at the first sign of another trick."

"Tell him it wasn't any trick. *Quickly.* We knew nothing of that damned fool there. We guarantee him access to the radio."

Kajima spoke in rapid phrases. Simura eyed the speaker suspiciously, waiting.

Yelland squeezed his transmit button. "Major Stevens! Pull your men back and order them not to interfere with that Japanese!" He looked at Kajima. "Talk to Simura. Give him my word as the captain of this ship. Release the girl and we'll escort him to the radio room."

Another rapid exchange in Japanese. "Captain, he doesn't believe me and he doesn't believe you."

A voice carried from the speakers into the bridge. They turned to look at the speakers. It was from sick bay. "This is Lasky! For Christ's sake, *get him to use that damned radio!* If he gets to his superior, it can save thousands of lives—including his own fleet, if he can get them to call off the attack in the morning! Answer me, damn you!"

They listened to Matthew Yelland's calm response. "We read you loud and clear, Mr. Lasky. The Japanese doesn't trust us and we're trying to get him to the radio room. What do you suggest?"

In the room charged with tension, Lasky turned to

Owens, but continued to talk loudly enough for the microphone to carry his words to the bridge. "I'm talking to Owens. This is his specialty. Do you all understand me? He's the historian on the attack tomorrow morning. Owens, damn you, you speak up so Kajima can hear you. Give him time to translate for Simura. Tell him things that are impossible for any of us to know. Do you understand? His carriers, the battle fleet, his superiors, the plans for the strike! Tell it to Kajima and he'll translate it for the pilot and then he's *got* to trust us long enough to get to that radio and send his message. Do it—*now*!"

Again Yelland's calm voice came to them. "He's right, Mister Owens. Those are my orders. Proceed at once."

Dick Owens moved forward slightly, just enough to separate himself from the group, but not so much as to panic Simura into a sudden killing. Owens looked at Simura with a solemn, steady gaze. "All right, Kajima. I'll give it to you in phrases, and pause long enough for you to translate."

"Yes, sir," came the answer.

Owens's eyes bored into the Japanese. He began a strange litany that widened the eyes of Simura and finally brought him to gasp in stark disbelief at what he was hearing.

"On the morning of November tenth, the lead units of the Nagumo Force sailed from Kure naval base on Honshu. The Imperial Fleet sortied from Kure, and met other units at Hitokappu Wan on Etorofu. This force took to the open sea on November twenty-sixth."

They watched Simura as Kajima translated and his voice carried through the sick bay ward. The Japanese literally turned pale before their eyes. Owens went on like the voice of God.

"The force of twenty-three vessels, to which Jiro Simura is assigned as a carrier pilot, is under the command of Vice-Admiral Chuichi Nagumo. There are twenty-three warships and support vessels in this force. You are part of the First Air Fleet."

Simura could have been struck with a thunderbolt as he listened with mouth agape.

"The First Carrier Division is made up of *Akagi* and *Kaga*.

"The Second Carrier Division includes *Soryu* and *Hiryu*.

"The Fifth Carrier Division includes *Zuikaku* and *Shokaku*."

Owens paused for the translation and a greater effect to allow his information to sink through the incredulity they saw. Then he went on. "The fleet also includes two battleships, two heavy cruisers, one light cruiser, nine destroyers, and three supporting vessels."

He added one crushing blow after another. The information on the secret battle fleet was bad enough. The names of the ships was worse. The killing blow came on a personal element.

"The supreme air commander of your Attack Air Group is Commander Mitsuo Fuchida. Lieutenant Akira Sakamoto will lead the dive bombers. Your own commander, who will lead the Zero-sen fighters in the first wave, is Lieutenant Commander Shigeru Itaya. The second wave of fighters will be led by Lieutenant Saburo Shindo."

Again the pause, and the final clincher. "On the morning of the second of December, Admiral Nagumo received from Tokyo the message: *Niitaka Yama Nobore*." He repeated the phrase: *Climb Mount Niitaka*.

Jiro Simura trembled visibly. But no less devastated by what he had heard was Senator Samuel S. Chapman, who had struggled to his feet, leaning for support against a bulkhead. "How . . . how in the name of God could you know all this? Who are you? What is all—"

His voice stopped. A hand shot out across the floor

and closed viselike about Simura's ankle. With a gasp of desperation, the wounded Corporal Kullman had seized what he considered his only chance, grasped Simura's ankle, and jerked with all his strength. Laurel threw back her arm to deflect the rifle, throwing Simura off balance. The woman had enough presence of mind to throw herself flat, and the marines at the doorway, seeing Simura bringing his rifle to bear upon the wounded Kullman, reacted instinctively. Several M-16 automatic rifles thundered in the confined space, hurling pieces of Jiro Simura through the air and splashing wetly against the bulkhead.

Lasky groaned. Time was getting more elusive as events ground their way inexorably into the future.

Sam Chapman sat on the edge of the sick bay bed, a doctor examining the angry bruise along his ribs. "You'll be all right, sir. It will hurt for a while but no ribs are broken. I think the best medicine for you right now is a medicinal brandy." He held out a glass, and Chapman downed the brandy gratefully in a single long swallow.

"Now, doctor, will somebody, for God's sake, get me some clothes!"

Captain Yelland stood in the doorway. "You heard the senator, doctor. I should say a size forty-two would do fine. Bring the senator a flight suit in that size. Immediately, please."

Yelland, Thurman at his side, came up to Chapman. "Senator, my apologies for taking so long to meet you personally. I'm Captain Matthew Yelland, commanding this vessel. This is my executive officer, Dan Thurman."

Chapman seemed a bit dazed by the introductions, but shook his head clear and clasped the hand of each man. "Captain, I don't have time for fancy words. What this man," he pointed to Owens, "was saying. Is it true?"

"It is, Senator."

"How in the hell could you have determined everything down to individual ships and even the names of the pilots!"

"It's a very long amd complicated story, Senator."

Chapman studied Yelland. "Is this some sort of game you're playing with me?"

"I assure you, sir, there is no game."

"I haven't got time, as I said," Chapman went on hurriedly, "and neither have you. If all this is true, I suppose you've notified the proper authorities at Pearl Harbor?"

Yelland paused. He forced himself not to smile. "No, Senator, we haven't. I don't think they'd believe us if we told them."

"The least you could do is try!"

"Senator, we're tracking the Japanese battle fleet. If it appears that they really do intend to launch that attack on Pearl Harbor, we're well equipped to disperse the attack and destroy that fleet."

Chapman looked at Yelland as if he were mad. "One carrier? One carrier against a whole fleet like this officer just described, and you can destroy it? Captain Yelland, what kind of an idiot do you take me to be, anyway?"

"Senator, there's a lot you don't understand—"

"I understand only too goddamned well! There's some kind of insane plot here to maneuver the United States into a war that nobody wants, and you people—" He took a deep breath. *"For the record,* Captain Yelland. You are the commanding officer of this warship, and I am a senator of the United States. I request—no, damn it, I demand to be provided with the proper radio facilities to call Pearl Harbor and sound the alarm myself."

An orderly approached with the flight suit. Chapman took the few moments necessary to slip into the suit. Yelland used the opportunity to keep himself cool and unruffled.

"Senator, if that's what you want, of course we'll

bring you to the radio room. We'll assist you in every way possible." During the brief interval while Chapman dressed, Yelland's memory had flashed back to the history of the tragic hours preceding the attack against Pearl Harbor. He recalled the name of Joe Lockard. An army radar technician who saw strange blips on his still-new radar set and reported them to his superior officer and was officially ordered to "quit having the jitters, for Christ's sake. It's Sunday morning."

"You mean that? You'll really do just what you said?" Chapman pressed.

"Absolutely, Senator. Mister Thurman, escort the senator to COMM. Set up everything he requires. I'll be along in just a moment."

They watched Chapman leave with Thurman. Lasky looked with amusement at Yelland. "I see you finally came to the same conclusion," he said.

Yelland nodded. "I remembered something. It's strange the way the past can point the way to the future. Do you remember the name Joe Lockard?"

"Yes," Lasky said.

"Then you know what I was thinking."

"I do."

Owens looked at them strangely. "Begging the captain's pardon, I wish to hell I knew what you two were—are—saying."

"In due time, Mister Owens. It will all be very clear. You're the historian. See if you can dredge up the name Lockard from your mental files and you'll catch up with us very quickly. And now I suggest we join the good senator in COMM and listen to his sounding of the alarm."

"He's no Paul Revere," sighed Lasky. "Did Kaufman really rig his equipment to talk directly to Pearl?"

"He did," Yelland confirmed.

"And after Chapman makes his, ah, attempt?"

"I learn quickly, Warren. After that, one step at a time."

Lasky nodded slowly. "Got it. Just like walking through a minefield."

They entered the radio room to catch the end of a strange discourse between Chapman and Commander Dan Thurman. Chapman was obviously studying the executive officer with a measure of outright disbelief.

"You've been in the navy *how long?*"

"Sixteen years, sir."

"And you're a commander? That's incredible. In fact, it's absolutely unheard of." Chapman looked up as Yelland and his group came up to him.

"You find my exec's rank to be something strange, Senator?" Yelland said.

"I certainly do. I don't know a single Negro officer in the entire active line of the navy, and this man says he's been in uniform for sixteen years."

"He's also a graduate of Annapolis, senator. First in his class, by the way."

Chapman shook his head, started to respond, and changed his mind. His world was spinning about him. He was grateful for the interruption from Kaufman. "Senator Chapman, we've established contact with the duty officer at Pearl. If you'll take this seat, please? I've set up the speakers so everyone present can listen to both sides of the exchange, if that's all right with you."

"Fine, fine," Chapman said, sitting before the microphone. He turned to look at Yelland. "All right to start?"

Yelland nodded. "By all means, Senator Chapman. And good luck to you."

☆ 17 ☆

"This is Senator Samuel Chapman of the United States Senate. I am at this moment on board the aircraft carrier *U.S.S. Nimitz*, with Captain Matthew Yelland, the commanding officer, here with me. Please acknowledge and provide your name and rank. This is a matter of the utmost urgency. I repeat, this is an emergency. Do you understand? Over."

The hiss and crackle of radio static burbled from the speaker. Chapman waited, impatience growing, frowning. "Calling Pearl Harbor! Calling Pearl Harbor! Damn you, answer this call! This is Senator Samuel Chapman aboard the aircraft carrier—"

"Whoever's calling on this frequency, stand by." Chapman remained quiet. Then the radio speakers hissed and crackled again. "This is Lieutenant Perry Wade, officer of the deck. Go ahead, please."

"It's damned well time you answered!" Chapman shouted. "Now you listen to me, Wade. There's a big damned Japanese fleet on its way to Pearl Harbor at this very minute, and they're preparing to launch hundreds of fighters and bombers against you people the moment we get the first light of day. They have six carriers and two battleships and—"

He heard the shouted interruption. "Hold it! Hold it, for Christ's sake! Who are you and—"

"Never mind all that!" Chapman was turning purple

178

in his desperation to alert the American forces at Pearl. "Didn't you hear me? Sound the alarm, for God's sake. I said there was a whole Japanese battle fleet right now on its way to attack Pearl Harbor and—"

". . . and I remind you that use of military channels by unauthorized personnel is a felony under federal law. This is a poor idea of a joke, whoever you are, and—"

"I told you who I am! Senator Sam Chapman! I'm aboard—"

The radio voice overrode his pathetic protests. "There is no aircraft carrier named *Nimitz*, and we've also checked with personnel, and there is no Captain Matthew Yelland in Pacific Command, so whoever you are, you idiot, get off this frequency! You're wasting our time and you're not funny." The radio line went dead.

Chapman stared, speechless, at his mike. Slowly he made a fist and banged it very deliberately against the table. He looked as if he were about to suffer a stroke. His face twisted, he turned to Yelland. "In the name of God, Captain, tell them, *please*, tell them who you are—"

"You heard the man yourself, Senator Chapman. He won't believe you and he won't believe me."

Chapman's voice was badly strained. "He . . . he said there was no *Nimitz* and . . . and that they had no record of a Captain Matthew Yelland."

"That's what he said, Senator."

"But—but—"

"I know. You're not crazy, sir. I'm here and you're aboard *Nimitz*. The man on the other end of that radio just doesn't know about us."

Sam Chapman looked at Yelland and the others as if they were ghosts. "Who are you people . . . ?" There was no answer and Chapman looked about him frantically, settling his eyes finally on Lasky. You! You're a civilian! What the hell is going on here?"

"Senator, my name is Warren Lasky, and I'm an advisor from the Department of Def—sorry, I meant the War Department. I'm on board to test some new celestial navigation equipment for this ship."

"Then maybe you can answer a direct question. What kind of damned charade are they playing with me?" Chapman was no longer the belligerent politician. Even his legendary reserves of willpower and determination were beginning to wane in the face of one staggering blow after another. Everything he had ever built and everything that had been real about him seemed to be wavering as if it had all turned to rubber on some shaky foundation. He was buffeted by things and events that hammered at his sense of reality.

Warren Lasky spread both hands, palms outward, courteously yet unquestionably easing out from under. "I'm sorry, sir," he said calmly. "I'm here just as an observer. There's really very little I know beyond the navigational system I'm here to study under line operations."

Chapman eyed him warily. "Navigation, you said?"

"Yes, sir."

"Are we really two hundred miles off Pearl?"

"More or less, yes, we are."

"What about all these crazy machines I've been seeing? Those airplanes without propellers and those whatever-they-are that took us out of the water? Where the hell did they come from?"

"I'm not allowed to answer anything like that, sir. The papers I signed before I came on this ship stated very clearly that I'd be violating military security if I discussed anything I saw here. It's a standard form, Senator. Surely you're aware of that requirement. If I answered you, I'd be breaking the law, and I won't do that."

"What about those goddamned Japanese!" The voice was shrill again.

"Senator Chapman, you've made more speeches about the Japanese than anyone I know. You have the ear of President Roosevelt. You're in defense appropriations committees, and *you're* asking *me*, a technician, about the Japanese? You saw everything I saw. You were there the whole time. What could I tell you that you don't already know? I will tell you one thing else, Senator. No one aboard this carrier, no one, has lied to you."

Chapman was sagging visibly. "One more thing. That officer, Owens, I think, how could he know the names of those Japanese warships? How could he know when they sailed? How could he know the names of officers and pilots? How in the name of God could he know all *that?*"

"Senator, Senator," Lasky said softly, "do you believe there's a Japanese battle fleet about to strike at Pearl Harbor in just a few hours? Does Washington believe an entire Japanese force could sail the entire Pacific and nobody would know about it? You talked to the duty officer at Pearl Harbor—he thought you were crazy when you told him about that fleet."

"He said there was no such warship as *Nimitz* and they'd never heard of Matthew Yelland!"

"Then, Senator, he's incompetent or a fool or maybe both. Because you're on the *Nimitz* and Matthew Yelland is right here in front of your eyes. And now, sir, if you'll excuse me, I'm scheduled to do some tests with my equipment. You know, Senator, another day's pay and all that."

Stalemate.

Chapman looked at him with a gaunt expression as Lasky walked by. Lasky stopped before Yelland, and they left the radio room together. Thurman would take care of Chapman for the moment.

"That was very neatly done, Warren," Yelland said after a thoughtful pause.

"I know," Lasky replied. "I almost believed it myself. Let me drop one on you, Matt. Time's running out. That fateful hour is almost at hand. What do you do now?"

"I think. I think hard and carefully and then I will decide. And not until then."

Dick Owens knocked on the door to the small isolation ward. Laurel opened it personally. "Clothes!" she exclaimed. "Three cheers for the navy. God, will I be glad to get into something fresh and clean." She closed the door behind him. "What's the latest style?" she queried with a grin.

"Would you believe, Miss Scott—"

"Laurel, please."

"Good. The name on this side of the fence is Dick."

"All right, what am I supposed to believe?"

"We have a tailor on board who is very fast and fancy with a sewing machine. We gave him your size. You have your choice of bell bottoms, loose blouses, or what was once a flight suit, now tailored to you exactly and adorned with all the little things that make women happy and look great."

"You're quite the salesman. Why don't I try the flight suit, or what it is now."

"Jumpsuit. I think you'll like it." He placed the clothing on the table. "I'll wait outside while you change."

She motioned for him to stay. "Dick, please don't go. I'll guard my modesty by changing behind this screen. Right now being alone is the most frightening thing I can imagine. I'm confused, I've nearly been killed twice today, men have died all around me, I don't recognize what's happening, and even old Rock-of-Gibralter Chapman is frazzled to tatters." She moved behind the screen. "Make small talk, Richard. Whatever. We'll let me worry about my reputation."

He laughed. "There's hardly any need to worry about your reputation."

"Sure," came her voice from behind the screen.

"You must snatch stray girls out of the ocean all the time. Happens every day, right?"

"Well, not every day. Your case is different. We don't always rescue fair damsels in the company of a United States senator."

She didn't answer immediately. "Richard, would you mind if I were very blunt about something?"

"Not at all. Officer and a gentleman and all that."

"Well, let me tell you something, then. I'm an ambitious and a very capable young woman. You've been very decent with me and that's why I'm saying this. I'm rough in the clinches. I'm a better politician than most people on the Hill. I'm much too smart to be a girl. All these are elements not much appreciated in our day and age, so I've also become very good at being a chameleon where people don't even know I'm around. It's a man's world out there, Commander Richard Owens. I assume you'll agree to that."

He almost laughed aloud. She didn't know there was a choice of worlds, really. "Okay, I'll agree."

"You're too patronizing."

"Try honest."

"Your point. I wasted a lot of years trying to hide the way I look. I even wore glasses I didn't need, and tied my hair in a bun, and flattened my bustline. All sorts of things in the hope that some of the men I had to work for might notice brains instead of body."

"From what I saw of you, dripping wet and frightened, and imagined how you'd look otherwise," he said slowly, "my guess is that it didn't work out too well."

"Let's just say," she answered carefully, "that in the long run I found out I was losing on both ends of the candle. So I decided to use what mother nature gave me freely—womanhood. And if that helps to open the doors I want opened—well, they say that God helps those who help themselves, and I'm on a full program of self help."

"Does God help them, whoever they are, when you're through with them?"

Her laughter was like the tinkle of ice in a glass. "I never stayed around long enough to ask. Are you ready for my debut? Your tailor is a master, by the way. I've never felt a material like this before. What is it?"

"Something we're testing at sea," he said to sidestep the issue of synthetics that didn't exist in 1941.

"It's wonderful. All right, Dick, ready or not. . . ."

She stepped out from behind the screen and he was almost breathless with the sight of her. Her hair flowed in shimmering gold well below her shoulders. She wore no makeup and didn't need any. And that jumpsuit. . . . "My God, it looks like he measured that thing to fit you like a hand in a glove." He had no idea of that full and straining bosom. "You, Laurel Scott, are absolutely a knockout."

She studied the genuine admiration on his face. "Thank you, Commander. I am flattered."

"I also had a thought."

"Which is?"

"Maybe it should be a question, Laurel. Like, God help the senator?"

She laughed and started to reply, holding her words when they heard a knock on the door. "Come in," he called. A marine orderly stepped inside and snapped to attention. Commander, the captain requests you and Miss Scott to join him in his inport cabin."

"Please inform the captain we'll be right there."

Owens wanted to laugh as they walked along the corridor. Crewmen stared in disbelief and did everything but drool at the sight of the stunning young woman in the tight-fitting jumpsuit.

"To pick up where we left it before, Dick," she said as they walked, "Sam Chapman is going to be not just a very important man in this country, but one of the most important men. I realize that being out to sea as much as you are may make such things seem unimportant, but they're not."

"Then I'll have to take your word for it," he said.

"Would you really do that?"

"Of course. Why wouldn't —?" he asked, puzzled.

"Men rarely listen to what a woman has to say," she said matter-of-factly.

He had to force himself to think in her time-frame and not his own. "Whether it sounds real or not, Laurel, I'm listening, and what's more I'm learning."

"Then you're a rare breed." She smiled. "I keep to a goal, and that's to be where the decisions are made. That's the top of the heap as far as I'm concerned. And what I'm trying to say without seeming like too much of a dragon, that is, is that I've learned that the only way upstairs is by brainpower instead of shape."

"You, I will quickly admit, lack nothing in either department."

She slipped her hand through his arm. "You, Commander, are a charmer."

Sam Chapman was in an intense conversation with Captain Matthew Yelland and several of his staff when they entered the inport cabin. They smiled in recognition and appreciation at the sight of Laurel Scott in her new jumpsuit. "Miss Scott," Yelland smiled, "I'm glad we were able to bring you safely back into our midst. You're a beautiful woman."

"And you, sir, are very gallant. Thank you," she said graciously.

"May I add you've acted as if you had the strength of ten men, Miss Scott," Yelland added. "It is a rare trait."

"Is that meant as a compliment to a woman, Captain?"

"It is a compliment to *you*, Miss Scott."

"Captain, your crew is fabulous. I feel as if this is the first time I've been with a group of men who appreciate someone for what that person is, and sex doesn't matter."

"You might say we're just a bit ahead of our time," Yelland said with a smile—causing Warren Lasky almost to choke.

Chapman broke in. "My apologies for going right to business, Laurel, but the word time is extremely relevant here," he said by way of explanation. "I'm still not sure I know what the devil is happening in terms of a Japanese battle fleet, but there's no doubt in my mind that the Hawaiian Islands are in grave danger, and there's no time to waste. I've asked Captain Yelland to fly us as quickly as possible, directly to Pearl Harbor. I won't get the crap on the ground I had from that idiot on the radio." He turned from Laurel back to Yelland. "Captain, I really must persist, and I ask your every assistance."

"You have it, sir," Yelland replied. "Mister Owens."

"Sir?"

"A helo is being raised to the flight deck right now and the crew is standing by. You will escort the senator and Miss Scott to the flight area, make certain they are equipped with everything they need, and waste no time in flying them to navy headquarters at Pearl. Any questions?"

"No, sir."

Laurel gestured, concern on her face. "I know this seems a small matter, captain, but—well, it's my dog, Charlie. He's still on board somewhere."

"Laurell Forget the goddamned dogl" Chapman shouted. "We're talking about a warl"

Lasky slipped smoothly into the breach. "Miss Scott, we'll take care of him and we'll get him back to you. You have my personal promise." He smiled. "And that of the war department, too."

"Thank you, Mr. Lasky." She squeezed his hand.

"Laurel, damnit, let's go."

Chapman nearly dragged her from the cabin. A moment later Dick Owens reappeared and went directly to Yelland. "They're being taken to the chopper, sir. I'll catch them without wasting any time. But I had to talk to you for a moment."

"Go ahead."

"Sir, anything that man tells the authorities at Pearl Harbor is just going to add to all the confusion already stirred up."

"It won't matter very much then, will it?" Yelland said with a trace of a smile.

"May I make a point, Commander?" They glanced at Lasky. "There's not much they can do at Pearl, even if they believed his story. You know what happened. We fired on Japanese submarines hours before the planes left their carriers, and no one reported it to headquarters. Joe Lockard, that army technician, even tracked the Japanese planes coming in on his radar, and he was ordered to ignore what he saw. Even before Pearl itself was hit, Japanese fighters planes were shooting up aircraft from the carrier *Enterprise*—and shot down a bunch of them. You're the historian among us, and certainly you remember that those planes from *Enterprise* never fired a single shot in their defense. Time has an ally we should have recognized before, Owens."

"He's right," Yelland said. "It's name is inertia."

Owens looked doubtful. "Yes, sir," he said noncommittally.

"Listen to me, Dick," Yelland said, his face serious. "You do *not* fly them to Pearl. I would have told you this by radio, but it's better right here and now. There are several small islands off the main shoreline, west of Pearl. You remember them?"

"Yes, sir. I've flown over them many times."

"Then you'll have just enough time to deposit the senator and that woman on one of those islands. Find one that's deserted. Leave them provisions, and get the hell out of there. Time has become an enemy. What time did the Japanese planes leave their carriers?"

"Oh six hundred, sir."

"Then you'd better shag ass, Commander. Just drop them off and get back here, pronto."

"Matt, you just can't dump them like that!" Lasky protested.

"Oh?" Yelland's brows went up. "You have only seconds to tell me why."

"Damnit, it would be a terrible mistake, that's why. Senator Sam Chapman was killed on December 7th, 1941—and it will be December 7th, right past midnight, very soon now. If he had lived, then he almost certainly would have become president in 1945 when Roosevelt died. Now, with what you're doing, he will be killed. You're putting him on an island but he's still in the bullseye. We need him with us today—not dead somewhere."

Yelland eyed the other man thoughtfully. "I'll keep this short. My job is to make decisions here, and right now, not with an eye to what some senator *might* be in the White House years from now. This ship is about to engage in all-out battle and I do *not* want those two civilians aboard." He turned to Owens. "Move it, Commander."

"Captain, Owens will support what I'm saying," Lasky said desperately.

Yelland was ice. "Commander Owens will carry out his orders, Mister Lasky. Commander, do not say another word. Get the devil out to that chopper. Be back aboard this vessel at oh five hundred. I want my best man leading that strike force."

Owens took off at a run, and Lasky fixed his gaze on Yelland. "You said two civilians, Captain. You were wrong. Make it *three*."

Yelland began an angry rebuke, thought better of his words. "Warren, you'll learn that there always comes that time when all the rationalizations in the world aren't worth one ounce of action. You're standing on that moment right now. You are free to go with the senator, but I advise you to move your tail to that flight deck as fast as you can run—or you'll see them leaving without you. And, Warren, whatever—and whenever—good luck."

Lasky ran after Owens.

He reached the helicopter on the windy deck as they were about to slide the cabin hatch closed. The chopper was ready to lift as Lasky ran up to the door, shouting. The door slid open and Owens stared down at Lasky.

"What the hell are you doing here, mister?" he shouted above the wind and thunder of engines.

"I've the captain's permission to go with you!" Beyond Owens's form, Lasky saw Laurel staring at him, questioning.

"To the devil with permissions! You're not coming aboard this aircraft!" Owens started to close the door.

"You can't do this, damnit! It's vital I go with you!"

The door stopped. "Lasky, just what will you try to do when we get there?"

"No one else will know how it all ties together, for God's sake. I'll be the only one who knows both ends of the tunnel! I want to be certain we get everything just right!"

Owens smiled coldly. "That's just the trouble, Lasky. Anyone who works to have everything set up for time to follow is more dangerous than an atomic bomb!" The door slammed shut in Lasky's face. Furious, and as helpless as he was angry, Lasky stepped back quickly as the helicopter went to full power, crashing wind and thunder back down upon him. Then it was gone. Lasky watched the lights flashing as the chopper dwindled into the darkness. He started back for the bridge.

"Where's Captain Yelland?" Lasky asked.

Commander Damon had the bridge. "He's in COMM. He's preparing to talk to the crew. You can just make it before he starts if you hurry."

Lasky entered the television room with a minute to spare. Yelland looked at him with surprise. "Warren, you pop up everywhere. I thought I'd never see you again. How come you're not on that chopper with the senator?"

Lasky shrugged. "You know how it is, Matt. Birds of a feather, I guess. Besides, I thought you might get lonely. Who are you going to get to talk to about warps in time and space?"

Yelland smiled. "I'll take that up with you as soon as I talk to my men. Have you seen Black Cloud?"

Lasky sensed something serious. "No, sir, I haven't. Has anything unusual come up?"

"You're damned right it has. Hard to tell what it is, but that smudge that drove our weather people crazy, just before the storm that slung us back here, seems to be showing up on the radar scopes."

Lasky's jaw dropped. "That could mean—"

A sharp gesture cut him short. "Not now," Yelland said quietly, but with a cutting edge to his words. Lasky nodded.

"Sir, we're ready," a technician told the captain. Yelland looked into the camera of the closed-circuit television system. Where there were no monitors aboard *Nimitz* his crew would hear his voice from speakers. A hand pointed to Yelland and a red light flashed on the camera.

"This is your captain. During the last few hours I know many of you have been confused and perhaps even frightened by the strange events in which this vessel has been involved. You have heard rumors of all kinds and I want to dismiss the rumors and the scuttlebutt. Nothing could approach the truth of the matter. You all remember, some of you painfully, that storm through which we passed less than eighteen hours ago. No one aboard this ships knows exactly what that storm was, where it came from, or how it started. What we do know is that it had an effect upon us all that can't even be described as incredible.

"You may have heard of twists or warps that affect both space and time. Apparently such effects are real in the universe. The amazing truth is that eighteen hours ago we were in 1980. Right now the world in which we are sailing is the world of nearly forty years ago. The date is the sixth of December 1941. At twenty-four hundred hours it will be the seventh of December, and you all know what that means. In the history books, Pearl Harbor was attacked on the morning of Sunday, the seventh of December. We're now back in history.

"I have made my decision that no matter what has happened to us, no matter what we understand or do not yet understand, we are first and last a fighting ship of the line of the United States Navy. Our sworn duty is to defend the United States. I intend, with the help of every one of you, to do just that. Understand what this means. We are about to fight a battle that was fought long before many of you were even born. We know what happened when Pearl Harbor was bombed. I do not know by what intervention we have been given this chance to prevent that terrible slaughter, but I assure you, this time it is going to have a different ending. *Nimitz* is going to take on the entire battle fleet now preparing to attack and destroy Pearl Harbor. We are going to take them on and we are going to whip those people so badly the war may never really have a chance to get started. Let's keep the theory and the philosophy for later. Right now we go by the book, all of us. Gentlemen, *Nimitz* is now at General Quarters."

Yelland nodded to the TV crew and the red light winked out. Lasky was nearly overwhelmed. Yelland had cut the mustard in such a way he had a hyped-up fighting team on his hands that already was itching to tear the Nagumo attack force to shreds.

At the same time, Matt Yelland recognized the fears and uncertainties lurking in the minds of so many of his men. This was the moment for the ship's chaplain,

Commander David Gleason, to speak to the crew. The chaplain was already at another seat before another camera, and his face and voice carried through the carrier. Lasky listened, or half listened. A grizzled chief petty officer stood beside Lasky. He had come in just as Yelland began his talk. They stood in silence as the chaplain invoked God and piety for the benefit of the crew, and the only remark Lasky heard from the veteran by his side was a grumbled "Bullshit."

The chaplain completed his message, turned to look at them. It seemed he'd known the CPO for a long time. "Chief Duncan, you were here for my message?"

"Aye, sir."

"Good, good. I thought the men would appreciate a word or two of comfort—"

"Meaning no disrespect, Father, but most of them don't much give a damn. Those who are too young won't understand and those who are old bastards, like myself, think it's so much guff."

Chaplain Gleason's face hardened. "The war has made you cynical, Chief."

"Which war, Father? There've been so many I've lost count. And yet you still prattle on about God being on our side, and you talk nonsense about the sins of war. We're going to fight, Father, not pray. What the captain had to say made sense. What you had to say just confuses everybody."

"War never settled anything, Chief."

"That's where we differ, sir. I fought through a lot of wars and even though I can't understand how the hell all this is happening, I fought all the way through the one that's starting in just a few hours. I was lucky. I was at Pearl Harbor, on the *Arizona*, in fact, but I left about two weeks before the Japs creamed us there."

"I'm sorry," the chaplain said. "It's just that I once gave a memorial service there. On the *Arizona* itself, I mean."

"Tell me, padre," Chief Duncan said with naked sarcasm. "A whole bunch of my friends are still in that hulk. Twelve hundred men in all. You know what, padre? You ought to fly over that thing. You can still see that long, twisting oil slick. The oil's been leaking from that hull ever since she went down. Maybe it'll be leaking for a hundred years more. You're right, padre. It's a memorial service that never quits. And just think. If the captain is right, then we can prevent Pearl Harbor and the *Arizona* and Wake Island and Kwajalein and Tarawa and Okinawa and all the rest of it. We could have prevented it the first time, but we didn't have the balls to do it."

"I'm—I'm not sure I understand," the chaplain said, hesitating.

"You talk to God. Maybe He can explain it to you. Me? Like the captain says, we go by our book, and I'd follow that man to Hell and back again if he says go. Better get your flak helmet on, padre. It's likely to get real interesting when daylight comes. And now, sir, excuse me." He spun on his heel and left.

Yelland stood behind the chaplain. A smile played on his face and then vanished. "Mr. Lasky. I have an urgent call from Black Cloud. I want you with me in the weather office *now*."

☆ 18 ☆

"I don't have much time," Yelland said to open the conversation in the weather office. "Spell it out fast."

Black Cloud glanced at his captain. "Sir, we're getting the same phenomena we experienced just before that crazy storm hit us and knocked us back in time. Electrical interference up and down the scale, radio transmissions going in and out, even the first signs of surges from the nuclear reactors."

"Does it cover the same area?"

"Yes, sir. The outline approximates what we experienced before, as best we can tell on our scopes."

"Let me see for myself."

"Right here, sir." Black Cloud led the way to a hooded scope. Yelland peered at the glowing lucite. He saw what his weather officer meant. *Nimitz* was represented clearly on the tracking board. He saw the familiar signs of distant clouds, even the small bright spots of his night patrol over the carrier. Well to the rear of the carrier's position the radar scope showed a strange blur. Yelland kept his eyes on the scope while talking.

"When did you first see this?"

"Twenty-eight minutes ago, sir."

"Is it moving?"

"It sure is, Captain. And it's moving toward us."

Yelland finally looked. "You mean that thing is following us?"

"Captain, I'm way over my head with this business," Black Cloud said. "It seems to be following us. I don't know for certain. I have no way of knowing. That could have been its original course, but I got a strange feeling that somehow we, well, we're *attracting* it."

Yelland looked at Lasky, who was deep in thought. "Don't theorize any more than you have to, Warren. Let's hear it."

"I think he's right," Lasky said. "Whatever were the conditions that first time, I don't know, an electromagnetic signature from the nuclear systems of this ship, whatever, it could be repeating. That storm could also be having a rebound effect. You know, like the overpressure wave of an explosion. It creates a partial vacuum and you get a return pressure wave to make up the imbalance. That's the best I can do."

"Sir, if we change course we'll know a lot better," Black Cloud offered.

"You mean we might just get out of its way," the captain said.

"Yes, sir."

"Damnit, I don't know if we should even be trying to escape it."

They all stared at him. "Jesus," Yelland swore. "We're right back to that closed circle of knowing *not* what to do. To the devil with the theories. Right now I have a mission to launch. John," he said to Black Cloud, "you stay glued to this room. You don't leave it. You keep a record of everything that's going on. I'll hold an open line between the bridge and you. If it looks important, you get on that horn to me right away, understand?"

"Yes, sir."

"Good. Mr. Lasky, join me on the bridge. We're about to start or to stop a war, and I'm afraid I don't know which it's to be."

Owens stood between and behind the two helicopter pilots. They were flying with all running lights, beacons, and strobes off to avoid drawing attention from the military installations or patrol ships off the main Hawaiian Islands. The three men studied the radar screen displayed dead center in the cockpit. It had been switched to land contour mode to bring into glowing lines the shapes of small islands off a major land mass.

"Two o'clock position," Owens said. "See that one island off by itself? Take this thing into there. It's uninhabited, so when we get real close bring her down slow and use one landing light. There's a good beach for about a hundred yards without any trees or obstructions. Take her in and put her down there."

The pilot glanced at Owens. "Sir, we were told to take the senator to Pearl Harbor."

Owens nodded. "I know what you were told. Other people were supposed to hear your orders. Now I'm giving you a direct order, Lieutenant. Land on that beach I pointed out. Any questions?"

"No, sir." The pilot set his lips grimly and began the steady descent toward the radar target growing steadily larger as they eased from the sky. "That's it," Owens confirmed. "Radar altimeter shows a hundred feet. Hold this until you're over the beach and take her down gently."

"Yes, sir."

Owens returned to the cabin and went through a ritual of fastening his seat belt. Chapman and Laurel could hear the best of the rotors changing as they descended. Moments later they felt the big helicopter lurch slightly. "We're down, Commander," the pilot called back.

"Very good. Keep everything running," Owens ordered.

"Wait a damn moment!" Chapman said angrily. He was peering through a window. Everything outside was dark. The only lights he could see were far in the distance. He turned to glare at Owens. "This isn't Pearl Harbor. Where the hell are we?"

Owens met his gaze without flinching. "My apologies, Senator Chapman. My orders were to put you down here where you'll be safe."

"What orders?" Chapman shouted. "You heard the captain talking to me! He said to fly us to Pearl!"

Laurel showed fear at the unexpected exchange. "What's happening? Is there something wrong?"

Owens and Chapman ignored her questions. They were in a contest that Owens controlled and they both knew it. "I'm sorry, Senator," he said. "This is the only way for us to go. Like I said, you and Laurel will be safe here."

Owens turned from the enraged man before him and addressed the crew chief. "All right, you know what to do. Get those supplies outside on that beach. We're running out of time, so let's move it."

Owens pulled open the sliding door and stepped down on the sand. Air whistled about him from the idling rotor blades. Behind him two men carried out several small crates of supplies.

Chapman stared at what was happening. He made an instant decision. "Laurel, get Owens to help you down. Do it, quickly!"

For the moment Owens and the crew were occupied. Chapman turned behind him, pulled open the safetly catch on an emergency flare kit. Covering his movements with his body, he snapped a thick shell into the chamber, closed the flare gun, and stuffed it inside the flight jacket given him before leaving the carrier. Then he turned, hands in the jacket pockets, watching the men on the beach. Laurel had grasped Owens by his arm.

"Will you please tell me what's happening, Richard? I don't understand any of this!"

He looked at her with more than regrets for just following his orders. "Laurel, I'm sorry. My God, you don't know how sorry I am about all this. But you're safe, and that's all that matters right now. Please don't ask me any more because I can't give you the answers. Trust me, I—"

She pulled back from him, the one landing light illuminating her face just enough to show sudden anger. "Trust you? I *don't* trust you. Not now! You lied to him and you're lying to me, and I don't believe a word you're saying. I don't take orders from you, Commander!"

Owens looked at her with sudden exhaustion. Damn, he had to get back to the carrier, because— But he couldn't leave her like this and he ran after her, reaching for her arm. In the cabin Chapman could just make out her words. "And keep your damned hands off me!"

Chapman made his decision. He would never have a better opportunity than right now. Everyone among the crew was busy. The senator brought the flare gun from his jacket, moving slowly toward a crewman securing tiedown straps. The crewman turned, startled, and the heavy flare gun crashed against his temple. The crewman collapsed like a poled ox, unconscious. Chapman spun about and ran to the cockpit. The flight engineer was talking with the pilots when he felt the muzzle of the flare gun against the side of his head.

"Just freeze right where you are," he was told.

The pilots stared at him. "If you follow orders, he lives. If you make one wrong move, I squeeze this trigger and I'll burn his brains right out of his head. Do you understand me?"

The pilot stayed very cool, very calm. That flare gun was a bomb inside his machine. "I understand."

"Then you take this thing straight up, *and right now*, or this man dies." He glared at the pilots. "You goddamned traitors, do it!"

"Yes, sir, we'll—"

"Shut up and get into the air, damn you!"

The pilot nodded. A moment later the sound of the engines increased and the great overhead rotors threw off their blatting thunder. The ground fell away slowly. The pilot shouted over his shoulder. "Mister, be careful. You shoot that thing off in here and we *all* burn."

"That's the price of this ride, buster," Chapman snarled. "I'm willing to pay the ticket. Keep going!"

On the beach, Owens stared in horror as the Sikorsky spun up its rotors and began a slow ascent. Cursing, he ran frantically toward the helicopter, reaching the rising machine as it climbed. He couldn't make the cabin door and in an act of desperation he threw himself at the hull railings. He clung precariously to the chopper as it moved across the water. Then the pilot increased power, the Sikorsky pitched forward for speed, and the downblast overwhelmed Owens. He fell away from the accelerating machine, only a dozen feet above the water, and crashed into the surf.

Chapman looked ahead toward the brighter lights. "That's Pearl over there. I know that harbor. You make straight for the navy base and you land at headquarters."

The pilot nodded grimly. "You got it, mister. I don't know what your game is, but—"

"Shut up. *Fly*."

Behind Chapman, the crewman knocked out by the blow to his head had regained consciousness. He struggled to a sitting position, unheard by Chapman in the crashing sound of engines and rotor blades. The crewman steadied himself, and then hurled his body at the civilian with the gun. Chapman gasped from the blow, but he was desperate and like a wild animal. He flung the man from him and turned to face his adversary. The moment the gun moved from his head, the flight engineer slammed a fist against Chapman's head. The senator gasped, his body jerking from the blow.

His finger squeezed involuntarily.

A blinding flash speared at them as the gun went off. The flare slammed into a hydraulic line.

Dick Owens stood in the surf, looking after the helicopter moving across the water. He saw a flash of light inside the cabin. Before he could try to understand what the light might be, an enormous white-yellow ball of intense flame mushroomed outward in all directions. Blazing wreckage spewed into the water.

Behind him, Owens heard Laurel screaming.

Captain Yelland glanced at the digital clock on his bridge command console. The figures read 0528. Yelland turned to the radarman across the bridge. "Have they started back yet?"

"They're in the air, sir, but—I've lost it! It just went off the scope. It's down, sir!"

"What the devil do you mean, it's down?"

The radar operator looked up, shaken. "Sir, it looks as if they crashed."

Yelland cursed beneath his breath. Dan Thurman was by his side immediately. "Captain, we can launch a rescue helo in seconds."

Yelland looked up again at the clock. The lines on his forehead deepend. "There's no time. It'll have to wait." He leaned forward, looking across the great flight deck in the gloom, dull lights of many colors identifying planes and launch crews. "Mr. Perry," Yelland said quietly, "bring her into the wind."

The huge warship began her turn into the wind to increase the air flow across the deck for the catapult launches.

"Plot, this is the captain. Report on the Japanese fleet."

"Aye, aye, sir. Two hundred miles out from Pearl, holding course, and—sir, they're starting their turn."

Yelland looked at his staff, Warren Lasky with them. "Two cruisers are set to launch four Zero floatplane fighters at 0600. That starts them all. The first planes will leave their carriers at the same time and start forming in the air. Less than ten minutes to go." He squeezed the transmit button again. "Plot, give me the weather with the Japanese."

"Aye, aye, sir. No change. Six thousand feet overcast, winds out of the northeast."

"Captain." Yelland turned to Lasky. "Would you mind a question?"

Yelland hesitated a moment, watching the afterburners blazing on a Tomcat as it catapulted into the night. "Go ahead, Mr. Lasky."

"In just ten minutes the Japanese will launch a hundred and ninety fighters and bombers."

"I know that."

"I'm wondering why you didn't go after their carriers before they launched. It would reduce the chances of a successful attack by—"

"Those carriers can't hurt us at Pearl, Mr. Lasky. Until they launch those planes and they're in formation and on their way to attack, there isn't any attack. They need daylight. They'll launch at six o'clock and they'll work their way into formation. They will not drop their first bomb until shortly before eight o'clock. I will not accept a war situation until those planes are on their way and committed. Then we shall intercept them. Those planes are like clay targets to our aircraft. Then, and only then, after we have engaged in the air, will we go after Nagumo himself. Have no fear, Mr. Lasky. There are twenty-three ships in that fleet and we will send all twenty-three to the bottom."

He fell silent as two more fighters crashed into the night sky. One after the other the powerful fighters and bombers thundered into the fading darkness.

Yelland's earphone buzzed. He punched in the line to weather. "Sir, weather here."

"Go ahead."

"There's no question, Captain. It's the same kind of

storm, maybe even the same storm. It's moving up on us. And, Captain, when we turned, it turned with us like we were a magnet."

"Keep me informed. How far out is that thing from us?"

"Thirty miles, sir."

"All right. Give me any changes as they occur."

Spears of flame tore across the deck. In the first touches of dawn Yelland watched the powerful jets, seen by their position lights, taking up formation. The combat controller's voice came across his headset.

"Victor Two One Zero, this is Zulu Five. Assume your planned course. You will pick up visual for target intercept at zero six four zero."

"Plot from the captain. Report."

"They're in the air, sir. The scope is cluttered, but we count one hundred and ninety bogies. One zero niner aircraft, on course for a direct approach from their fleet to Pearl."

Yelland looked at Lasky. "Right out of the pages of the history books, Mr. Lasky."

"Weather to the captain."

"Let's have it."

"Sir, that storm is picking up speed. We're getting much stronger interference. Captain, I thing it's going to be as bad as before, maybe worse. And we've got all those planes out—"

"Thank you, Mr. Arthur. Stand by."

Yelland listened to the radio exchange between his aircraft and operations. "Zulu Five, this is Strike Leader Victor Two One Zero. We confirm radar contact. Bandits at one eight zero miles. We're closing fast. Request permission to arm all weapons. I repeat, request permission to arm all weapons. Over."

The controller looked at Commander Dan Thurman. For a long moment Thurman paused, then he nodded. "Go."

"Strike Leader from Zulu Five. That is affirmative. I repeat, you are affirm to arm your weapons. Over."

"Roger, Zulu Five." Several seconds went by, then the voice ghosted through the airwaves. "Strike Leader to Zulu Five. We're hot. Confirm all aircraft are hot. Over."

"We read you as all aircraft armed, Strike Leader. Continue as planned."

The sky had started to lighten along the horizon. They looked from the bridge toward the stern of *Nimitz* and beyond. Already they could feel the deep throbbing pulse beneath them as the seas began to heave. The greenish cast to the sky increased with every second.

"Captain! Weather here. It's overtaking us, sir."

Yelland turned to the helmsman. His voice cracked like a whip. "Steer one eight zero. All ahead, flank speed."

"Aye, sir!"

Nimitz veered away from the storm bearing down on her, an enormous cauldron of violence seemingly intent on snaring a running prey.

Two minutes went by. Three. Four.

"Weather office to the bridge!"

"This is Yelland."

"Sir, it's no joy. That damn storm is coming after us, Captain. It's changed course and it's on the precise track we've taken. We're getting heavy lightning along the horizon—"

Yelland could see that for himself. The wind was already making its banshee cry heard on the bridge and terrible clouds boiled along the horizon. "—and there's no way we can outrun it. Captain?"

A low moan of despair came from Yelland. He banged his fist slowly against his console. He looked up at Lasky, despair stamped on his face. "Full circle, Mr. Lasky. It's all coming full circle. We can't outrun that devil storm. We may have tripped over a glitch in time, but nature repairs its own wounds. Damn!" He took a deep breath. "There's no choice. We've got to recall our aircraft."

Lasky turned white. "My God, Captain, *you can't do that!*"

Yelland turned the speakers from the weather office full up. "Mr. Arthur!"

"Sir?"

"Classify your situation as to the storm bearing down on us."

"Captain, I—" Black Cloud hesitated, then threw away his restraints. "Sir, it's worse than the last one and closing fast, and the situation is critical. Full emergency, sir."

"Thank you, weather," Yelland said calmly. "Pass the word to secure this vessel for violent weather. Full emergency conditions." He hit another button.

"COMM, the captain. We have just moved into full emergency weather conditions. Scrub the mission. I repeat, scrub the mission. I'll stand by on open line. I want to hear full confirmation from Strike Leader personally. Do it."

Lasky stared, searching desperately for the right words. How in the name of God could he do this now, of all times! "Matt," he said softly, "you're wrong, you're *wrong*."

"Oh, for God's sake, Lasky. . . . how little you know sometimes. We can't outrun that storm. You've got the same gut instinct I do. We're committed to it, linked for all eternity to that damned thing. And I've got to get those planes back here. Do you understand?" He shook his head. "No, of course not. How could you? You never flew a jet in hellish weather trying to reach a carrier deck that's gone mad. Their only chance is to return immediately."

Lasky had regained his self-control and Yelland saw that smile show on his face. "Nice try, Matt. We both know they're not going to make it in time. Look at that weather. The way this thing is rolling, the wind. Just like before. Maybe worse. You're right. I never flew a jet onto a carrier deck that's gone mad. But I know that no one could do it in this kind of storm, when even the carrier can't be controlled. Sail her into the wind? That's a joke. You're just trying to keep her from going down, that's all."

Yelland's eyes were slits. "What's your point?"

"Suppose they don't make it—back here in time to land before that storm engulfs us." He looked up. "They won't, either. What do we have, then? Men with degrees in physics and chemistry and nuclear engineering and aerodynamics and ordnance and all the rest of it, enough knowledge among those men, between them, to build the atomic bomb and reach the moon and develop jets and all the rest of it years before it's supposed to happen. . . ."

Yelland nearly shouted into his mike. "COMM! Where's that confirmation from Strike Leader?"

"Sir, we're having trouble getting through. Everything is scrambled. We're staying with it."

"Standing by," Yelland said, turning back to Lasky.

"That's quite a picture you're painting," he said.

Lasky's smile flickered, was gone. "Yes, it is. A terrifying prospect, Captain?" He paused just long enough to hear a drum beat of time washing through them. "Or a tempting one?"

Matt Yelland laughed in his face. "You want a terrifying prospect, Warren? I'll give you one, then. Let's not deny we're going back into that space warp or time tornado or whatever the hell that thing is. Now, you tell me where we come out—and when."

Lasky stood rooted to the deck. "I . . . I don't know."

"You're damned right you don't. And neither do I." His face showed sudden anger at the long silence from the air controllers, but in the same breath the speakers boomed out at the bridge.

"Strike Leader, Strike Leader from Zulu Five. Abort! Abort! I repeat you are under orders to abort the strike mission. Confirmation code Foxtrot Eagle

Six. That is Foxtrot Eagle Six. Return to home plate immediately, return to home plate immediately. Confirm voice and Foxtrot signal code. Over."

The pause in response was pregnant with anger. Yelland studied his console. Strike Leader would confirm in two ways. First he would activate a coded electronic signal that read Foxtrot Eagle Six to confirm the validity of the two-way transmission. Then he would report in voice. His words were barely audible over the rising interference from the storm.

"Zulu Five, this is Strike Leader. Code signal transmitted. Verbal confirmation your order to abort strike." Then, to the other flight leader en route to intercept the Japanese. "Strike Leader to all aircraft. You all heard the man. The mission is canceled. I repeat, the mission is canceled. All aircraft start your return to home plate immediately."

Another pause and then a single last angry voice before communications were ground to hash by the storm.

"You mean we're going to let the goddamned Japs do it *again*?"

☆ 19 ☆

The sun broke through low clouds on the horizon, sharpening the world into glowing focus. Commander Richard Owens, USN, looked up at the skies, waiting. His clothing was spread on a low tree just above the beach, and he rested on the sand, wrapped in a navy blanket. Owens was both astonishingly settled within his own mimd, to his almost complete surprise, and shared at the same time a keen anticipation at being witness to what, until a few moments from now, yet to happen, was only an historical record. *To live what had been lived before and to live it as a participant, locked downstream in the flowing river of time.* He wasn't certain where that thought had created itself within his mind, or when it solidified sufficiently so that he might remember it as an entity, later to be treasured, but he knew he had come to this moment with absolute peace within himself. No regrets, no self-imposed pity or piety at having been wrenched from his own straw of time. Somehow he knew that whatever had wrenched him back four decades had, somewhere, gone CLICK! and the door back was closed forever. But it could be goddamned well fascinating! The thought brought a chuckle to his lips.

He watched Laurel unpacking their provisions. She had been through so many devastating psychological and emotional shocks during the past day that she recovered with speed and strength from the yellow-white fireball slapping across the ocean and sending the broken wreckage, with the body of Sam Chapman, hissing into the sea. Perhaps the full effect had yet to be told on her psyche; God knew she'd had enough this past day and night to break a dozen men. Now, the tides having washed away even the remnants of the big Sikorsky, she buckled down to her own immediate reality. The supplies and provisions had included clothing and blankets, and she helped the shivering Owens from the surf when he waded back ashore. Out of the wet clothes and into a blanket. He'd warm up when the sun rose. Emergency rations was what they both needed for strength. Owens gave no objection when Laurel insisted she would do the unpacking of the supplies. She was in for a very rude shock once more and he knew of no better way than this for her to comprehend what had happened these past hours. He watched her, intent in her work, holding a food container. As he had expected, her body went rigid, and she turned very slowly and deliberately to face him.

"Have you seen these before?" she asked. He understood her manner of treading these new waters so carefully. He nodded.

"Yes, Laurel."

"This is no joke." Question and disbelieving statement at the same time.

"It's real," he said quietly.

She stared at him, at the can, back up to him. "Richard, this is impossible."

"Why?"

"Look at what it says!"

"Read it to me, Laurel. Go on, please."

"It says Inspector 118 and the date is July—" She hit a mental block.

"Read it, Laurel."

"The date is July, 1979." Her eyes were wide as she

looked up to him. "But, Richard . . . that's impossible."

"I used to think so, too. I was wrong. It's not only possible, it happened. It's real."

She came to him, kneeling before him, gazing into his eyes. "That explains all those things I could never understand, then," she said in wonder. "That great warship of yours, those airplanes that have no propellers and are so fast—"

"Faster than the speed of sound, Laurel. Twice as fast."

"But that's impossible! I—" She giggled, hiding her mouth with her hand. "I've got to stop saying that, musn't I?"

"Only to me, Laurel."

"What Sam was trying to do, I mean, get to the navy at Pearl Harbor—you know what's going to happen, then."

"Yes, I do."

"He was talking about an attack—"

"Don't even get started, Laurel. We've learned a lot these past few hours. About time, I mean. Think of time as a great elastic sheet that curves back in upon itself. Four dimensions, maybe more. You can bend the elastic out of shape, but the overall shape won't change that much. Time allows minor errors to creep into its structure, but not major ones. That's why I'm here, pushed forty years back into history, but the major events that happened will always happen, no matter what we do to alter them. You see, history records that Sam Chapman died on the morning of December 7th, 1941. It also speculates that had he not died on this day he would have become Roosevelt's running mate in 1944, and when Roosevelt died in 1945—"

She paled.

"Damn, I've got to remember that a small historical fact to me is the whole world to you," he said with self-anger.

She squeezed his hand. "No, no; we'll both adapt."

She smiled. "Did you ever see me before? In that future of yours, Richard? How far ahead were you?"

"1980."

"It's going to take a while to get used to that."

"Laurel—"

"Has the world changed much by then? *Please.*"

"Laurel, we tamed the atom and created artificial brains. We've walked the moon and taken closeup pictures of Saturn and Jupiter and landed ships on Mars and Venus and—" He stopped himself short and saw the hope in her eyes. "No, honey, we didn't change the character, the nature of the beast. There are wars up and down the planet, just like always before. But there's more hope than ever." His eyes widened. "I just thought of something," he said, with a tone of reverence in his voice.

"I know," she said, her eyes bright. "There's a reason for your being here. *You're a guide.*"

The words sobered him, as effectively as having ice water poured over him. "I don't know if I could handle that sort of thinking, Laurel."

She took his hand. "I know today. I don't think the future will be a problem, and—"

She turned at the sound of dull thunder. "I don't understand," she said. "There's no storm in sight and. . . ." Her voice fell away as she glanced at his face. The sound grew into a hard, droning roar. "Oh, no." She saw the small shapes in the distant sky, growing larger. "Oh, dear God. . . ."

"Hang on, kid." He pulled her close to him as the opening waves of the great aerial armada from six Japanese carriers closed in against Pearl Harbor. "You're an eyewitness to the beginning of the Second World War."

It was happening again. The mountainous waves beyond the carrier deck, the strange greenish glow that kept brightening steadily, the screaming wind and that unnerving yaw of the great ship, the static electricity that crackled everywhere, and the booming crash of thunder: the crew had known all these effects not so long ago.

Matt Yelland strapped in tightly, knowing as well as any other man what to expect. "Plot!" he roared, "where the hell are those planes!"

A voice gasped from radar plot. "Captain . . . we can't pick up a thing in this stuff! The scope is crazy. We can't get any returns and, oh my God, *my ears.* . . ." Yelland heard the man sucking in air; he also felt the same stabbing pain as they'd known before.

The pain in his heart was inconceivably greater. He had fifty fighters and bombers out there in this horror, and he didn't even need to look at the deck to know that no airplane could ever set down safely on that berserk surface.

They were on their own. Then memory trickled in to him. The last time they'd come through this storm they had an A-7 out there, and it went through the warp with *Nimitz* and reappeared still on its final approach for landing. Yelland flicked his eyes upward. *Keep one more miracle for us, please. Those are good people out there.*

He turned with a smile to Warren Lasky. "Are you frightened, Warren?"

"Jesus, I was scared out of my wits before, Matt. I think this time it's just a bit closer to stark, naked terror."

Yelland couldn't help the short laugh at Lasky's own biting sarcasm of his fear. "Mr. Lasky, you'll do just fine. Hang on."

Nimitz rushed toward the waiting Time Dragon.

There wasn't one among the 5,482 souls aboard the carrier who lacked fear for a companion. Men who had survived shrieking typhoons and emerged from beneath tidal waves, who had been battered by towering waterspouts, who had suffered collisions with icebergs and felt the crunch of bombs and torpedoes—not one of them could dredge from their past experiences any confidence for what they were now entering. These same men who had endured even the time funnel that had hurled them violently back to 1941, who *knew* what it was like to be in the midst of a storm the physical effects of which derived from vast and enigmatic electromagnetic and space-time forces, also knew that what they now were entering was much worse than what they had known before.

It did not take place with shocking suddenness; that might have helped. It came as a steady gathering of might. The effects they had known before met those levels and then increased. Static electricity appeared in the form of St. Elmo's fire; the entire carrier was turned into a generator and bearer of electrical forces so mighty they could not be drained away. Lightning sparked by the ship itself crashed from the deck to the radar masts, leaped along corridors, sent glowing whorls of blue luminescence racing up ladders. Thin forks of flame in every color danced along wings, lifted hair from the necks and backs and heads of the crew. The entire bow was bathed in a ghastly green glow that expanded and contracted as the electromagnetic field became ever wilder.

Matt Yelland took her straight into the teeth of the ultimate fury. One mistake and they would become a broken chip flung away with contempt by the storm. Yelland sat strapped in his chair, his seat belt and inertial-reel shoulder harness securing him to the backrest. His interface with his ship brought him a feeling he had known only rarely in his many years at sea. *Nimitz* trembled through her entire structure, a phenomenon that doesn't happen often with a ship and almost never with a vessel as enormous as this carrier. There are different sensations when a ship takes the brunt of a storm: sudden heeling, a wallowing yaw, a sickening plunge, fierce rolling and violent pitching, even shudders and groans and agonized twisting. The trembling is something else. It is a tremor such as one might see in a dog that is either cold or trembling from some inner fury. It is the signature of a ship that seems to know—through some intelligence of the ship itself—that it teeters on the brink of unimaginable disaster.

And there are only a limited number of options. You secure everything you can. They had done that. You seal every watertight compartment. The compartments were dogged; sealed. You have your damage-control parties ready and waiting. Damage control was razor-poised. You expect trouble. They were ready for hell itself. You keep her straight into the wind. If they could, they would, and they were holding dead-on into the maelstrom. You have everything set for emergency systems: power, pressure, electrical. They had redundancy upon redundancy poised. The fluctuations of energy from nuclear reactors was more frightening than the storm itself, so the only thing to do was grit teeth, hang on, be ready. They clung grimly.

You hope and you pray.

There was a lot of that going on.

Last but never least, you talk to her. You whisper and cajole and you plead and you tell her how absolutely damned great she is, and the ship will sense it and know what it is doing, what is happening, and then you bite the bullet.

Together.

Theirs was a world of natural madness that was punctuated by the recurring sanity of voices and digital readouts. Ahead of the carrier, the swells were heaving two hundred, perhaps three hundred feet high. The ship rose and fell along the slopes of these gargantuan waves, not even her size and structure allowing her to avoid being compared to a floating cork. A voice came loudly above the thunder, the crashing of water, the scream of wind, and the very hissing in a man's ears from the fluctuations of pressure. The voice cracked through speakers about the bridge: "Bridge from plot. We are now five minutes from rendezvous with the storm center."

The voice swept through *Nimitz*. Yelland had decided that every man must know what was happening at each moment, especially during this countdown into the worst and then the expected peaking of the violence. Normal procedures didn't mean a damn right now.

"Plot from the captain. Continue your indications without further request and send it out on every channel you've got."

"Aye, aye, sir."

The ship rose and fell in sickening plunges; as she crested the enormous waves, she seemed to twist about on a balance point like a gyroscope, but without its balancing protection. Then would begin the slide downward, the crew struggling to keep the vessel bow on lest she slide sideways into a trough, which could crack her steel as if it were merely brittle wood.

"Combat plot here. Four minutes thirty seconds."

Men licked dry lips.

Throughout the ship most of the security measures were holding. Not all. Some equipment broke loose, whipping through the air like enormous missiles.

A fire broke out on number three deck. A lieutenant, who was bound securely to his control panel, punched buttons. Fire-retardant foam gushed out in great smothering billows to choke the flames.

"Four minutes to rendezvous."

Men blinked. Something weird was happening. Vision was becoming distorted. The air seemed filled with electricity. They couldn't see straight. That icepick was back in every ear, starting to shrill within every brain.

"Three minutes thirty seconds."

A great radar mast snapped like a toothpick. The wind seized it greedily and flipped it into the air like a child's kite. It disappeared in the snap of a finger.

"Three minutes."

On the weather scope the curving line they had watched so intently brightened swiftly. "Oh, Jesus," a man said, "there it comes."

Black Cloud leaned to one side and nodded. He started to speak, biting his tongue as the carrier crashed into a trough. He ignored the salty taste of blood, took a deep breath.

"Bridge from the met room. We're picking it up on the PPI, Captain."

Yelland set his lips grimly. "Very good. Keep me informed."

Behind Yelland, Warren Lasky stood against a bulkhead. Rather, he was secured to the bulkhead by powerful strands of cargo webbing that left his arms and hands free. He had a perfect view looking forward and his eyes widened as lightning forked hellishly along the crest of a great swell, tumbled down the trough, and sent up a screaming plume of steam.

"Two minutes thirty seconds."

Every radio and electronic system on *Nimitz* became useless. The electromagentic field had gone wild. Lights flickered, dimmed, brightened. They became eerie beacons to some terrible unknown. The piercing screech on the edge of the ultrasonic worsened.

"Two minutes."

The voice from plot was barely audible. Static made a hash of everything.

Unconscious of the motion, Yelland cracked his knuckles. Behind him he heard Lasky's voice. "Careful, Matt. You might get arthritis."

Yelland turned his head, managed a death's head grin. "I hope it hurts like hell—tomorrow. How are you doing, Warren?"

"I thought you'd never ask. How do I get a transfer from—"

"Ninety seconds. Ninety seconds."

"I was thinking, Matt." Lasky had to shout to be heard. "I was thinking of poetic justice. I used to have a wife. Divorced. She, uh, could never understand why I could never keep track of time, so she divorced me." He grinned like a lunatic at Yelland.

"Well said, Warren. I—" Yelland gasped for breath. A knife seemed to be twisting inside his brain. His mouth opened like that of a fish out of water gulping to breathe.

Every man on the ship felt the same terror. A voice barely gurgled on the speakers. Few men understood the words. They didn't need to. They knew what they were.

"Sixty seconds."

They fought to breathe, suck in air through tortured lungs, gasped, blinked their eyes in the pain that rose and fell like invisible waves through their bodies.

Nimitz went up the side of a mountain made of black water. The carrier hung, poised, on the thin edges of eternity.

Yelland tried to see the chronometer on the panel before him. The sweep hand moved like a rubber band being pulled a dozen ways at the same instant.

How much longer?

Seconds?

Centuries?

Forever?

No time?

They fell out.

Lasky found his mouth opening like an idiot's. A scream began down in his gut and tore up his throat, a primordial shriek that had no sound. It filled the universe, unspeakably loud in its silence. It was heard-felt-sensed?

Time stopped. It was forever and no-time together.

On the bridge, the helmsman rose slowly in his harness, a boneless puppet in slow, slow motion, his arms reaching upward and outward in supplication of forever. The sounds still came to them, but they were wrong, like a 78-rpm record turning slower and slower, the pitch going ever lower into a groan that was impossible.

Did God play a bass viol?

Space-time wrenched in upon itself.

The helmsman began to float down gradually, unreal, real, floating, his eyes wide, blank. His body distended, stretched longer and longer. An elastic gasp of life.

The deck of the bridge rippled. Steel shimmered like a thin veil, gossamer, dreamlike.

They were at the bottom of everywhere.

They began to fall upward.

It was an impossible acceleration, like being shot upward in a catapult, beginning with endless slowness and going faster and faster. Eyes bulged, muscles strained, bones began to break.

They fell upward faster and faster. There was no world, no sound, no reality.

Only acceleration.

Lasky stared, frozen in his webbing, pulled taut against its strands, as the lines holding Lieutenant Artemus Perry to his seat snapped like threads, and Perry's body began an awkward ballet, a pirouette through the air, as if gravity had been banished.

He fell, slowly but faster, upward, and then he twisted impossibly in on himself and began a sideways arc across the bridge; he sailed against the thick Plexiglas on the other side of the bridge, the side of his face touched the Plexiglas, and his skin flattened and slowly his cheekbone collapsed and his nose broke and still the inexorable pressure, seeming to last forever, crushed his teeth and his skull without any sound of the blood and liquids glowing from within splashed outward in all directions like iridescent foam.

From somewhere, from everywhere, the universe screamed.

The light from inside the belly of the sun exploded silently in their brains.

Instantly the light went out.

Darkness became theirs.

And in darkness Time is forever.

☆ 20 ☆

The storm ripped them the early morning of December 7th, 1941. Daylight. The sun.

Darkness fell away from them but there was no sun. They wiped blood from ears, noses, mouths, realized the terrible pounding was gone. The savage knife-sound . . . *gone.*

Nimitz sailed on a smooth sea under the stars.

Throughout the carrier everything came alive. Not just men stirring, but the machinery *and the electronics.*

Machines gurgled and clattered to life. Teletypes clacked frantically. The systems tied in to satellites leaped into furious action. Digital clocks everywhere through the ship blurred, then snapped into focus with the time *and the date.*

July 16, 1980.

Yelland threw off his harness. He banged his hand on a transmitter button. "Plot! The bridge here. Do we have contact with that strike force?"

"No contact, bridge. But we still have equipment coming on the line. Sir, everything's working again! We'll stay with it."

"Keep trying," Yelland said unnecessarily.

Lasky groaned, worked his way to Yelland's side. "If they were within the boundaries of the storm, they'll be here. But they could be a thousand miles away, Matt. No way to tell."

Yelland nodded. If all systems were operating again, then radar would be working, and they could pick up a transponder code from—

"Plot to bridge! We've got them!"

"Report!"

"Yes, sir! Twenty-four miles out and we count fifty radar targets, sir. That's every last one of them."

Yelland pressed another button. "All hands, prepare to recover aircraft. Look alive down there. We've got fifty coming in. Let's go, let's go."

He didn't need protocol or officious announcements. The word that the planes had wrenched back into the future with them was more than enough. Yelland busied himself, checking for damage reports, assuring the reactors were sound, feeling the pulse of the carrier. Corpsmen removed the broken body of Artemus Perry. His neck had snapped. Yelland felt better there hadn't been any long suffering.

He thought of time twisting like a rubber band. One never knew, he thought, as he watched Perry's body leaving on a stretcher.

One by one the fighters and the bombers came in with their crash-landings on the deck. Helicopters hovered in recovery positions. Lights gleamed everywhere on *Nimitz*. Then the last fighter was on deck.

Lasky sipped from a mug of hot coffee. "Do you recall how long we were back in 1941?" he asked Yelland.

"Strange question. You were there. About nineteen or twenty hours. Why?"

"That's close enough," Lasky replied. "Oh, I was just thinking of the job you've got ahead of you. I don't envy it."

"What job would that be, Warren?"

"We were in 1941 less than twenty-four hours. I came aboard *Nimitz* on July the thirteenth. Today's three days later. You've been missing, *Nimitz* and everybody and all her planes have been missing, with no contact, *for three days.*"

Lasky smiled. "You're going to have a hell of a time explaining that to the Pentagon."

Matt Yelland nodded. "It will be interesting, won't it?" He laughed. "The best part of it is that they won't be able to tell anyone else. Who'd believe them?"

☆ 21 ☆

Nimitz towered above the bleak gray quayside. A sense of the ominous received impetus from the high wire fences and barbed wire emplaced hurriedly only hours before the enormous carrier slipped into Pearl Harbor. The ship and its personnel were sealed off from the world by drastic security coverage.

Captain Matthew Yelland stood by Warren Lasky on the dock. Lasky carried his attache case and, especially incongruous under the conditions, restrained a dog by its leash. Laurel Scott's animal. Someone in the White House had been in touch with the chief of naval operations. No one knew the source of the powerplay, but the navy had been ordered to provide a car and driver to pick up Warren Lasky as he departed *Nimitz*. They watched the car's lights as it went through two separate security checkpoints before it could reach the aircraft carrier.

Lasky looked beyond, across the water, his gaze shared by Yelland. They held their eyes on the memorial to Pearl Harbor: the hulk of the *Arizona* with her dead crew entombed within the battleship's armored sides.

"It still doesn't seem real," Lasky said finally.

"Everything's real, depending upon your point of view," Yelland responded.

Lasky sighed. "I'll be reading history books until I'm blue in the face."

"We'll all be going in mental circles for a while, I suppose," Yelland offered. He watched the car pull up. The driver opened the door for Lasky, waiting.

Lasky clasped hands with Yelland. "What does one say at such a moment?" Lasky asked, smiling. "It's been a great trip?"

"An interesting one, Warren. Somewhere, soon, I believe we'll meet again to compare notes."

"I hope so."

"In the meantime, wherever you are, whenever you have doubts as to your own sanity, keep one thing in mind," Yelland offered. "I'm sure it will help."

"By all means, Matt, tell me."

The captain pointed to Charlie. "Right there is the youngest forty-year-old dog you're ever going to see in your entire life. Good sailing, Warren."

"Driver, where are we going?" From the back seat of the car, Lasky made out the silhouette of the navy enlisted man at the wheel. He had seen something else when he climbed into the car, the dog following a bit reluctantly. The man was armed.

"Sir, I only know the address. It's an estate up in the hills. My orders were to drive you there."

Lasky thought for several moments. "Those navy orders?"

"Yes, sir. The only kind I get."

"How come this car hasn't got any markings on it? You know, serial numbers, U.S. Navy, stuff like that?"

"We're a special group, Mr. Lasky. Top VIP's only. We pick them up and drop them off and that's all we know, sir."

"I see." He didn't really, but what the hell. "Mr. Lasky, there's a bar there if you'd like a drink." A red light glowed on a panel, he heard the hum of an electric motor, and a bar slid out from the seat before him.

"Sir, your martini is on the right side of the bar. All mixed just the way you like it. You'll find ice on the left if you prefer it that way."

Lasky picked up the drink, added two ice cubes and sipped. It was perfect. "All this part of your orders, sailor?"

He almost heard the chuckle. "Yes, sir. It is vodka instead of gin, isn't it, Mr. Lasky?"

Lasky nodded to himself. "It is," he told the other man, and the martini disappeared in a long, slow swallow.

Forty minutes later they turned off the main highway. A narrow road wound and twisted along a steep slope and the car stopped before massive metal gates. Lasky watched with interest. He knew security systems and there was a lot more backup to this gate than met the eye. He picked out the TV scanners, which meant that likely the gate area was covered with automatic weapons and the road ahead was mined, the devices to be detonated by remote control. What in the hell was this? They drove through and continued along the winding road.

The car emerged from between heavy growth to either side of the road. Ahead of them stretched a magnificent garden and lawn, and a curving driveway to a building he never expected. He would have paid little attention to a great colonial home with white columns, or even a massive wood-and-stone structure of modern design. The last thing he ever expected to see here was an enormous black cubicle rising from the curving hill, dominating a magnificent view of the islands and communities far below. "We're here, sir," said the driver. He remained behind the wheel. Before Lasky could open the door, a figure stood by the car to open it for him.

"It's good to see you again, Mr. Lasky."

Lasky climbed out. "I don't remember—"

"I saw you off on the helicopter that took you out to the *Nimitz*, sir."

Lasky nodded. "I remember. You're Harold Elliott. Executive assistant to Richard Tideman."

Elliott took his attache case and shook hands. "Mr. Tideman said you never forgot names, places, or positions," he said easily.

Lasky glanced up at the formidable structure. "Is Tideman here?"

"Yes, sir. Mr. and Mrs. Tideman are expecting you. If you'll follow me, please?"

He walked slowly behind Elliott. "Mind a question?"

"Not at all, Mr. Lasky."

"We just docked tonight. *We* didn't even know when we were getting in. How could *you* have known?"

"It's an interesting thought, isn't it, Mr. Lasky?" . Harold Elliott managed a smile. "Really, sir, I'm not putting you off. My instructions are to let all such questions wait until you're with Mr. and Mrs. Tideman."

Lasky chewed on the answer. "All right," he said simply.

They went through another security check at the entrance to the great cubicle, much larger than he had estimated at first glance. An elevator took them eight stories up, and they stepped out into a wide foyer, plushly carpeted, with glowing walls. Not a picture or a sign or anything. Except for a single massive door. Elliott handed him back his case.

"This is where I remain, Mr. Lasky. You're expected. Through that door, please?"

Lasky took the case and went forward slowly. He had expected Richard Tideman to be secure from outside interference, but this was beyond anything he imagined. He opened the door and walked in slowly, the dog moving cautiously beside him. He moved forward on thick carpeting. On the other side of the room, standing by wall-to-floor windows, waited a man and woman. "Warren Lasky," he heard the man saying his name. "We have waited a long time for this moment."

Before Lasky could answer, the dog let out a yelp and tore the leash from his hand, bounding forward. Lasky looked at the man. "Are you—"

"Forgive the security measures," the man interrupted, still in shadow. "Yes, of course, Lasky. I'm Richard Tideman, and this is my wife."

Lasky strained to see, but he couldn't make out the details. "My pleasure," he murmured.

They walked forward, their faces now in the light. Richard Tideman extended his hand. "Hello, Warren."

Lasky shook hands with the strong, silver-haired man before him. His smile was electric. He—

He felt the icewater rush through his veins. *"My God, it can't be—"*

"Oh, but it is, Warren."

"Dick Owens!"

"I'm sure you remember Laurel." He stared at a beautiful—no, a stunningly elegant woman, holding an ecstatic animal in her arms.

"Hello, Warren. It was only yesterday when I last saw you and you promised to take care of Charlie for me. Only yesterday," she said with a dazzling smile. "Forty years ago."

"Laurel. Laurel Scott," Lasky breathed.

"The same," she said.

He turned back to the man. "But . . . you're Richchard Tideman!"

"You need another drink, Warren."

They had talked through almost all the night. "So in the long run," Owens-Tideman said, "it appears that time serves itself. Until yesterday, I was Richard Owens, navy commander, assigned to *U.S.S. Nimitz.* But after what happened—that time warp—the paradox was established. I could not be in two places at the

same time. I could not be a man on a small island off
Hawaii in December of 1941 and also be the person
who would suddenly reappear in the future. When
Nimitz was enveloped in that storm a second time and
warped back to *now*, I couldn't be aboard. People's
memories or recollections don't affect time, only physically causative elements. In other words, when *Nimitz* went through the warp to reappear in its own time
and space, the person of Richard Owens, aged twenty-
eight, was not only not aboard the carrier, but he no
longer existed.

"Let me put it another way. Time serves itself, but
history can and does accommodate a paradox, just so
long as it doesn't stretch the elasticity of reality too far
in any one direction. It's flexible, in other words. Laurel and I are living proof of what otherwise would
have to remain a theory."

Tideman—and Lasky was forcing himself to accept
this man as Richard Tideman—sipped from a glass of
dark red wine. "I've waited many years for this moment. I confess that Laurel and I had often wondered
how it might turn out, but now we *know* beyond any
and all questions. *Nimitz* returned through time. Richard Owens did not. The tear in space-time was re-
paired. And yet, Tideman, the man I am at this instant, really did not know until you walked through
that door how it must turn out. Charlie is one more
wedge of the new reality." He leaned back in a wide
chair and sighed. "So it all fits. It was both yesterday
and it was decades ago. That paradox *is* accommodated. That is a fact of the most overwhelming im-
portance."

"It must have been a, shall I say, strange, forty
years?" Lasky ventured.

"Interesting, and informative. There is, well, it so
happens there are small ways in which you can influ-
ence events. For example, your own career was nur-
tured and directed by Laurel and myself. Your

computer work, your analytical programs, were all part of a plan."

"You mean I had no choice in the matter?" Lasky felt a touch of anger.

"Of course you did. We didn't maneuver you, Warren. We simply helped you, from behind the scenes, in what *you* wanted to do."

"Yes. I can understand that."

"It's no surprise to you—you knew it *before* you went back to 1941—that I am a very wealthy man. Indeed, the word wealthy is inadequate. I am worth more than we can easily compute. It is in the tens of billions of dollars, and I literally control hundreds of billions more. It's hardly surprising, when you consider that I knew everything that would happen in the future ahead of me. I knew what moves to make, what stocks to buy, what properties to obtain, what small companies to control, what power politics to play. Laurel's the true master at that, as the years have established. Above all, though, I made certain never to rock the time boat, never to introduce elements that were inflexible, or even grossly out of proportion with events I knew were supposed to occur. So long as we moved with the time stream, I was safe, we were safe, and history would accommodate us. There is no changing history as would have happened, let's say, if the planes from *Nimitz* had shot down the Japanese planes on their way to Pearl, and then wiped out the Nagumo fleet. Said simply, gross alterations are not permitted by changing the past, but subtle alterations are accepted. I don't think I could write you a formula for that, Warren, but I don't need to. Here I am. The proof. There's one more proof. History recorded that Sam Chapman died in 1941. He did."

"You didn't—"

"No. He tried to force the chopper crew to take him to Pearl so he could sound the alarm about the attack. He got into a fight, probably using a flare gun. It went off in the helicopter and the machine exploded and killed everyone aboard. The crew could die because they didn't affect the main thrust of time or history. Sam had to die because any change in *his* life that way would have been a big bump. Since it could not happen—ergo, it didn't."

Lasky sat quietly for several minutes and they respected his need for unbroken thinking. Finally he leaned forward to face both people. "I wondered. With what you knew, if you might have prevented the next big war. Hitler, all that."

"You mean a crusade to stop that war? You can't do that without massive interference with lives and events. And since you're operating from what would be predestiny you've got to do good, because you're trying to prevent bad. It sounds very cut and dried, but it's true. It's also a hopeless cause. The world doesn't recognize good or bad, Warren, and it offers neither of those two conditions any advantage. The world needs performance. History has proved that over and over, and, well, that's reality. Do-gooders are held in contempt by history, I'm afraid."

Lasky again held court in his own mind. Slowly but surely he had come to realize there was a lot more here than simply all these explanations. "You said something, before, Mr. Tideman—"

"None of that with you, Warren. Of all people in this world who are close to us, none is closer than yourself."

"Thank you. You said before that the paradox—the time discontinuity—could be accommodated. You also made a point that this was terribly important to you."

"It is," Tideman said. "And to you as well. You're going to be in it right up to your ears, Warren."

He waited.

"History accommodates. Forward and backward," Richard Tideman said. "Do keep in mind that the United States won the Second World War, that we were the first to harness atomic power, that we were the first to build computers still far ahead of anything the rest of the world knows, that we were the first to walk on the moon. I could go on with a very long list. Time allows me a nudge factor, as it were. Laurel and I played more than a small role in those affairs."

Lasky nodded. "I can imagine."

"Yes, of course. You of all people would understand. But there's more. I have some truly incredible laboratories. Not even Warren Lasky, my top computer scientist, knew of them before this moment. We possess power systems unknown to the world. We are, how shall I say, dabbling with the affairs of time."

Lasky felt dizzy. "You don't mean you're. . . ." He couldn't get the words out.

Tideman looked at him with compassion and with honest warmth. "Yes, Warren. We are literally on the brink of being able to control movement in—through— time. The return of *Nimitz* was the final confirmation of being able to move *mass* through time. Now that we know we're right, that the capability of movement in the time stream is within our grasp, we will move in that direction."

Tideman stood before him. "You need rest, and you need to do a great deal of thinking. We would have you accept our hospitality and stay with us in our living quarters right here. Everything you need is in your apartment, already waiting for you."

"Yes, yes," Lasky murmured. "Of course I will." He also climbed to his feet, met Tideman eye-to-eye. "One more question."

"Of course."

"You intend to travel through time . . . and be able to control that travel."

"Yes. The legendary dream come true. We are, you are."

He couldn't speak for a moment. "The past? The future? Where?"

"Not where, Warren. *When.* That's the key word. Not elsewhere, but *elsewhen.*"

Lasky's voice was a painful scratch. The truth struck him a numbing blow. "You've been into the future."

There was no response.

"*Please*. You know I'll never sleep unless you tell me. . . . *What was it like?*"

Richard Tideman and his wife smiled at him.

"Alien, my dear friend. *Alien*."